Death
DANCES

Death
DANCES

A Novel

J.M. CURLS

THE DANCING WORDS LLC

www.thedancingwords.com

Jacket design by Brandi Doane McCann

Library of Congress Control Number: 2018942111
ISBN: 978-1-73215-063-8 (hardcover)
ISBN: 978-1-73215-064-5 (paperback)
ISBN: 978-1-73215-061-4 (ebook)

For more inquiries regarding this book, please email:
thedancingwords@gmail.com

For my family, the one I was given and the one I have chosen, I love you all more than you could possibly know.

CONTENTS

MY DANCE CARD

Death comes to us all. It is simply a matter of time. Since time is the only reality we know, all that we know exists within it. We know nothing outside of it. Life and death do their dance to the music of time—always together—they dance with each of us as partners until the music stops. Each life, like music, moves through tempos such as grave, adagio, allegretto and prestissimo, giving us partners with which to pace our steps and measure our beat.

Time, like music, is an arbitrary thing, subjected to any of a variety of agreed upon conventions. I count time in the dances I have danced, the songs I have sung, and the partners I have had. I say reality is how I did the time-dance with life and death and the women who fill my dance card.

A Year

Each life lives as it does and then demises. Life and death measurements are not subject to interpretation. But in our physical world, time is. If time measurement is a social construct that can be decided by things such as the sun, the moon, the stars, the seasons, Caesars, sundials, and clocks, then I select for myself a new convention to measure a year. I say a year will be measured in the songs of the women I have known. Women who gave my life strength, definition and texture. Women who stepped onto the dance floor, giving themselves to the rhythm of life and death. Women who, at some moment in time, allowed me into their universe, filling my dance card and leaving me richer for the dance.

DANCE NUMBER ONE: THE BUNNY HOP

The Song: "The Bunny Hop"
The Dancer: Lorraine Brown

The Observance

There it is, clinging to the crease of the card, the obituary, pristinely clipped from The *Call newspaper*. Lorraine Marshall, née Brown, of Kansas City, Missouri, passed away on the twenty-eighth of April at the Morning Star Healthcare Center. Born in 1944, Lorraine attended Booker T. Washington Grade School and Lincoln High School. She took college courses at Penn Valley Junior College. Lorraine worked as a practical nurse at Queen of the World and St. Joseph's Hospital until she retired. Lorraine loved to bake and work with deaf children at the Silver Lining Home for the Deaf. Lorraine was a deaconess at the Pleasant Oaks Baptist Church, where she had been a member for fifty-five years. Lorraine is survived by three children (Paula Marshall Hendricks, Felix Marshall, and Sherman Marshall), nine grandchildren, two great-grandchildren, and a host of family and friends. Her home going has been set for Saturday, May 5, at 10:00 a.m. at the Pleasant Oak Baptist Church. That was that. A life confined to eight sentences.

I have not seen Lorraine since high school. I went away. She stayed in the neighborhood. In the picture, I see a woman with a plump face peering through glasses. She does not smile. Her hair is a short bob. After reading the obituary, I slip it back into the spine of the card, put the card inside of its envelope, and drop a life in the trash.

The Dance

It's a Small, Small World

And so, with the reading of the obituary, it began. The unwrapping of my world for almost three-quarters of a century, traveling back to a place that time had buried beneath the strata of a million memories. The excavation took a while, but then there she was. Lorraine Brown. The Lorraine that I knew lived across the street. Her hair was two black braids; her manner was delicate; her friendship was true.

We talked every day, shared every secret. Lorraine told me the first dirty joke I ever heard. She took my hand, stealthily guided me inside her garage, and whispered, "This is top secret. I shouldn't tell you this. My brothers told me, so cross your heart and hope to die you will never, ever tell."

I raised my hand and swore on my imminent death. Lorraine was pleased with my pledge. Her tone grew even more hushed.

"Well you see, a little boy is looking for his little red wagon. So he goes into his parents' bedroom without knocking, and guess what?"

"What?"

"They're in bed together."

"Uh-oh." I was shocked.

"Wait, wait,"—she was hopping up and down—"and they were both naked."

"Oh." I inhaled, unable to exhale.

"I know. I know. And the little boy sees them, and he looks at his dad and points at his you-know-what."

At this, Lorraine points her finger between her legs. I wasn't sure if I knew what, but whatever it was had to be shocking.

"And he says to his dad, 'Daddy, what is that?' and his dad says, 'That's my flashlight.'" With that, she sputtered a laugh. I joined her. Lorraine continued.

"Then he points to his momma's you-know-what." I felt certain I did. "And says, 'Momma, what is that?' and the momma says, 'That's my cellar.'" We put our hands to our mouths and tittered.

"So, the little boy says, 'Dad, could you take your flashlight and look in Momma's cellar and see if you can find my little red wagon?'"

We stared at each other for a moment, as the proposition seemed anatomically impossible, but then simultaneously erupted into peals of laughter. We weren't quite sure why, but we understood that what we had just shared was very adult and therefore very dirty.

That was life east of Twenty-Seventh and Prospect in the late '40s and early '50s. People lived in comfortable, neat homes. Some were large, some not. All had been recently vacated by Whites fleeing the Black migration moving up from the south. The homes had manicured, maintained lawns. Many lawns had hedges and flowers. Children played ball in the street, played hopscotch on the sidewalk, jumped rope, and rode bikes. The local drug store, Parkview, sold lots of cards for Father's Day because, for the most part, people lived in nuclear families.

Children played outside unmolested and unabducted. The two rules that governed most children were: (1) you could have a nickel to buy a treat when the ice cream truck came jostling, playing music, and (2) you had to report home when the street lights came on.

Fathers held jobs and supported their families with income as laborers from construction, the stockyards, the railroads, and the coveted post office. They were maintenance men, icemen, trash men, milkmen, and laundrymen. Some owned small businesses. They had fish markets, gasoline stations, and cleaners. Big businesses to us were the Palace and Consolidated cab companies, funeral homes, and The *Call newspaper*. Some people passed for White and worked in White businesses, undetected, morphing back to Black when the 5:00 p.m. whistle blew. Lorraine's dad was one of those. The Black middle class were teachers, nurses, lawyers, and doctors, in that order, as other professions held little promise for employment. There was also the occasional outlier who graduated college with a major he could never practice.

While it was a segregated society, it was not monolithic. The local grocer's name was Hoffman. His family knew everyone in the community. When women bought their groceries, Mr. Hoffman required only that they sign for them. They could pay later. The Parkview Drug Store was White-owned, but the lunch counter was ours with cooks who for fifty cents would give us a spectacular cheeseburger and a twelve-inch strawberry malt. One sales clerk was Black; one was White. The pharmacist was Black; the postal worker who sat selling stamps and money orders was White. Once a week a Black man came into the neighborhood to collect for the Atlanta Life Insurance Company. Every day a White man pushed a cart down Prospect Street selling Mexican tamales.

We could not eat at Myron Green Cafeteria or the Jones Department Store downtown, but no one gave a shit. The workers said the food tasted like sour dishwater. Anything worth having was always smuggled home anyway. Besides, who wanted that food when you had Gates's and Bryant's Barbecue or could order Chicken in the Box that would be delivered smoking hot to your door?

Some women worked. If they wanted to work at will, many did what was euphemistically described as day work, which meant cleaning White people's homes. A woman could have as many or as few days as she chose. Women also worked in the laundries, as elevator operators, as cooks, and in a variety of plants. People, if they sought it, could find decent work that paid a living wage. So the Great Migration continued, pouring people into the city from the south. Big homes had roomers, people who lived with the homeowners until they got on their feet.

Friday night, at our house and many others, meant watching the fights on television. Saturday night, for adults, meant dressing up to go out to a club for drinks, cigarettes, and dancing. Sunday meant going to somebody's church.

For a child, a good time meant going for a Sunday ride in a car and ice cream cones. There was the occasional visit to Swope Park, and on the Fourth of July a picnic on the segregated Watermelon Hill. The weekly admission price of fifteen cents could get you into the Saturday afternoon serials at the Carver Movie Theater.

Rhythm and Blues could be had any day on the Black radio station, KPRS (for Keeping People Really Satisfied). I'm sure there were police but

I rarely saw them. When people died, one of the three main funeral homes took them under.

This was the world Lorraine and I inhabited. It was safe, sound, and most of the time fun. But that was then, before public accommodations, integration, the Civil Rights Movement, social upheavals, and economic downturns made landfall into our world, irrevocably altering it for better or for worse.

The Dolls

Lorraine wanted to play with the dolls. We both had them and named them after movie stars we saw on the silver screen and magazines we read at the Parkview.

My doll was Audrey, named for Audrey Hepburn. Hers was Susan, after Susan Hayward. It was misting, and so we sat on the porch having ventriloquist conversations as those two alter egos.

"I'm planning to go out tonight with Carey Grant, when he finishes making *Room for One More*. We are going to dinner. Then we are flying to Niagara Falls for a honeymoon," my Audrey said.

"Did you get married?" asked her Susan.

"Not yet, but I will soon."

"You need to if you're going on a honeymoon. Where is Niagara Falls?"

"I think it's in Paris."

"Well, that's nice. Clark is taking me to the *Hit Parade*. That's in New York. I'm going to meet Snooky Lanson and Gisele MacKenzie."

Not to be outdone, my Audrey boasted, "Well I'm going to make another movie."

"What's it called?"

"I think it will be called, *Tomorrow Is Just Another Day*. I don't know. I may make a western and call it, *The Sun is Hot*. It won't be in black and white like your movie. Mine will be in Technicolor."

Lorraine's Susan countered, "I'm making a movie. It's a scary movie called, *The Mummy's Cousin*. The mummy comes out with all the bandages and holes for eyes and…" It was then that Lorraine whispered, "Look, look who's coming."

I turned in the direction that Lorraine was looking and saw Ernestine. Ernestine lived near the other end of the block in her aunt's house. They had come from Louisiana, so my mother said. I had muted a laugh when I first saw her. She talked funny, and her clothes were labeled, by our neighbor, as "mammy made." They were poorly constructed and never seemed to fit.

"Hi, Ernestine, where are you going?" Lorraine asked.

"Goin' to Kaufman's. Gotta git beans and salt pork for Momma. She wants to boil a pot."

"What did she just say?" I asked.

"She said her mother is sending her to the store to get beans and salt pork to make dinner," Lorraine replied.

What was Lorraine doing? Even then I understood class and did not want to be a part of Ernestine's social group.

"Well, you better get going" was my suggestion.

"Say, we could walk with you. Then when we come back you can play dolls with us."

What? No! Had Lorraine lost her mind? What kind of a unilateral decision was that? First, I did not like the way Ernestine talked. Second, I did not like the weird dress she was wearing. It had no belt and was not starched. And third, I intuitively knew two people playing dolls was far better than three. But there was Lorraine, up and moving toward Ernestine, motioning for me to follow. Grudgingly I did. I was right about twos and threes. The two of them walked and talked while I followed, grumbling to myself.

How could Lorraine even understand Ernestine without an interpreter? I heard Ernestine say something about being "Geechie," which I later learned had something to do with African descendants from Sierra Leone. To be honest, I really had no clue what she was saying. Good lord, how could Lorraine tolerate it? Her speech pummeled my ears. I decided to wait outside the grocery store and watch the people get on the bus.

When they emerged from the store, the three of us began skipping down the street. Skipping was perfect. It was not a team sport and was hard to do when talking.

My house came up first, and that should have been the end of it. Lorraine and I should have stopped and resumed our doll playing, and Ernestine should have taken her beans and salt pork six houses down the street. But no, Lorraine wanted more.

"Would you like to play dolls with us?" she sunnily invited. The nerve. Lorraine was now inviting a nonnative speaker to my home—not her home, my home.

"S'okay?"

"She said…"

"I know what she said."

"Well, is it OK?"

How awkward. Thanks, Lorraine.

I twisted my mouth, searching for a response. "Well, you know…her momma's beans…"

"'Sides, I ain't got no doll," Ernestine confessed. I looked at Lorraine. Case closed.

"We can make you a doll," proposed Lorraine.

"We can?" Was she serious?

"Ya can?" Ernestine asked, overjoyed.

"Sure we can." Lorraine smiled. "Right?"

"Sure. Why not?" I conceded.

"We can get some rags, and does your momma have any old hose?" Lorraine was addressing me. Lorraine had not only appropriated my front porch. Now she intended to repo my mother's nylons. I was too overwhelmed to object.

"Let me see. I'll ask."

Ernestine was as happy as I had ever seen any human being. She flung down her grocery bag and began this spontaneous hugging thing with Lorraine and me, speaking a tongue that has not been used since the tower of Babel.

With socks, rags, and nylons riddled with runs, Lorraine rendered a doll. Admittedly it was slightly terrifying, unnatural, and asymmetrical. But for Ernestine, it was spellbinding. She kept trying to articulate her gratitude. It was what Lorraine did next that practically paralyzed me. She gave Ernestine her doll.

"Here, you take Susan," she insisted. "I am going to play with Elizabeth."

Womanhood

Was I thirteen? No, twelve and a half. Lorraine and I did not go to the same school. She was Protestant. I was Catholic. Catholics, at that time, were discouraged from fraternizing with Protestants and were forbidden to attend Protestant churches. In Kansas City, this would equate to self-imposed social isolation, as most colored people were not Catholic. The enforced education separation was almost too much for Lorraine and me to bear. Our separated school circumstance forced us to reconvene after school at the Parkview lunch counter over a limeaid or a phosphate soda.

These rendezvous were critical to our sustainability. The Parkview was where we deliberated and discussed the major events that comprised our world: the latest Frankie Lymon and the Teenagers' records, the Mickey Mouse Club, the disgusting and unsanitary kissing practices of the French, the hoop and the crinoline under our skirts, and the scandalous but ever-so-exciting pelvic movements of that singer from Memphis who said he was White but sounded Black.

It was in the throes of one of these life-altering conversations that I felt the warm wetness in my underpants. What was that? Maybe something. Maybe nothing. Whatever it was, it couldn't be that significant. When I stood from the stool to leave, I heard Lorraine from behind.

"Did you sit in something?"

"I don't think so?"

"Well, there's a big spot on the back of your skirt."

"Yeah, maybe." I did feel something.

"I think you should go home."

"I think so, too." I felt another surge. I was growing concerned.

"I'll walk you home." We walked an ominous walk. Each step told us things were changing. I had heard about menstruation from my other friends at school. They tried to describe it. Some said it was painful. Some said messy. Some said it made them feel different. Others said it didn't change anything. Together Lorraine and I went to the bathroom, where I pulled down my pants. Lorraine gasped and clasped her hand across her mouth.

"I think this is it," I announced, staring at my pants crumpled around my ankles.

"What do you think we should do?"

"I think I'm going to have to get supplies."

"I think you should tell your momma."

"I think so, too."

I next stepped out of my underpants, with pinched fingers lifted them like a flag of surrender, and marched with Lorraine to my mother in the kitchen.

"Momma, look, look!" My voice began to break as she turned to see what had me so distraught.

"What is it?" Momma turned, examined my cotton cluster, put her hand across her heart as if to make a pledge of allegiance, and then declared,

"Child, you have just gone into womanhood." Womanhood! On the stool at Parkview!

"Now let me tell you, child, and you must understand. You listen, too, Lorraine, because you're probably next." Lorraine took two terrified steps backward.

"When you go into womanhood, there are things you have to know, so listen and believe what I have to say. For one thing, this is going to happen every month, and you may not know the time or the place."

It was beginning to sound a lot like the second coming.

"And another thing,"—her finger was waging now—"you can never take a bath or wash your hair during your time of the month, or you might catch your death of cold and go right on away from here, just like that." Momma snapped her finger.

Things were going from bad to worse, but there was more.

"Most important, and I mean most important, no messing around with boys. Do you know what I'm saying?"

Dead silence. Was that all she had to say about that?

"Do you understand me?" Her voice escalated, and she seemed anxious.

"Yes, I think so." I had to say yes. The glare from her eyes was so intense I thought she might lapse into an advanced state of apoplexy or just melt like the witch in Oz.

"Do you know what I mean, Lorraine?"

"Yes, ma'am," Lorraine reflexively spat out.

"Good. Then enough said about that. So now you have to go to Parkview and get yourself a green box of Kotex. Not a blue or pink box but a green box of Kotex and a sanitary belt. That's how you take care of yourself. What color did I say?"

In concert, we repeated "Green."

"Green. That's right. Now let me get you some money."

"No." I followed Momma as she searched her purse. "No, no, Momma. I cannot go to Parkview and buy a green box of Kotex. Everyone knows me there. Everyone will know I'm in womanhood. There are men there, and they will know." I was begging. I was crying, wiping my eyes with the bottom of my blouse.

"Momma, please. I can't do it. I just can't." That's when I heard the other frightened voice in the room.

"I'll do it. Give me the money. I will do it."

From that day until I left for college, Lorraine would go to Parkview each month with seventy-five cents and buy me a green box of Kotex and bring it to my house in a brown paper sack.

A Is for Adolescence

In my sophomore year, Momma took a job for two days in a private family. The family she worked for lived near the Country Club plaza, that incredible outdoor mall designed in a Seville Spanish style by J. C. Nicholas.

Up to this point in my life, going to the plaza had been a destination. Though it was only five miles from our home, it was like going to Topeka. Colored people didn't regularly go there. The plaza's shops and boutiques displayed only the best of what Kansas City called haute couture. They flaunted brands you never saw downtown. If Negroes were there they were probably working as stock or janitorial personnel.

On Thanksgiving Day and throughout the entire Christmas season, the tile roofs and Spanish architecture of the plaza became a blazing light spectacle that was astounding to behold. The light display wasn't limited to the retail center. The surrounding neighborhood also got into the act, illuminating the night sky with a rainbow of colors, making each residence an electronic canvas. It was magical, and everyone was invited to view. All you needed was a car.

We had one, and our parents would treat my sister and me to a one-night ride through the gala, which was the plaza. We would all ooh and ah. Dad would slow down, when he could, so we could better appreciate anything fascinating. This evening we took a long pause in front of the home where Momma worked.

"This is Miss Lottie's house," she announced as if it were her own. There were lights in trees, and on the roof Santa was darting for the chimney with a sleigh full of toys.

"It has five bedrooms. Isn't it beautiful?"

"I thought you said they were Jewish." Dad was staring at the roof.

"They are" was all she said. Lesson learned—belonging can trump religion.

The money Momma made came in handy. That Christmas Momma asked Miss Lottie to purchase Daddy a tie from the high-end store, Jack Henry. Momma bought my sister a doll from Parkview, whose hair could be permed, and me a portable radio from the pawn shop.

By that summer, however, I wanted to fall in love. Every evening when I would retreat with the phone under my bed covers to talk with Lorraine, I would vociferously complain of my romance deprivation.

Lorraine was at the all-Black high school, Lincoln. I was at the all-White Catholic high school, St. Patrick's. This is the way it worked. Each year when Negro kids graduated from Saint Augustine's Mission School, Father Henley would divide them up and parcel them out to the White Catholic schools that were also pretty much divided by ethnicity. Three or four children went to the Italian high school, St. Joseph's. Three or four went to the German high school, Saint Gregory's. Three or four went to the Irish high school, Saint Patrick's. Usually, there were two or three families in the parish with greater means. These would send their boys to De La Salle or Rockhurst and their girls to St. Theresa's or Loretto. If you were considered extremely well-off, you probably had become a Presbyterian convert.

Father Henley had selected two other girls and me to go to St. Patrick's. The first year was difficult. We clung to one another for comfort and support. It just was not easy. In gym class, we were the last girls to be picked for anyone's team. We all sat together at lunch, and although others were at the table, we only talked among ourselves. In choir the nun had an affinity for Stephen Foster songs, which lauded the South. She was particularly fond of "Old Black Joe" and "My Old Kentucky Home."

Girls would sometimes snicker, whisper, and cough when they passed, making us feel we were the object of their conversation. When we went to class, people sat beside us only if there was no other desk available.

By the beginning of my sophomore year, one of my classmates defected to attend Lincoln High School. The other one contracted tuberculosis and was dispatched to a sanitarium. This abandonment left me totally isolated. While there were three Negroes each in the junior and senior class levels, the one thing more verboten than integration was speaking to underclassmen.

Lorraine knew my dilemma and tried her best to keep me from becoming socially stunted. She enrolled us both into the Johnny Mathis Fan Club, which met every other week. When we came together, all the girls would write love letters to Johnny, get professional black-and-white photos signed by our Adonis, endlessly play his records, and dream of the day he would ask one of us to marry him.

But Johnny was not enough. I wanted more. Lorraine had real suitors. In the spring, while walking home from Parkview, I saw a boy in a crew neck sweater and penny loafers carrying her books. She had turned to go to her house when she remembered them. When she swiveled to reclaim the books, Lorraine caught sight of me waiting alone on the opposite corner. I saw her lower her eyes. She could sense my despair.

It was understood that we girls could not date until we were sixteen. For Lorraine that would be in two months. Planning ahead, Lorraine had begun trolling her high school waterways, lining up prospects. At Saint Patrick's, the boys were all White. As if that weren't bad enough, the nuns had imposed other enforcement actions. Boys and girls could not go steady. Students who went steady could not play B team or varsity sports. They could not be cheerleaders or hold office. There was a Catholic KGB system at the school, where unidentified informers would submit the names of any offenders.

Students attended Mass and confession weekly to be provided the necessary vaccine against sins of the flesh. To combat teenage angst and to fortify socialization, students were encouraged to join the booster club and scream, to play sports and realize the meaning of community pain, and to attend the monthly sock hop, where the girls danced with one another and the boys stood on the perimeter of the wall.

Each and every night I would climb into bed and complain to Lorraine about my abysmal situation. She would listen sympathetically until she had to go in anticipation of her next scheduled call from another active suitor.

The summer began to show some promise. The boy across the street and eight houses down had convinced my dad to let him mow our lawn. Dad consented. He came to our house pushing a lawn mower, with a rake and scythe strapped across his back. The boy's name was Jesse Banks. I was always future-focused, and his last name sounded promising.

I made it my business to sit on the front porch every time he mowed. I would also bring out my portable radio and place it on the porch banister with the volume loud enough for him to hear. We would listen to different songs and countdowns, giving thumbs up to the songs we liked and thumbs down to the songs we didn't. One day I even brought him out a glass of grape Kool-Aid.

When he went to the side of the house to mow where there were peonies and no windows, I trailed behind him as if to suggest I might take soil samples. When we were out of everyone's view, Jesse propped me against the stucco siding and kissed me on the lips. It was awkward. He had been standing on my right foot, and the stucco caught my hair. It wasn't exactly *Splendor in the Grass*, but it would have to do. That very night I told Lorraine all about it.

"Lorraine, Jesse Banks kissed me today on the side of the house."

Lorraine squealed. She had been kissed a total of six times, so she reigned as an expert.

"Was it wet?"

"Well, you know I honestly can't remember."

"Well did...did he open his mouth?"

"You mean that French stuff? Oh God, no. But I can prove it really happened. He had been mowing and touched my face; my upper lip is green. You wanna see?"

"Oh yeah."

"Well, come over tomorrow morning. I won't wash my face until you come. I'm going to say something I never thought I'd say, but Lorraine, I think I'm in love."

The evaporating nature of love! Daddy did not like the way Jesse trimmed the shrubs or his complete neglect of the parkway. Jesse was fired, and my love life was retired.

The Debutante

In June, Lorraine turned sixteen. Her parents had friends over to celebrate. It was a garden party. The guests ate ham and potato salad in the backyard. I was invited along with several boys and girls from her Baptist church. Unlike the Catholics, who grew stronger with such activities as dancing, drinking, and bingo, Lorraine's Baptist congregation eschewed such displays. Even so, her mother had bought the 45 rpm song of the summer, "Sixteen Candles," by The Crests, for Lorraine to dance her debutante dance. As dusk began to stretch across the sky and call the evening, her mom brought the record player to the open kitchen window and spun the song. Lorraine and a boy danced to sweet applause.

When I turned sixteen, I was home alone. My isolation was voluntary. Momma swore she was looking for something better, but she was still doing two days for Miss Lottie. My birthday was one of her work days. The prior evening, as atonement for having to work on my birthday, Momma had presented me with the gift of a teal-green ruffled dress made of organdy. It was a gorgeous thing, purchased at the posh Harzfeld's boutique. There were three ruffles that made the skirt, reminding me of curtain valances. They fell from the waist in tiers like overlapping flower petals. The dress had belonged to Miss Lottie's middle daughter, but it appeared to have seldom been worn. Early that morning, Momma had made me a strawberry birthday cake upon which she had planted sixteen candles.

"Ask Lorraine over," Momma suggested. "We'll celebrate this weekend."

Momma headed for her bus stop. My sister walked the three blocks to a YWCA girl's summer camp. I climbed the two flights of stairs to indulge in a serious self-pity spa. I first drew myself a warm bath using Momma's Duz laundry detergent to get a bubble effect. Next, I brushed my hair into a smooth ponytail applying her Royal Crown pomade. After smearing my face with Pond's cold cream, I basted my body with Jergen's lotion. Momma always kept an atomizer on her dresser to spray herself when she went out on Saturday nights. I couldn't resist and squeezed my pulse points just as she did. Wednesday was the day before, so all the clothes had been washed. This meant fresh underwear. When I was properly prepared and undergirded, I slipped into that diaphanous teal-green birthday dress. I was ready now to mourn my abysmal life.

When Lorraine arrived, I was slumped in Dad's easy chair. The cake was on the coffee table. I was flipping through a *Screen Gems* magazine.

"Knock, knock!" Lorraine bounded into the living room. "Is this where the birthday girl lives?"

I drew myself up, giving her a blank stare.

"Wow, you look so pretty! So what's wrong?"

"This, Lorraine, is the season of my discontent. Look at this. Do you know," I mounted my grievance, "two girls from my church were in a debutante ball?" I grabbed a glossy booklet from the coffee table. "Can you believe this? We contributed money to this sponsor book and printed sentiments like, 'Congratulations to the very sweet and beautiful Melanie.' Melanie isn't sweet or beautiful. She has a horrible overbite, but she danced in a gorgeous gown with her dad and then with some boy I never heard of. She was being presented." I paused and emphasized the word again. "Pre-sen-ted. Next week it will all be written up in the *Call Paper* with pictures. But me? I have no party, no date, no dance. I think I should take something."

"Like what?" Lorraine asked.

"I'm thinking arsenic, or maybe I'll just go in the backyard and find myself an asp."

Lorraine approached to feel my head. "This is bad."

"Yes, it is."

"Listen, it's not the end of the world."

"Yes, it is."

"No, it's not." Lorraine was emphatic.

"Yes, it is." I was more so.

"No, it isn't." Lorraine slammed her foot to the floor. "We are going to celebrate."

Before I knew it, she had escaped to the kitchen, made Kool-Aid, and returned to the living room with two glasses, a pitcher, two plates, a knife, and a box of matches, supported on my mother's striped plastic tray.

"It's time to celebrate!" she shouted. "Someone just turned sweet sixteen!" Like a military martinet, Lorraine marched to the fireplace mantel and turned on my portable radio. The countdown was on. We listened every day, and so we knew its approximate position. Numbers fifteen, fourteen, thirteen, twelve, eleven, and ten had played. We now were in single digits—nine, eight, seven, six—and there it was, number five. The Crests were singing "Sixteen Candles."

As the soft harmony began, Lorraine stepped to the center of the living room and like a faithful courtier heralded, "Presenting the most beautiful girl in the land!"

With that, Lorraine strutted over to me, one hand across her waist, the other behind her back.

"Madam," she asked, "may I have this dance?"

I stood and extended my arm. Lorraine took my right hand. She clutched my waist with her left hand. It was the loveliest slow dance ever. I had been presented.

Graduation

By the time I graduated high school, my life had taken a decidedly upbeat turn. Junior and senior year had proven to be incredible. I was entering an age of self-discovery and had found another life path. I was seeing less and less of Lorraine. There were different life magnets pulling us apart.

In her senior year, Lorraine became engaged to Jimmy Marshall. He had graduated two years earlier and had a good job at Railway Express. Her plan was to go to junior college and become a practical nurse. They wanted to marry and buy a house. I had other plans.

I did not go to her graduation, but she and Jimmy came to mine. It was Mother's Day. When I took off my mortarboard and gown, Lorraine pinned a red carnation on my dress.

"I'm proud of you. I love you, and I'll always be there for you." With that, she kissed my cheek and joined my family at Gates' BBQ to celebrate my rite of passage.

It is at this point in time that the image of Lorraine's face, in my memory, begins to blur. Things become sketchy. Dad finally landed that coveted post office position. Mom passed the federal exam and was hired by the General Services Administration. She still worked late afternoons on Thursdays and Saturday mornings for Miss Lottie. But things were changing. The Great

Migration had opened up scores of homes for Negroes in the south of the city. Negroes had now rebranded themselves as Blacks. The old neighborhood was decaying. We moved that summer, farther south, on a tree-lined avenue called Benton Boulevard.

The obituary confirmed Lorraine had married Jimmy Marshall. I do not remember when they married. I did not go to the wedding. I cannot say why. The woman in the picture I do not know, but the eyes are indisputably hers—round, brown, warm, and kind. Kindness was her gift, silent but effusive. Without me even knowing it, she had taught me to try and be kind. It doesn't hurt; it only helps.

The dance ends.

DANCE NUMBER TWO: THE STROLL

The Song: "The Stroll"
The Dancer: Sister Patricia Ann a.k.a.
Sister Teresa O'Malley

The Observance

Spring is coming unseasonably late to Atchison. It is mid-April, and the ground is rock hard. It doesn't help that my feet are killing me. The shoes are over-the-top classy. When I walked into the store, they called to me in a siren song. I answered. It was a to-die-for sale at Neiman's last call. The shoes are mine. But why would I buy a half size too small? What was I thinking? No part of my body is getting smaller. It was the hypnotic trance of the shoe siren song, and now I am paying the price.

Less than two weeks earlier I had been at the Mount, shorthand for Mount Saint Scholastica. For 152 years, Mount Saint Scholastica was the mother house and convent for the Atchison, Kansas, Sisters' Order of Saint Benedict. In 1863, these nuns opened a school for girls and, in 1923, its college. This college was the sister college of St. Benedict's. The Mount was the nexus and the incubator that grew young girls into religious women. As the convent grew, the work of this religious order expanded, spreading to other towns in Kansas, Missouri, Iowa, Nebraska, and Colorado. These women were teachers, staffing Catholic high schools and a junior college in Kansas City, Kansas.

When I was introduced to the Mount's campus in Atchison, it housed an elementary school, high school, and college. The convent, administration building, dorms, student center, various houses, gardens, miscellaneous other buildings, and a cemetery comprised the campus. The vibrant world of nuns, as I knew them then, has today become a dying star. In 1965, there were one hundred and eighty thousand nuns in the United States. Today there are fifty-six thousand. Their average age is seventy-four. For the Benedictine nuns at Atchison, their high schools are gone. Mount Saint Scholastica's administration building and dorms have also been demolished. What remains is the convent, a retreat center, and a recently remodeled complex called Dooley Center that houses their aging and invalid sisters.

One should, however, never imagine this to be a bleak or dour environment. Nothing could be further from the truth. These amazing women are astonishingly adaptable and have reinvented themselves in ways hard to imagine. These are extremely well-educated, assertive women who are on a mission. Their mission is ministry, service, education, and social justice. Their resilience and vitality are palpable. They go to their death committed to and working for what they believe in, and I am here today to bury one. Her real name is Teresa O'Malley, but when I met her, she was Sr. Patricia Anne.

I follow the procession that trails her casket as her religious community, family, and friends make their way to the nun's burial grounds nestled behind the Stations of the Cross. With its rows of headstones, the cemetery is startling. Clearly, there are more sisters dead than there are alive. Everyone gathers around the gaping ground. The wind is taking little slices out of my face.

The priest intones the prayer. I begin to drift away. Wasn't it two weeks ago that I had come to see her for her birthday? I had gone to Sr. Teresa's bedroom, where she was sitting and ready. I knocked on her cracked door. She was expecting me.

"Hello, my lovely." Sister smiled, and I was sixteen again.

"Hello, Sister."

"Come, sit beside me." I did as ordered.

"Whose woods are these?" she began.

"I think I know," I responded.

"His house is in the village, though." Her eyes twinkled as we picked up the tempo. Sr. Teresa loved Robert Frost, especially this poem. She claimed the last line for herself.

"But I have promises to keep, and miles to go before I sleep." She clutched my hand.

"And miles to go before I sleep."

"Happy birthday, Sister." I leaned into her emaciated cheek and kissed it.

"Is it my birthday?"

"You know it is."

"And so it is."

"I brought you something."

"Oh, how you spoil me. You know I need absolutely nothing." She was opening the wrapped box. Then she conceded.

"But I will take this. It's so me, don't you think?" The gift was a blue-and-white silk blouse. I had to buy it two sizes too large to accommodate the hump that had widened across her back.

"OK. Let's get me all gussied up, and then we will go to the dining room for lunch."

The dining room was the eating space for the nuns who lived in the convent or for the ones who resided in Dooley Center who did not require special assistance. Sr. Teresa seldom ate in the dining room, but today was her birthday. Fortified with the determination only nuns can muster, Sr. Teresa was committed to eating there.

I put on her new blouse and combed her gun-metal-gray hair. I even put a little of my lipstick and blush on her face for color and contrast.

"Now that's a hoot," she chortled, holding the mirror. In my opinion, for ninety-six, she looked pretty damned great.

I put her in her wheelchair and pushed her to the dining room. When we came through the door, most of the nuns were seated, but upon seeing her, they rose and applauded. Food in the dining room was served à la carte. I went through the food line and got her what she requested, but she didn't eat it.

There were prayers and reflections during lunch. A parade of sisters kept stopping by the table to greet her, wish her happy birthday, and tell her how pretty she looked.

"You know they're jealous." Sr. Teresa chuckled in my ear.

The prioress approached the podium and announced it was Sr. Teresa O'Malley's ninety-sixth birthday. Another standing ovation and a robust singing of "Happy Birthday" followed.

It was a week to the day when the call came.

"This is Sr. Michelle. We have been sitting vigil all night with Sr. Teresa. She is slipping fast. We want you to tell her it is all right to go. Here, I am going to put the phone up to her ear."

What I heard next was labored breathing that gurgled.

"Sr. Teresa, it's me. There are no more promises. You have kept them all. Every single one. It's OK now. Go to sleep."

Thirty minutes later the phone rang again.

"Sr. Teresa is now with her loving God. Thank you."

Yesterday I came to Atchison. I wanted to be in the foyer when the funeral home returned her body. The entire available community of nuns and friends had gathered to receive her. Her casket was taken to Scholastica Chapel, where she lay in repose. At the appointed time we were admitted for the visitation. There were prayers and songs. Then came the time to view the body. When my time came to process by, I stopped and looked down at my teacher, my mentor, my light walker. That devilish smile was blooming on her lips, and she was wearing my blue-and-white silk blouse.

After the visitation, all guests gathered in the sisters' dining room for supper. When the meal concluded, the prioress approached the podium as she had a little over a week ago.

"Tonight we remember Sr. Teresa O'Malley. What a lady!"

The agreement was audible. "What a lifetime!" For me, it felt as if the room was levitating.

"And so tonight we will share stories of our friend, and we will call on all and any who wish to say how she impacted their lives."

The Dance

Sophomore Year

My assimilation began my sophomore year. The third period was biology, taught by Sr. Mary Thomas. I had had general science the prior year, but after all the brouhaha about Sputnik, nothing else was very exciting.

That was not the case with biology. It spoke to the natural world, to plants, animals, and humans. Sr. Mary Thomas was an engaging biology teacher who used words like photosynthesis and metamorphosis to explain incomprehensible events in nature. I was alone now; my two classmates were gone. I sat in the back of the class, but Sr. Mary Thomas had the voice projection of a bass drum, so I missed nothing.

This day she was explaining tadpoles, which we were later going to the lab to dissect. Sister was saying that scientists now believed that tadpoles had at one time been fish but over thousands of years evolved, developed feet and lungs, which enabled them to leave the water and walk onto land.

A hand waved in the air.

"Yes, Bobby. Stand and state your question."

"Sister, I thought the Bible said God created the world in seven days. How does that work if it took thousands of years to get a tadpole?"

"A good question, Bobby."

I certainly thought so. With that, Sr. Mary Thomas pushed her glasses back on her face, planted her feet apart, and bellowed her defense of God.

"Listen, people. It needs to be understood that seven days to God is not the same as seven days to us. What we do know—and I want you always to remember this—is that true faith and true science never contradict." Her finger underscored the point. "Never."

So sit down, Bobby, I said to myself, but please forget that answer. In my opinion, God had overreached with the creation. It was like selling Girl Scout cookies. You set an unrealistic goal, and before you know it, you've swept the neighborhood, and you still have thirty boxes left to sell. So you go to the next block and the next. On each block, it gets harder and harder to sell. Finally, you go to your parents and dump what's left on them. I get it. You try to do something, and you screw up. Trees, peacocks, and elephants are beautiful. But some things just don't work. I think God got overconfident; he did a lightning bug, wow, but with his second attempt he got a house fly. Not so great. He tried again and got a beetle, wow. In his next attempt, he got a water bug. Shit happens! Things don't always work as you plan. If you're God, you have prerogatives that humans don't. God can just redefine what constitutes a week. Politicians redefine terms all the time.

In my neighborhood, God would have been unemployed. Colored people knew they had to deliver the work to get paid, to make ends meet, to combat the prevailing stereotype that they were lazy. There were always new recruits arriving from the south who would work. There was no way Miss Lottie would wait five hundred years for her laundry.

The creation story was a turn-off. But then Sr. Mary Thomas introduced Charles Darwin. The tadpole got it—the ocean wasn't working. If it wanted a better life, it had to do something and did it. No one said it was going to be easy growing legs and lungs. That fish was probably a lot like me, lonely but determined to survive. It would have to adapt. Survival, Darwin said, was for the fittest. Things that did not change would become extinct. At that moment, in that class, with that Darwinian introduction, it became brilliantly clear that no matter how painful the process might be, I would have to adapt or become extinct.

Junior Year

By the time my life became linked to Sr. Patricia Ann's, I was a work in progress. It was the beginning of my junior year. In my sophomore year, I initiated the painful process of adapting. I studied harder and raised my hand. When I got more answers right than wrong, I raised my hand even more. People were taking notice. Some began to smile. A couple of times I was called to the board to diagram sentences or work on an algebra equation.

In my gym class, I was now only the third last person to be selected for a team. When I beat the other girls in the second running of our indoor track meet, the girls cheered.

In chorus, when we sang "Zippity Doo Dah" from Uncle Remus, I was loud and animated. Sr. Phillip was so impressed, she asked me to sing "Somewhere Over the Rainbow" solo in the spring madrigal. I stayed after class and practiced. The next day I sang it before the class. Everyone applauded. Two classmates cried.

As my junior year began, I was ready to grow longer, stronger legs. I moved toward the front of the class. Mary Cecelia, one of the honor roll girls, sat beside me. Momma had bought me three new uniform blouses, which meant I had a fresh blouse every other day. I was ready for the world.

What I was not ready for was Sr. Patricia Ann. I knew who Sr. Patricia Ann was in the solar system of nuns who orbited our school. She was the sister who taught speech, drama, history, and English. Sr. Patricia Ann directed the annual senior play and the spring musical. She coordinated the intramural speech meets with other Catholic schools throughout the state. Sister did not teach religion but was over the Sodality, a confraternity dedicated to the Blessed Virgin Mary. Little did I know that before she was finished with me, I would be immersed in all these things.

Our beginning was benign. I picked up my class schedule, and there was Sr. Patricia Ann's name. My academic performance at the end of my sophomore year had been impressive enough to elevate me to advanced English. Sr. Patricia Ann taught it. I was scheduled for American History. She taught it. I was taking speech. She taught that. I looked at my schedule again. This woman was also my homeroom teacher!

The first day of class, Sr. Patricia Ann made her entrance. She did not just walk into the room. She owned it. The door opened. We all stood. The atmosphere altered. The air grew lighter, lifting her black veil. Her arms were extended from her sides as if she had just descended to earth. Sr. Patricia Ann's voice was a melody.

"Good morning. Good morning, children."

"Good morning, Sister."

"My name is Sister Patricia Ann. Shall we now make the sign of the cross?"

I had done this drill a hundred times before—the sign of the cross, the prayer, the Pledge of Allegiance—but with Sr. Patricia Ann, it all seemed like grand theater.

After prayers and pledges, we took our seats for a brief roll call and a few announcements. The bell rang, and everyone was off to their class. I was taking speech and remained in the room with Sr. Patricia Ann. My next class was geometry with Coach Schmidt and then back for English with Sr. Patricia Ann. French was with Sr. Marcita and then back for American History with Sr. Patricia Ann. Sociology was with Sr. Mary Raphael. My last class was typing with Sr. Sharon and then back to Sr. Patricia Ann for roll call, prayer, and dismissal. That was my junior year schedule.

I had just given my first speech when Sr. Patricia Ann asked me to remain after class. She wanted to talk to me. For our first speech, Sister had given us three topic options: what we did the past summer, what it meant to be Catholic, or a famous person we admired. My speech topic was a no-brainer. I certainly did not want to recall and give voice to the summer of my discontent. Frankly, I wasn't sure what it meant to be Catholic. Dad was a Cradle Catholic, and Momma, a convert. I had observed that being Catholic meant different things for both of them and probably something still more different for me. The process of elimination nailed it. My first speech would extol a famous person I admired, Abraham Lincoln. He had freed the slaves. That was pretty admirable. When delivering my speech, I had projected my voice, filling it with passion. I had made eye contact, scoping out the whole room, and my presentation had a central idea, a beginning, a middle, and an end. I must have really impressed Sr. Patricia Ann.

The room emptied. I was still sitting at my desk when sister called me.

"Come here, my lovely, and sit down."

It was two weeks into school. If you were in Sr. Patricia Ann's homeroom, she had by now assigned you a pseudonym to which you would answer at roll call. There was Michael, her archangel, Delores, the sprite, Mark, the defender of the faith, and Mary, Catherine the Great. I was her "lovely."

"Sit here, my lovely." She gestured toward the chair beside her desk. "Let's talk about your speech."

"Didn't you like it, Sister?"

"Oh yes. I liked it very much. I don't mean that. I'm referring to your speech."

I was bewildered.

"The way you talk, my lovely."

"Oh, my speech. Is there something wrong with my speech?"

"Yes, there is."

"What's wrong?"

"What's wrong is that it's not right. You lose syllables. You drop endings. Some of your diphthongs are a disaster, and you often fail to enunciate."

It sounded terminal. I was humiliated.

"Let's look at this." She was scanning the written speech I had just given.

"Here. Read this line."

I took the paper and began to read the sentences she had underlined in red. My voice cracked slightly.

"You can't hear that, can you?"

"Hear what?"

"What you just said. 'Lincoln feed the slaves.' Lincoln did not 'feed' slaves. He fr-eeee-ed slaves. Can you hear the difference?"

Everyone I knew spoke the way I did. "You mean, you want me to speak like White people?"

"No, my lovely. I mean I want you to speak correctly. Language is the instrument we use to communicate. When you play the piano, and you hit a flat note, it offends the ear of the listener. If you continue to play that way, people conclude that you can't play the piano and stop listening. The same is true with language. Words are the tools that we use to communicate. To be an effective speaker, we must use them properly. As a nation, we speak English. When we speak English, we have agreed on certain conventions as to how the words we speak will be sounded out. This is important, so people don't think when we say one thing we mean another. That is not to say that all the students in the speech class speak proper English. The great benefit that will accrue to you, in the world in which we live, is this—if you can speak English correctly, it will advance others' perception of you exponentially. The value of language improvement for the other students, because of who they are, is important, but for you, my lovely, it can be a life-changing skill." Sr. Patricia Ann stood up. "I see clearly what God needs me to do," she announced. Smiling, she patted my cheek and floated out of the room. "Close the door and turn out the light when you leave, my lovely," I heard her call from the hall.

The combat training began. My tadpole legs were growing longer and stronger. Speech met five days a week. Each week everyone gave a different type of speech: original oratory, persuasive, informative, speeches for special occasions, group presentations, and dramatic readings. My speech class, however, was extended. Sr. Patricia Ann incorporated private elocution lessons, twice a week, into my school day. It wasn't punishment. It was practice. I equated it to rehabilitation. Sister had me recite passages from any number of books. I delivered the speeches of Brutus and Franklin Roosevelt. I read Anne Frank, Elizabeth Barrett Browning, and Emily Dickinson aloud. I was in Wonderland with Alice and voiced both Romeo and Juliet. Then there was Robert Frost (always Robert Frost): his early works, "A Boy's Will," "North of Boston," and "Mountain Interval."

Sometimes, Sister would bring a metronome into the room. Other times she just swatted the side of her habit with a ruler. "Please," she would insist, "let me hear that ending. Again. And again. How does *t-h* sound? The word is *with*, *t-h*, not *wid* with a *d*. Let me hear the *t-h* sound. How does *e-d* sound? Sound it out, my lovely. Let me hear the *e-d*. What is that sound you just made? It should sound like *y* as in *py*, not a as in *pae*. Try it again."

For those not in Advanced English, there was some reprieve, but I was in Sr. Patricia Ann's Advanced English, where she began most class sessions with the preamble:

"Students, this is Advanced English. Not just English, not remedial English—Advanced English. We do more."

With that directive, she would preview the coming attractions. There would be no English mechanics for us. Diagramming was a thing of the past. We would read four books that year and write four book reports. We would explore great literary works: *Beowulf*, Dante's *Inferno*, and Chaucer's *The Canterbury Tales*. We would experience Dickens beyond *Great Expectations* and be introduced to Louisa May Alcott's *Little Women*. Poetry had a more elastic format. A student would begin the class by standing, giving a brief biography of the poet they had selected, and then reciting the poem. A discussion would follow. Reading aloud for a part of the class was expected, and Sr. Patricia Ann would call upon students, at random, to do so.

In Sr. Patricia Ann's world, the Olympic Games were defined as intramural speech meets. These were public speaking contests that occurred each spring between the Catholic schools throughout the state. Students who participated in these events competed before judges in such categories as dramatic readings, poetry, children's works, and original oratory. The finalists within any given category contended for first-, second-, and third-prize ribbons. The winning schools were awarded trophies memorializing the categories and levels that were attained. I did not volunteer to compete. I was conscripted. When Sr. Patricia Ann informed me I would be participating in these contests, I was nervous and unsure.

"Sister, I don't even know what category I will be able to compete in." I pleaded for mercy.

Sr. Patricia Ann wasn't having it. "What do you mean? Poetry, of course. It's poetry."

Practice for these competitions added another evening to my school week. Initially sister selected "Birches" for me to read. I had begun the recitation, "When I see birches bend to left and right, across the lines of straighter darker trees…"

Sister interrupted. "No, no it's not right for you. Not right."

Next, we tried "The Lady of Shalott": "On either side the river lie, long fields of barley and of rye…" I loved this poem. It was music. But Sr. Patricia Ann did not.

"No, no! It's not right for you. Not right!"

I read Carl Sanburg, too rough; Edgar Allen Poe, too macabre; Shelley and Keats, too prim; Gwendolyn Brooks, maybe but maybe not. I was in an echo chamber of no's, seeding me with the hope that I might still escape the entire thing.

But hope faded the afternoon Sr. Pat came charging, book opened. "My lovely, competitions are about winning. We don't compete to reduce our time in purgatory. Ejaculations are for that. We compete to win. I have an idea that may make you a winner. This piece is usually recited by a man, or a boy with a deep voice. But what if we flipped the switch and gave it to a girl, a very skilled girl, who knows how to turn a phrase with emotion and use a pause to punctuate? A girl who has the stage presence, vocal range, and dialect versatility to pull this off."

Her eyes shown with demonic possession. Was I that girl she was talking about, or was someone else in the room? She had never spouted words like this before. It was as if she had entered into a compact with Satan. Sister thrust the book into my hands. "This, my lovely, is what I want you to memorize. It's time to begin." I was staring at James Weldon Johnson's poem, "The Creation."

On April 23, before a panel of six judges and clad in a dark blue dress with sweeping sleeves, I delivered, from memory, the powerful words of Johnson's Genesis. I won the blue first-place ribbon.

Senior Year

High school is about cliques. In the world of girls at St. Patrick's, I can remember three. There was the popular girls' clique. They were usually cheerleaders or very pretty. There was the smart girls' clique. These girls were in the National Honor Society and most of the boring clubs, and they held a lot of the school's offices. There was the snotty girls' clique. Only three girls achieved this standard. These were girls whose fathers commanded middle-class incomes or were some kind of professionals, but the families often had too many children to afford the lives of their Protestant counterparts. These girls were just haughty and resentful that their financial circumstances did not elevate them to the social status they believed they deserved. Even so, they had cars to drive, sneaked cigarettes in the john, and took out-of-state vacations when the school year ended. What other cliques there were, I am not sure, but I am certain there were others.

I had maneuvered myself into the smart girls' clique. We called ourselves the Electric Eleven. *Ocean's Eleven* had been released the past summer. There were similarities. There were eleven of them, and one was a Negro. There were eleven of us, and I was a Negro. We leaned on one another for cohesion and survival. By senior year, we took most of the same classes, compared notes, studied together, ate lunch together, and shared secrets. When I was invited to a sleepover at a friend's house in Raytown, my dad balked, but Momma and my sister intervened. Dad grudgingly allowed me to go.

All eleven of us spent at least an hour together after school each day, five days a week, and four hours on Saturday. It could have been a catholic girls' herd mentality, but I was happy. It was early October. We were rehearsing for the senior play. The play was broadcast as the seniors' gift to the school. This year the senior class would perform *Our Town*. My character was Julia Gibbs.

Sr. Patricia Ann was the director. The stage was in the gym. The football team was winning, and everything was totally about homecoming. These were my awkward moments—those public *exposés* when I realized I could only adapt so much. Girls, even smart girls, were being asked to the homecoming. I had undertaken my amphibian transformation, but I was a different type of tadpole. Tadpoles that looked like me didn't get asked to homecoming. The hardest part was only I seemed to notice.

My ten friends were lounging across the stage, waiting to do what was assigned: read a part, carry a prop, or focus a spotlight.

"Michael asked me," one of them secretly announced in a stage whisper.

"No way." Squeals.

"What did you say?"

"I said yes." Squeals. Squeals are like the tide. They're either high or low. This one was high.

"Mary Pat, aren't you going with Jerry?" And so it went. The roll call and pairing of names followed by high squeals.

Everyone had left. It was getting dark. Dad was coming to get me. Only Sr. Patricia Ann and I were left. She was bent over the stage lip, counting collected scripts.

"What's wrong, my lovely?"

When had she stopped counting scripts and come to me? "Nothing."

"I don't believe that."

"Well, nothing you would understand."

"And why not?"

"Well because…"

"What is because? Because what?"

How could I say this? "Because, well, you're not a young person. And you're not normal. You're a nun…and you're not a Negro."

She paused, took my hand. "Let's just sit here on the ledge of the stage." We did.

"Well, let's see. I have been young, and I have been normal. I do admit I haven't been a Negro. Can you tell me how all that intersects?"

I looked at Sister, confused.

"You know. How does all that come together?"

"It's simple. If I were White, I'd have a date to homecoming. Did you ever go to homecoming?"

"Yes, as a matter of fact, I did. His name was Mark."

"Did you dance with him?"

"As a matter of fact, I did. I even kissed him."

"Oh God!" I was horrified.

"Not God, my lovely, him. Frankly, it doesn't matter if you are Negro or White. Homecomings, proms, these are important times in the lives of young girls. Even young girls who grow up to be Benedictine Sisters." Her smile was packed with empathy. "Here is what I want you to do. First, remember that God knows all things and can do all things. All we have to do is ask. Next, I want you to practice the line from Luke 1:37 that says, 'For nothing will be impossible with God.' Can you say that?"

"Yes."

"Of course you can. For you this is easy. You're the girl who memorized 'The Creation.' So say it."

"For nothing will be impossible with God."

"Next, I want you to go out front and meet your father. So let's jump down from this stage, walk to the door, and say good night."

As I got in Dad's car, I wanted to slit my throat. Why was I spilling such a delicate confidence to a nun? What made me ever think that an abnormal nun would understand being young and Negro?

A week passed. Sr. Patricia Ann and I never again spoke about that conversation. But the next Sunday, Wesley Carpenter, a senior from De La Salle Academy, approached me as my family left 10:00 a.m. Mass.

"I'm sorry," he said, halting us. "I know we haven't talked much." That was the truth. Not since eighth grade. "And this may not be the right time or place. I didn't have a phone number, but I knew for certain you would be here. What I wanted to say was, would you go to your homecoming with me? I have a car."

He seemed to be speaking from a prepared text, but it was working. All I could say was, "You have a car?"

"Yes. Father Henley said I could use his."

Homecoming was great. It's really about the dress. Mine yelled class. Another smart frock from Miss Lottie's collection. I had a loaner date, and he had a loaner car. Most of the time I danced with my girlfriends while he talked sports with the boys whose dates were dancing with their girlfriends. When we did dance, it was fast. At one point the whole dance floor made a line and did the Stroll. That was fun. I didn't plan to kiss Wesley that night. He didn't seem to care. As I glided past Sr. Patrician Ann, who was chaperoning, she smiled but didn't say a word. We both knew two truths: compromise is an art, and nothing will be impossible with God.

Senior year meant status elevation. We were upperclassmen. We ruled. All the underclassmen wanted to be us. My elocution lessons were over. I could now hear when other people didn't speak as I did. Classes were rigorous but not intolerable. French II was an extension of French I. European History expanded American History. More books, poetry, reports, and term papers were required in Advanced English. We read *Lysistrata* as a chorus. Psychology was the individualized version of Sociology. I was not lunatic enough to take Trigonometry. God forbid I carry a slide rule in my notebook all day. Typing and shorthand continued, just in case one of the three career options, teaching, nursing or a secretarial career, that the GATB Test slated for most females, really materialized. Religion class, of course, was always there.

My senior yearbook picture should have read "joiner." I was on the girls' volleyball B team, in the book club, the camera club, the school choir, and the drama club. I was a roving reporter for the school newspaper, and I had proven electable as senior class secretary. Although Sr. Patricia Ann was not my homeroom teacher, I felt closer to her than ever. It was hard to explain, but she seemed to know things. Several of us seemed drawn to her presence. We reflected the light from her star.

When Sr. Patricia Ann asked if we wanted to join the Sodality, all four of us answered yes. This society placed young women under the protection of the Blessed Virgin and chose her as their patron. After our Thursday Sodality meetings, the girls would go to the all-purpose room, where Sister stocked soft drinks and usually had a pizza. While we ate, Sr. Patricia Ann told us beautiful stories. She was a one-woman show, voicing and gesturing for every character. Sometimes we girls would make up stories—the four of us. It was our version of Catholic school improv. Someone would start a tale of some kind, and the next person would continue it, acting out the parts.

When Dad picked me up one Thursday, I could tell he was concerned.

"What are you all doing in there every evening?"

"We're telling stories."

"Well, that sure sounds like one to me."

When spring arrived, almost everything was coming up roses. In March, I won the religion contest delivering a contrasting and comparing oration on the Roman and Orthodox Rites of the Catholic Church. In April, I won the State Intermural speech meet in the category of original oratory for a piece I wrote and delivered on "Social Justice Realized Through Public Accommodations."

May in Kansas City is like June in Illinois, pleasant without humidity. The month began with the Spring Festival. Sr. Patricia Ann had selected *Robin Hood* for us to perform. I had tried out for Maid Marian, but the part went to Sonia Barton. The role required a soprano. I was a mezzo-soprano and so was chosen to be Dame Durden, an innkeeper. Instead of Robin Hood, I would play opposite Ben Grotosky, who portrayed the sheriff of Nottingham. Sr.

Patricia Ann said our two roles provided the comic relief in the operetta. Ben was a linebacker on the school's football team. Sweet and blemished, I wondered if he detected the nuanced type casting here. The Negro girl and the Polish boy providing the comic relief. I had seen those movies with Alfalfa in the *Our Gang* episodes on television and Rochester with *Jack Benny*. I wasn't sure how I felt about being comic relief. Was the casting intentional or me just being overly sensitive? Ben probably wasn't digesting the subtleties of it anyway. He was all absorbed in being a linebacker. It hadn't escaped me though. Recently, I had begun to hear the whispered jokes about his tribe, and boy were they ever funny. How many Poles did it take to screw in a light bulb, or hang wallpaper? I had laughed at those jokes, even told a few myself. It made me feel as if I were a member of the club, that I belonged. After four years as my classmates, several students held the conviction that they had earned the privilege to tell me the joke about why Negro people had white feet. I had laughed, but it wasn't funny. At least the Polish jokes weren't about me.

I sized up Ben again. No, he didn't get it. He was a linebacker on the varsity football team. That was all he knew. Ben and I had a dance routine together. The scene was outside of the inn that I ran. It was one of those numbers where the acting ensemble was on stage. Ben and I were out front. The music began. I went through the paces. I took several steps, a twirl with Ben, and then I sashayed stage right. Ben whistled, and I ran back into his arms for a lift. Sr. Patricia Ann stopped everything.

"No, no, no. What is that? Please stop pointing your toe. Who do you think you are, Maria Tall Chief? Your dance is comic relief, my lovely, comic relief, not Swan Lake. Here is the scene. You are both a little tipsy from the brew. Everyone's a little tipsy. You are not prancing around the stage like an Arabian pony. You are staggering. Ben, you whistle. She comes back. You grab her and roll her across your chest. You roll her, don't lift her, and when he rolls you, your legs and feet flail in the air, not point toward the sky. This is comic relief, people. Do you get it? Comic relief."

I guessed I could play comic relief and not be oversensitive about the role. When Momma saw the dance, she said I reminded her of Ginger Rogers. My sister said it was like American Bandstand. Dad insisted the movie, *The Adventures of Robin Hood,* was better.

The next social item of my senior year to check off was the prom. Wesley was back on board. It would be a sequel to homecoming. Wesley, once again, drove Father Henley's car. For me, it was all about the gown. I picked a formal that weighed more than me. It was strapless, which meant, for the sake of modesty, I would have to find a cover-up. I selected a stole with cap sleeves. It came in very handy when Wesley spun me around. I moved, but the dress remained stationary. The stole preserved my virtue. At points, several kids asked if we were going steady. To the uninformed, I only smiled and shrugged my shoulders. Still, the question made me feel so very assimilated. The tadpole adaptation had worked.

It would be our last Sodality meeting of the school year. After her closing prayer, Sr. Patricia Ann announced that those of us who could, should adjourn to the all-purpose room for a vital project. The usual girls responded. The tables in the all-purpose room were pushed to its center, making one work space. In the middle of each table was a stack of folded sheets.

"We've been asked to send bandages to Molokai for the lepers. Some of us will tear the sheets into strips, and the rest of us will roll the strips into bandages and place the rolls in one of these boxes."

We had all done this several times before. In grade school, I had seen *Ben-Hur* and felt sorry for the lepers.

Sister continued, "Since we want to keep the bandages clean, we won't have pizza. Also, instead of impromptu stories, let's do rounds of poetry." We all agreed and set about our work.

Sr. Patricia Ann began reciting John Donne's poem, "For Whom the Bell Tolls." Anyone who wanted could join in. We had gone through several poetry rounds. Gloria Bailey was delving deeply into being dark and dreary, weak and weary when Sr. Rose Calahan stepped in. She bent and whispered to Sr. Patricia Ann. Sr. Rose Calahan next walked over to Mary Pat, who was stuffing boxes.

"Come with me, child" was all she said.

Several days later the senior class was wedged together in Saint James's Church for the funeral of Mary Pat's mother. Several of the Benedictine Sisters were there as well. At the beginning of the year, I had attended a sleepover at Mary Pat's. She was one of eight siblings.

"We almost take a whole pew at Mass," her baby sister had proudly proclaimed. All ten of the Electric Eleven were crying, some audibly. Saint James was only four blocks from school, and so the entire senior class walked back. I ran to catch Sr. Patricia Ann, who was walking alone. Her eyes were stained pink from crying.

"Gosh, Sister, this is just awful."

"Yes, it is, my lovely."

"I wouldn't know what to do if I lost my mother."

"It is, without a doubt, one of the hardest of all losses."

It was incomprehensible to me that a young person could lose a parent. I was traumatized.

"Sister, I'm not sure what to do. This just seems that it shouldn't have happened."

"You have been dedicated to the Blessed Mother. Recite the Memorare, my lovely. That should help you."

I needed to know. "Sister, will Mary Pat ever be happy again?"

"She can be."

"You mean with time, when God washes away her tears?"

"I mean whenever she chooses to be. Happiness is a choice."

Kansas

Atchison is only thirty-five miles from Kansas City, but to me, it seemed like light years. The people I knew when I was a young girl rarely traveled. There were not the super highways then that exist today. For Negro people, car travel was hampered by inaccessibility to hotels and motels, making sleeping, eating, and relieving oneself extremely challenging. People filled with wanderlust would take the occasional good-time trip to Saint Louis for jazz, gambling, and whatever. But people only went to Kansas when they had to. The state's geography is overwhelmingly flat. In the summer, it's a skillet. It is frequently slashed by tornadoes in the spring and is the chamber pot for snow in the winter. There is just not a lot to love about Kansas—except for Atchison. The birthplace of Amelia Earhart is puffy with hills and sits on the Missouri River. Staring out the window of Dad's station wagon, I could see the train station in the center of town. Students were arriving from everywhere. Boys came to attend St. Benedicts', the all-male school at one end of town. The girls came to attend Mount Saint Scholastica on the hill at the other.

There had been a robust conversation around the dinner table on what college I should attend. Dad wanted me to go to Lincoln University in Jefferson City. It was a historically Black college: an exposure Daddy felt I desperately needed. Mom was promoting Oberlin, a well-known college culturally sensitive to Black learners. She believed that my hybrid education would make me a perfect fit. What was more, she had gotten a new job and could help shoulder the expenses. My sister wanted me to go to Spelman. She contended that I was an all-girl-school type who didn't function well around boys.

I was having none of it. "It's my life," I protested, "and I want to go to Mount Saint Scholastica. It's Benedictine. I know the Benedictines, and one of my friends, Mary Cecelia, is going with me as my roommate. If I can't go to the Mount, then I will accept the job offer at the telephone company."

That shocked them all.

We all batted around the pros and cons. In the end, the triumvirate yielded to me. I would be the first college graduate in the family. Why start me out stressed? They further concluded that Mount Saint Scholastica would be cheaper, would be closer, and would be all girls. All these reasons were true, but I had reasons of my own. Mount Saint Scholastica was the wellspring that bred and nourished the likes of Sr. Patricia Ann. What an amazing place it had to be. I wanted my voice to sing like hers. I wanted to be where she had been, to study and to grow where she had come of age. I wanted to be sheltered in a place filled with care and concern, a place that might answer the gnawing question I was asking.

"Hello, my lovely, hello my North Star."

There she was, materialized before my very eyes. It was my second day at the Mount. Mary Cecelia and I were wallowing in homesickness but had gone to Ricardi Center, as instructed, to register for our classes. We were processing down a line of tables facing one black habit after another when that indelible smile stopped us. It was Sr. Patricia Ann. She was beaming. I had asked Momma about what could make a person that happy. She replied, "Hadacol. The best vitamin supplement in the world. I feel like that when I take Hadacol. Two tablespoons will do it every time."

"Sister, what are you doing here? Why aren't you at St. Patrick's?"

Sister signed my schedule as she spoke. "I am here because, my lovely, Mother Superior reassigned me to the Mount. I am your English and drama professor and your spiritual advisor. Here is your schedule. Now move on." Be careful what you pray for!

It took Mary Cecelia and me two days to recover from the shock. But once we did, I interpreted Sr. Patricia Ann's presence as a sign. For the first time, I allowed myself to say something unspeakable to Mary Cecelia.

"C, I think I have a vocation. I think I may want to be a nun."

"Jesus, Mary, and Joseph," Mary Cecelia whispered. "A Negro nun."

"I know."

"You would be the first."

"I know. Is it crazy?"

"Yes."

"Is it insane?"

"But if you're serious, I'm going to do it with you." Mary Cecelia's comments were earnest.

"What are you saying?"

"I'm saying,"—she straightened her back—"that I'm going to be a nun."

"That's crazy."

"Listen. If I don't, you'll never make it through. You're just learning to eat White food. Remember the Borscht at my house?"

"Yeah, I do." A cold memory.

"And the quiche at Mary Pat's." It was true—White food was an acquired taste.

"OK, OK. Here's the plan. We spend our first year just like regular students, and our sophomore year, we'll enter the novitiate. That's the plan, and we tell no one."

"That's the plan, and we tell no one," Mary Cecilia pledged.

We hugged to seal our compact.

Freshman year at Mount Saint Scholastica had been remarkable. It had proven to be a time of discovery, freedom, friendship-making, and introspection. Sr. Patricia Ann was there but not with the intensity of high school. Her English class was excellent, but she could have been any exceptional English teacher. We sampled a host of drama works in that class from Tennessee Williams, to Edward Albee, and Anton Chekhov. Drama was only for a semester. I had hoped to take an advanced drama class with Sr. Patricia Ann but found, at the point of scheduling, that the class was not being offered. Sr. Patricia Ann was nowhere to be found on my second semester schedule. I rarely sought spiritual advice, since I did not want to betray my secret. With

parents would reciprocate with a week in the summer at the lake and a week over the Thanksgiving holidays in Chicago.

I could not explain why Sister kept invading my mind, but she was there. I had heard very little about the Mount once I had left. In time life layers over memory, so much had to be forgotten. The real world was about dealing with certain imperatives: finish college, get a good job, get a good husband, have children, buy a house. I knew where I had to go and what I had to do. To not achieve one of these milestones in the expected time frame would subject me to unending inquisitions by everyone's mother. The Bataan Death March paled against the questioning pursuit of these women. That was all behind me now. My world could again welcome Sr. Patricia Ann. There were things I wanted her to know. The day-by-day way she had grown my self-confidence and taught me poetry and speech had caused a sea change in my life.

When I mentioned going to the Mount, my sister's first response was, "Go where?" I think she thought I was considering hiking. But as I unpacked my memories, she got it.

"That's an easy trip. The roads to Atchison are much better now."

With that, I slipped into her car, prepared to journey back in time. But time is a ravisher. Atchison was a town on life support. The hustle and bustle had evaporated. The train station was there, but it appeared vacant. Downtown was a drying prune. When we tried to go toward Eighth Street, we entered decaying neighborhoods. There were mismatched chairs in the yards; barbecue grills were scattered here and there. My shock was audible.

"What happened?"

My sister did not try to explain. The song we had sung as students with such gusto, "High on a hill in Atchison there stands MSSC," seemed this day a faint, evaporating voice that matched the campus. Many buildings stood vacant or were gone. As we approached the abandoned administration building, a second gasp escaped.

"Are you all right?"

"I think so."

Mount Saint Scholastica's statue still stood sentry over the entrance driveway. The hill, with thirty years to refocus, seemed more like a mound. But the lawn was neat and green. Flowers were still vibrant but would soon fade in the autumn light. The modern library, dedicated the year I left, looked anemic. I was not sure what it was now, but surely it was not a library.

The car came to a standstill near the administration building. My heart did the same.

"Are we getting out?"

"Yes." My sister rested her hand on the door handle after turning off the ignition.

"When?"

"Now."

"Listen, we don't have to do this."

"Yes, we do."

With that, I opened the car door and ascended the granite steps. Our footfalls echoed like thunder as we entered the empty foyer. Across from me was the auditorium. I remembered now: musical performances, convocations, guest speakers. I cracked the door. The wooden chairs had disappeared, replaced with cushioned ones.

"May I help you?"

Both my sister and I had been peering into the auditorium and were now startled by the nun's question. We knew she was a nun because no one else dressed like that. They had mastered understatement. She wore a crucifix dangling from a chain. I was speechless.

"Yes, Sister," my sister replied. "We are here to see…" She looked at me. "Who are we here to see?"

"Sr. Patricia Ann."

"Sr. Patricia Ann?" I watched the confusion wash across the nun's face.

"Yes, Sr. Patricia Ann," I repeated. What was wrong? Had she died?

"Yes, Sr. Patricia Ann," My sister confirmed.

We were soon corrected in a manner that only a nun can.

"My dears, Sr. Patricia Ann is no longer Sr. Patricia Ann."

"She isn't?" I became fearful. What did that mean?

"We have now all assumed our birth names. Sr. Patricia Ann is now Sr. Teresa O'Malley."

My sister and I looked at one another, relieved. The nun's tone seemed to suggest she was in a witness protection program. I cleared my throat and asked, "Well, is she here, Sr. Teresa O'Malley?"

"Are you one of her former students?" Her eyes were searing our faces.

"Yes, Sister."

"One moment, and I will call and see if she's in."

After what seemed like forever, a shaft of light widened into an open door at the end of the hall. A woman, far shorter than I remembered, was walking toward me wearing a simple blue suit. The smile was still brilliant. The voice was still music. The air was lighter. She was making an entrance.

"Hello, my lovely. I thought I had lost you forever."

"You could never lose me." I began to cry. My sister appeared nauseous. I hugged Sr. Teresa O'Malley. I felt the hump in her back. When had she become human?

Sr. Teresa invited us to stay for Vespers and dinner. I had never been inside the sisters' chapel. There were opposing prayer stalls arranged like stadium seating. We sat beside Sr. Teresa reciting the psalms. After dinner, Sister and I began a conversation that would last for twenty more years. In the intervening two decades, Sr. Teresa O'Malley and I would experience seismic shifts from teacher and acolyte to the exhilarating experience of new friends discovering each other. There was so much about her, now that she was human, that I wanted to know.

Did the homogenizing spawned by the Second Vatican Council initiate an interior movement causing many priests and nuns to reassess their circumstances and exit their vows? Clearly whatever happened had profound impacts on the convent. Their numbers had shrunk. The median age of the nuns was rising with more and more sisters requiring health care and assisted living. The Catholic educational institutions they had staffed, scaffolded on low wages, were disintegrating. Most of their high schools had closed. The Benedictines, ever resourceful, had coalesced their resources, creating one coeducational university at St. Benedict's College and abandoning the academic and residential facilities at the Mount. Mount Saint Scholastica had become a major employer, as jobs once performed by novices, postulates, and professed nuns in the care and service of their community were now filled by Atchison residents.

With the demise of Catholic high schools and the college, most nuns moved into the public or private sector to work. Sr. Teresa had worked in Kansas City at the community college and at a private college in Saint Louis. Living in community away from the mother house had to be redefined because survival of the principal community was paramount. Some sisters accepted job offers as far away as Colorado and Minnesota. They lived alone and were indistinguishable from any other single woman. Whenever possible, they accepted jobs in towns and places where they could live in twos and threes.

Most had never imagined living this way. For many, it was too secular a lifestyle, and so they left. Others, like Mary Cecelia, would never become a postulate.

The deep lines pulled her face into a smile. "What a time," Sister remembered. "What a time."

"But you stayed."

"Yes, I stayed."

"Do you in any way regret it?"

Sr. Teresa O'Malley smiled and squeezed my hand. "Oh, my lovely, you must always remember, happiness is a choice."

The dance ends.

DANCE NUMBER THREE: THE TWIST

The Song: "Hit the Road, Jack"
The Dancer: Margaret Graham (Peggy)

The Observance

I sat behind Lester. He vacillated between nervousness and exhaustion. The day before had been the wake. I couldn't make that. There was a meeting with my regional manager that day. These meetings occurred every month. Trying to dispel all negative notions that I was an unqualified affirmative-action hire drove me to continually try and make a good impression. So I remained in Chicago.

I didn't love Saint Louis, but Peggy did. It undeniably had more going on than Springfield, her hometown, or Kansas City, mine. She was a teacher now, filling one of the GATB test's three dominant career options for women. Peggy had mulled over the possibility of grad school. She was intrigued with the role of the high school counselor. But other things happened first: the wedding, the house, the kids—death.

Peggy was only thirty-two years old when breast cancer claimed her. The trip to death had been hard and painful, filled with toxic medicines, mutilation, and charred skin. At our last visit, she lifted her hospital gown to show me the site. My beautiful young friend revealed a cavern in her chest and singed skin. In time, she said, there would be a prosthesis of some kind covering grafted, fresh skin. But time dodged Peggy and never came.

Here we sat. Lester, four kids, two sets of parents, and all the others they describe in the obituary as "left to mourn." These other mourners—friends, colleagues, and eclectic acquaintances—were seated near or behind me. Peggy died during summer vacation, so her fourth-grade class was not there.

Still, the church seemed full. Many, like myself, had come for the priest to attribute meaning to such a young and senseless death. For Catholics, everything is a mass. When one died, it used to be termed the Requiem Mass.

I don't think they call it that anymore, but it's still a mass. In the Catholic liturgy, ritual trumps innovation. It helps with learning disabilities.

Wearing a white chasuble, the priest celebrated Mass. How many people had this priest buried? How many times had he stood offering solace and an explanation? The church had tried to bracket our humanity, place us between the parentheses of baptism and the anointing of the sick. In the end, after all the millions of homilies, the question remained unanswered. "Why?" It was Father's job, yet again, to supply the congregates an answer. He would give it a try.

"Remember man that thou art dust. And unto dust thou shalt return."

Not a good liftoff, especially if you were Lester with an eight-, six-, four-, and two-year-old.

Father spoke about the cycle of life and the inevitability of death. Peggy's life, he said, was the endless reenactment of the divine plan. Now God had called her home to be with Him.

Why I asked, would God do that? And why now? I wasn't the only one questioning the timing. Peggy's mother had glanced down the pew at the four young children marooned with Lester, who was totally coming apart. The hallmark of Catholic funerals is that usually you can keep it together. If you didn't know it was a funeral, you might think it was a seminar. You never see the body during the funeral, unlike some Black Protestant denominations where everyone processes past the coffin for one last look and the grieving family can collapse in the casket atop their dearly departed.

Catholic funerals are very antiseptic. There are white cloths and drapes everywhere. Lester was trying to keep it together and was supported by Peggy's sister when he erupted into a sobbing shimmy. I knew what he was thinking: "How the hell am I going to manage these four kids?" I wondered the same.

The homily was drawing to a close. "Remember. God never gives us more than we can bear. And though it may seem dark today, and we are broken by our loss, our God has promised, and he does not fail. Joy will come in the morning."

Not tomorrow. Not for Lester.

I left the church after the recessional and walked to the family's limousine. Lester, the kids, and Peggy's parents were waiting to follow the hearse. Lester lowered the window. He dabbed his eyes.

"She was beautiful, wasn't she?"

"Beautiful," I answered him.

"I'm going to miss her."

"We all are."

Lester swallowed a sob to speak. "Are you going to the cemetery?"

"No. That's why I wanted to say goodbye now. I have to get back. But I'll keep in touch." I threw several kisses to everyone. Feeling the mounting pressure from people pressing behind me, I wiggled free of the mourners and drove to the airport. On my way there I replayed Father's homily. Father had it wrong. Peggy was not living out the divine plan. Had he known her, he would realize that Peggy was the Giving Tree. To all who knew her, she gave. When she expired last Friday, she had nothing left to give.

As my car pushed through the sweltering Saint Louis heat, I began to experience a deep separation anxiety. At that moment, I wanted to return to Mount Saint Scholastica, to continue the experience in which I was enmeshed before it was aborted. I wanted to know what Sr. Patricia Anne had known, to be anchored the way she was. But I wasn't Dorothy. I couldn't go back to Kansas.

I had transformed and transferred myself into another world. I lived there now, breathing in a different atmosphere. It had all come at a cost. It had taken precious time and extreme effort to become that amphibian in high school. During the bad times, there was always home—the neighborhood—where I could replenish my spirit and repair my self-concept. But the neighborhood couldn't hold. Where was Mary Cecilia, my friend with whom I had made a compact only to abandon it, never explaining the why? That promise couldn't hold. I had met Peggy at the Mount. She was fresh then and healthy. Sickness had ravished her body, decaying it months before she died. She couldn't hold. What did *holding* mean anyway? Apparently nothing.

The Dance

High on a Hill in Atchison

It was decided that only my dad would take me to Mount Saint Scholastica. I had boxes, luggage, sacks, and a foot locker. That was the reason we all gave why only he should come. There was not enough room for Momma and my sister in the car. It was a convenient cover to protect us all from the imminent breakdown that was sure to occur. My sister and I had already experienced a mini-seizure when I entered her room and asked her to safeguard my stuffed autograph hound that my senior classmates had signed. We began shaking and crying as if doomsday were upon us. Neither of us was capable of speaking; we just mumbled and shook. It took Dad to say, "Enough of this, already," forcibly separating us and stowing me in the car with my belongings. His stalwart armor did not last long. We had off-loaded my luggage to a designated senior class assistant and were saying our goodbyes when he commenced with sobbing and shaking. I immediately followed. The entire scene was nothing short of pitiful. It took a very stout, strong nun to pry us apart, assuring him that I would survive. I was toggled to another senior, who promised me that in a few days all would be fine. That senior steered me to my room.

Peggy lived in the room next door and stood watching as I came hobbling and eye swabbing. Her expression sounded an alarm, seeming to ask, "What happened to you?" I pretended not to notice her and turned quickly into my room. Several minutes had passed when a knock came to my door. I opened the door. It was she. "Hi, I just wanted to introduce myself. I'm Margaret Graham, but my friends call me Peggy."

Peggy was the other African American girl in our freshman class. Not the other Black student. There was also an African from Africa. She was Peggy's roommate. Her name was Adia. She and Peggy were our neighbors.

The dorm rooms were outfitted with two twin beds, two desks, two chests of drawers, a wall closet with sliding doors, and one sink and mirror. It was efficient and accommodated all our needs.

I told Mary Cecilia about our two dark neighbors when she arrived and was unpacking. I warned her that one smiled a lot. The other looked and smelled strange. I declined to rush and make friends with them, as Mary Cecilia didn't know anyone either, and my commitment was to her. There was another thing. If I paired Mary Cecilia and myself with the two of them, she would be the minority. White people did not know how to handle that. She would have to become a tadpole. Metamorphosis wasn't easy.

The girl who didn't look strange was constantly telegraphing smiles every time I saw her in the hall. I was in the hall often enough that first day, as that was the route to the bathroom, showers, and exits. Each girl was immediately expected to assume personal responsibility for her belongings. This expectation kept girls in motion, moving boxes, suitcases, and trunks. Without parents, the girls would instinctively learn to depend on one another.

I should not have been surprised when the smiler poked her head into our room.

"Hi, I'm finished. Can I help you guys?"

"Hi," Mary Cecelia responded, the first to return the smile. "No. I think I'm good."

I wasn't good. Sr. Mary Beatrice, the RA for the floor, had patrolled the halls, giving us room demonstrations on how to do a square fold with our bedsheets so they would remain flat and tight. I was failing miserably with my bed-making attempts.

"Hey, hey, let me. It seems complicated, but it's the way they make beds in hospitals. By the way, my name is Margaret, but my friends call me Peggy," she said, addressing Cecilia. "My mom's a nurse. She has us make our beds like this at home." Voilà! There it was. Peggy had produced a perfectly made bed and a picture-perfect smile.

Peggy was so easy to like, even if you didn't want to like her. In her mind's eye, it seemed we were all there in that place and therefore connected like beads on a rosary. So stop wondering who her dentist was, dispense with the formalities, and go straight to the friendship.

Even Mary Cecelia was drawn in. Peggy was a connector. Soon all eight of the rooms on our floor were friendship joined. We were sharing clothes, shoes, and doing communal hair backcombing to get that identical bouffant style. Adia's hair was a natural afro, but we backcombed it as well. We ate at the same tables, sat together at mass, watched the same soap operas, and shared the same package of cigarettes. When our radios played, Ray Charles singing "Hit the Road, Jack," we blasted the volume on every single one, positioned ourselves in the hall, and did the twist.

Each week I ran to the hall phone to call Mom and Dad and to gauge how much my sister was missing me. Each month I haunted the mail center, waiting for a care package from home filled with goodies that could be shared.

Undeniably I was drawing closer and closer to Peggy. There was something about her. She had excellent karma working for her. Every part of her being suggested an old soul. She was a beacon, guiding me through freshman year.

"You can't stay in your room all the time. This weekend you are going out with Lester and me. Remember he's the guy I met last weekend at the St. Benedict Sock Hop." Peggy was constantly scolding me about being a hermit. She did not know I was going to be a nun. I had equated that decision with self-imposed gender separation and did not venture out.

"You met a guy?"

"Yes. I met a guy." She was bubbling.

"Is he a Negro guy?"

"Is he a Negro guy? Let me see. Yes, he is."

"Wow. I haven't seen any Negro guys."

"That is because you are not seeing anyone. You don't leave your room."

"That's because I'm studying. You have no idea—metaphysics, biology—and you don't know Sr. Patricia Ann the way I do." Peggy was dismissing my words as I spoke them.

"That's not it. You're scared."

"Scared? Scared?"

"Mm-hmm."

"Scared?"

"That's what I said."

"Tell me, why would I be scared?"

"Well, that I don't know. But you are."

"And how would you know that? And would you please stop rummaging through my closet?"

"Maybe it's the clothes that frighten you. They frighten me. Give me a minute. I'll be right back."

Fifteen minutes later she was back.

"Here. Fitzpatrick said you could wear this."

"Joanne Fitzpatrick?"

"Yes." Peggy was unpinning a lemon-yellow wool pleated skirt. It had a matching floral sweater. The outfit was to die for.

"You're begging people for clothing for me?"

"Not people. Just Fitzy. You're about her size. For sure you can't go out with me with anything in there." She pointed to my closet. I couldn't believe it. She had just dissed my entire wardrobe. Revenge would be mine.

"Well, you don't seem to care about what that nappy-headed roommate of yours wears."

"You mean Adia?"

"Adia, Madia, whatever her name is."

"She's African. It isn't the same."

"It certainly isn't. Where does she shop, Goodwill? That get-up she had on today is Purple Heart Veterans' or something."

"Adia, for your information, is from a very poor village. Before she came to the Mount, she had to walk two miles one way every morning, collecting firewood and water so that her mother could make breakfast for the family. She is at Mount Saint Scholastica because the Kennedy Foundation selected several young people from her village and are paying for their college education. When she graduates, she's going to take a master's and a PhD in political science. Her dream is to return to her country, become involved in the political process, and help others to have a better life."

Could I have felt any smaller?

"I didn't know that."

"That's why you need to come out of your room."

I went with Peggy on her date. The date mates were Adia, Lester from Saint Benedict's, Peggy, and myself. We walked into town and caught the showing of *Breakfast at Tiffany's*. If Lester had a problem with the three-to-one odds, he never uttered a word.

Where did Peggy's wisdom reside, and how had she come to acquire it? On issues large and small, she seemed to have an answer. It was like having a friend who was an oracle. There was the day I stepped into her dorm room. She was standing there, still getting dressed.

"I'm sorry," I apologized, "but you said come in."

"Why are you staring at me like that? I'm not naked."

She certainly wasn't. She seemed to be wearing a full body cast.

"Peggy, why are you wearing that?"

"What?"

"That." I wanted to touch it but was frightened to do so.

"You mean my girdle?"

"That's your girdle? It's all the way down to your knees."

"Of course it is. It should be. Don't you wear a girdle?"

"No."

"That explains why your stomach pouts out. How do you hold up your hose? I mean when you wear them?"

"With a garter belt."

"Oh, girl, no, girl. That is all wrong. You want a girdle like this, and here's why. Girdles keep your organs in place, hold them exactly where they should be. You may think I'm kidding, but if you don't have a girdle, your stuff could fall out."

"What?"

"I'm serious. My mom's a nurse. She said she had seen it in older women. They get older, and out it comes. You need a girdle to keep it in place. A girdle makes your periods easier and helps with childbirth."

"Your mom told you that?"

"For real. And here's another thing—girdles keep you from shaking all over the place. I'm sure you've seen it when you're walking down the street behind some woman, and her butt looks like two boys boxing. That won't happen with a girdle. And look at this:"—Peggy lifted the lace trim that covered her leg—"I can clip my hose right here to these. A girdle is a miracle."

The next weekend Peggy and I walked to town, and we bought me my first all-purpose Warner girdle.

Peggy was that way. She just knew things. Like the fact that the tapioca pudding served perpetually in the cafeteria was there to fight any passion impulses we girls might feel, or that nail polish could stop runs in your hose.

I was even beginning to like Adia. There were cultural differences, I admit, but Joanne Fitzpatrick was from New Jersey, and she seemed odd as well. Peggy, on the other hand, accepted Adia and me as her self-improvement projects. For whatever reason, Peggy concluded we were off the fashion radar and needed to be reprogrammed and returned to the fold. For her to do this required major makeovers. She took us to the local drug store, where she bought Maybelline eyeliner and mascara to make our eyes stand out. In the end, Adia looked like a sarcophagus cover and I resembled a Keane painting. Whenever we appeared in public, Peggy endeavored to borrow clothing from the closets of others.

Sometimes in the evenings, I would go to Peggy's room to discuss major philosophical and social issues. Our conversations were stimulating, with both girls helping me perceive the world in different ways. Civil Rights was emerging as a social movement.

"Why do some people hate other people?" I pondered aloud.

"I think it's because people are afraid of people they have hurt," Peggy responded. "I think they know it's not right, and at some point, they understand that the people they have hurt will retaliate and hurt them."

"It's hard to know. My people say only the grass knows how it feels when the elephant stomps."

"Uh-huh," both Peggy and I rejoined.

"I think people are afraid of us because they don't understand us," I volunteered.

Peggy added, "It's because they are never around us. That is why they fear us."

"I think that is true," said Adia. "If a blind man pretends he is sleeping, what does he see if he is not sleeping?"

"Uh-huh," we repeated.

Another conversation addressed the issue of economic disparity. "Why do you think it is," Peggy wondered, "that resources are not proportionately distributed among people?"

"Do you mean," I inquired, "why some people have more than others, giving them a higher social class or status?"

"Yes," Peggy responded. "That's what I mean."

Adia, we could tell, had been thinking about it. "If you pound a potato on the top of a leaf and make soup in a peanut shell, the person who is fed will be full."

"Uh-huh," we reiterated. What in the world did that even mean?

On a more personal note, I observed one evening, "I wonder if Alice Tyson likes me? She sometimes seems so demeaning."

Peggy immediately understood. "Yeah, I know what you mean. She's made snide comments to me."

Adia reassured us, "Please don't be bothered by this. A tree that cannot support your weight when you rest on it cannot kill you when it falls on you."

"Uh-huh," we agreed.

One of our last memorable conversations was about women's rights.

"Do you think," Peggy questioned, "that women will ever achieve equal status to men? I mean equal jobs, equal pay, and equal acceptance?"

"It may take a while," I assured her, "but I think it should happen in ten years."

It was Adia who explained in ways we never could. "You cannot carry elephant's meat on your head and then dig the ground with your toe for cricket meat."

"Uh-huh." We were baffled.

Freshman year became a time of emerging expectations. Everything seemed possible. Ideas of freedom and opportunity were exploding in Atchison and the world. Voices were rising from the South and the North protesting racial injustice. The Second Vatican Council was ushering in a renewal of staid Catholicism. Adia was there to explain it all. The year had been so rich and rewarding, I didn't want it to end. But end it did. The last evening before I left the Mount, Peggy and I sat on the stoop of our Kremeter Hall Dorm. "I have a secret to tell you," she whispered.

My eyes popped, waiting to hear. "Lester and I are going steady," she confided.

"I have a secret to tell you," I confessed.

"What is it?" she prodded. "Well it's..." There it was, sitting in my mouth, the words ready to be said.

"I bought my kid sister a girdle, so her stuff won't fall out."

"Good for you. We have to take care of each other. Can't wait until I see you next year."

Till Death Do Us Part

Peggy's wedding was in Springfield, Missouri. Her family had long ago established a respected reputation in the Black community. Peggy's mother was a nurse, and her father, a mechanic who owned his shop. The generation before them had been land-owning farmers. The Grahams were reputed pillars who gave freely of their time and money to support several worthy causes.

The wedding was a village festival. An eclectic assembly of people were there, with everyone wishing them well. It was an afternoon nuptial. I was in her bridal party. After the rice throwing, everyone got into their cars to follow the bride and groom's car through the town in a honking parade. Peggy, radiant, was smiling, waving, and throwing kisses. Her sister was standing beside me as we watched Peggy and Lester dance their first dance.

"Aren't they the perfect couple?" her sister gushed.

"Oh my God, yes."

When the toast came, Peggy pledged to Lester, "You are all that I want and need. You complete me."

He replied, "Peggy, my dream every day will be to see you at my side, even when I am old and gray."

They hooked arms and sipped champagne. Glasses began to clang.

Lester was a chemist. An excellent opportunity presented itself in Saint Louis, and so they moved.

When I married three summers later, Peggy was there. She had one daughter and was pregnant with her second child. The night before the wedding, she came to my parents' home bearing a wrapped gift. With a sly glance and a devilish smile, she handed me the box.

"This is for you."

"What is it?"

"Let's go to your bedroom. I don't want everyone to know, if you know what I mean." I didn't, but the look in her eye told me I wanted to.

We sneaked up the stairs. Peggy closed the door, still smiling that Cheshire cat grin.

"OK, stop it. You're making me so nervous. What is it?"

"Open it," Peggy prodded. "Open it!"

I unwrapped the package and lifted the Emery, Bird, Thayer box lid. There, nestled in white tissue paper, was a piece of froth. I lifted it up by the scalloped neckline, which was all that I could see. As I held it, I recognized a hem.

"Is that the end of this?"

"Dangerous, isn't it? It's a negligee. Doesn't it get your blood pumping?"

"Who designed this, Frederick's of Hollywood? It's only a collar and a hem. You had this gift wrapped? You could've wrapped it in a Kleenex."

"What are you, nuts? It's a honeymoon. It doesn't get any better than this. Look how sheer this is. It looks like it was spun from angel's hair. What had you planned to wear, flannel pajamas?"

I was replacing the angel hair when my hand hit something else in the box. I pulled out a tissue-wrapped package. Peggy began to laugh.

"OK. So what is this?"

She drew a breath, then sprawled across my bed, shaking with laughter. "I swear, you're going to give me a miscarriage. I swear you are." The bed was vibrating from her shaking.

I opened the small box and saw its contents.

"You're insane. Completely insane." As I lifted the box of Blue Seal Petroleum Jelly, even I had to laugh.

"Just didn't want you to have to 'Stop! In the Name of Love.'" With that, we both sang a few bars from the Supremes' hit, halting as they did with outstretched arms.

As I walked down the aisle, I spied Peggy at the altar rail, in my brides-maid lineup. When I glanced at her, she returned a wicked wink.

As two married women, we resolved that our families would spend Easter weekends together. I had relocated with my husband to Chicago. Her family was in Saint Louis. The plan was to alternate the Easter holiday between the two cities. We were both couples who owned homes and held hefty mortgages.

It was everything to be young, gifted, and Black as well as gainfully employed. Peggy taught school, a profession that perfectly fit her require-ments to be home in the late afternoon with her children and her penchant for autumn pregnancies and summer deliveries. Peggy was pregnant with her third child that Easter when they came to visit. Peggy had a girl and a boy and was expanding with her third.

All our children loved the Easter holiday visits. Peggy's children were free spirits reared according to Dr. Spock. This gave them tremendous license to act out and question, to enter into adult conversations, and to demand expla-nations by the parents to the children.

My management career required a longer work day and no summer vaca-tion. This contoured my parenting style to be less accommodating and more direct. I found such phrases as, "because I said so" and "don't let me have to tell you twice," more efficient than extended explanations. When Peggy's kids visited our home, my children interpreted this as the Emancipation Proclamation. Control vanished. My children engaged with hers in con-tinuous 5K relays around the house, refused to eat the planned meals, and emitted primal sounds I had never heard. Each Easter, as I watched these children pummel stuffed bunnies, vie for plastic-covered Easter eggs, and jettison jelly beans, I wondered what had happened to the civilized, good old days when parents bought their children live, pastel-colored baby chickens from Parkview.

With Extra Strength Tylenol, I could muffle the cacophony, but nothing comforted my husband. Every Easter holiday caused him to grow more catatonic. During these episodes, only his eyes could move.

After that last Easter visit, I tactfully arranged for the joint family Easter holiday to be celebrated as a biannual event, giving Peggy time to get pregnant yet again. When Peggy told me she was pregnant for the fourth time, I detonated all political correctness.

"Why?"

"Why what?"

"Why do you keep getting pregnant?"

"What do you mean, keep getting pregnant? I'm pacing my children."

"With what, a ruler?"

"I can't believe you just said that. In case you haven't noticed, my children are all two years apart. That, Miss Know-It-All, is planned. I am using the rhythm method, approved by the church, which allows me to go to Communion and not be a hypocrite, like some people I know."

"Listen, I'm not trying to raise a moral question. It's a mental health issue."

"Whose mental health? In case you haven't noticed, we're happy."

They were.

"And I'm a very good mother."

She was.

"And we can afford the family we have."

They could.

"So your point is?"

No News Is Good News

The phone rang. It was Peggy in October. That could only mean one thing.

"Hey, I called to tell you something."

"Wait, let me brace myself for the news…OK, I'm sitting. When's the due date?"

The phone was silent.

"Peggy, are you OK?"

"They tell me I have breast cancer."

At that moment I entered a fog, a disjointed, unintelligible universe. Nothing she was saying made sense. I didn't know anyone other than Peggy who had cancer. Peggy was a young woman, only thirty-two. We were both only thirty-two. Women who were thirty-two did not get cancer. My words fell like blocks, clumsily stacking on one another.

"Are you saying you have cancer?"

Peggy's yes response was concise and complete.

"That's not possible." I was dizzy and confounded. "Peggy, that's not possible."

"I am so sorry to tell you like this, to be so abrupt, but I didn't know how else to tell you." Peggy's voice shattered. "They're going to do surgery next week."

"Surgery," I murmured. I covered my eyes, straining to push back my tears. But they came.

Peggy considerately proposed, "I know how demanding your job is, but I was wondering if you could come?"

I began weeping audibly into the receiver.

"Hey! What kind of friend are you? You're supposed to be comforting me!"

"I will be there. I promise I will be there."

I made that trip and six after that. The treatment regimen had been so difficult—nauseating chemo, scorched skin, disfiguring surgery, and loss of hair.

At first Peggy, following a period of initial illness, seemed to rebound. She returned to work and finished the school year. That Easter we traveled to her house for a bedlam of a holiday, with no one caring what anybody did.

Peggy attended the Good Friday Passion service. I sat beside her. I shivered when the gospel reading quoted Christ, who said, "Father, if you are willing, take this cup from me." I shivered again when he said, "My God, my God, why have you forsaken me?" Peggy clasped my hand.

"You OK?" she whispered.

"Hell no."

"Me either." Peggy squeezed my hand.

"The good news," she assured me, "is that now Easter Sunday will follow."

I smiled, but I could not help but wonder, what kind of God would sacrifice his only son for a species so undeserving? What kind of God would sacrifice Peggy, whose children still measured their ages in single digits? What could be the point? Hadn't the point been made before with Abraham and Isaac? We love you, you psychopath, we love you.

By June, Peggy had turned in her fourth-grade role book and her grades. She had lost weight and was requiring more bed rest. Her mother and sisters began spending long weekends with the family.

Three weeks before she died, Lester called.

"Peggy is at Barnes-Jewish Hospital. You might want to come if you can."

When I entered the hospital room, Peggy was a miniature of the woman I had known. Her cheek bones protruded, projecting her face in high relief. Her eyes, though deep, sparkled like jewels in a crater. Her wedding ring was on a gold chain around her neck, as her shrunken finger could no longer hold it. Morphine controlled the pain level in her body. Her white hospital gown and sheets swallowed up her diminutive frame. Her hair was a neat ponytail draped across her shoulder.

When I entered the room, Peggy attempted to lift her head, but it fell limp onto the pillow.

"Hey, girl."

"Hey, girl."

"You look so pretty."

"So do you."

"Liar."

My word bank was empty. I had nothing to say.

"I want you to know I'm all right." She was assertive. "Did you hear me?"

"I heard you."

"I want you to be all right."

Was she kidding? When your God is a nut job, how can you be all right?

"I mean it. I want you to be all right. Don't think I haven't asked myself the questions you have asked, like, why me? I'm so young. Who will raise my children if I'm not there? How will Lester manage?"

I was staring at the window. "Did you get an answer?"

"Yes."

"And?"

"The answer is that God isn't doing anything to me. This is me. Just me. What I must now do is remember all that I have ever believed and accept that this is the way my life should be. I must find the faith to know that life will go on, that there really is a higher power, and that all will be well. It's faith. It's always faith. Faith is the marker for hope."

I kissed her hand. The morphine had done its job. Two weeks later, Peggy died. Her family was with her.

Reconciliation

I broke my promise to Lester. I did not keep in touch. There would be no more Easters following Peggy's death. Our lives parted like two divergent streams. It would be ten years before I heard from him again.

When I answered the phone, the familiar voice sounded relieved.

"It is you. I wasn't sure I had the right number. Did you people move?"

"Yes, we did. I'm so sorry; I had planned to stay in touch, but…"

"Oh, I know. Believe me, I know. Those were tough times, girl. But listen, I have a favor to ask."

"Of course. Anything."

"Well, since I saw you last I have remarried. Her name is Thelma. I met her at this support group. Anyway, she had two kids, and we kinda needed each other. But here is the point. My oldest daughter, you remember her, she was eight then. Well, she's now going to college this fall at Northwestern, and we can't get there. Thelma has to go south on a family emergency and needs me. We sent her boxes ahead, and I was wondering, could you get my daughter from the train and see that she gets to school?"

I arrived at Union Station an hour before the train. I can't say why I felt uneasy. The Starbucks Caramel Roast wasn't making things better. My stomach did a somersault.

I began to churn up those insane Easter holidays. A sweet nostalgia caressed me. Without explanation, tears were streaming down my face. Puzzled commuters began to stare. This would never do, an old woman crying in her coffee. I was the generation passing the torch. Buck up. I dabbed my eye with a scratchy napkin and walked toward the gate.

It was mesmerizing when I first saw her, the high-voltage smile, the sparkling eyes, the personal poise and sense of direction. Good Lord, I thought, could it be Peggy heading straight for me? My initial instinct was to drop my cup and run. It was Peggy. It had been ten years. But she knew me. Arms outstretched, she marched toward me, and in her immutable way, hugged me.

"It's me, Faith. Remember? I've come back!"

I gathered her up, holding on for dear life.

"Yes, of course, I do. I'm so glad you're here."

The dance ends.

DANCE NUMBER FOUR: THE DC BOP

The Song: "To Be Young, Gifted
and Black"
The Dancer: Denise Scott

The Observance

"Shot herself?"

"Through the temple."

"This just sounds crazy."

"I know."

"I can't believe it. Are you sure?"

My sister gave me a look that said, "How many times do you want me to tell you this?"

"Listen, I didn't read the autopsy report or anything, but that's what Claire is telling me."

My sister and I are sitting at the rear of Bailey and Sons Funeral Home. I am home—not for this wake, but to make a popcorn visit on Mom and Dad. It's only after I arrive that my sister informs me that Denise is dead.

Bailey and Sons is located in Lee Summit and is poised to service those African Americans who are beginning to bleed into the area or are seeking something posher than the Black funeral brand from the neighborhood. Bailey and Sons is located on the rim of a park and conveys a sense of peace and serenity for grieving families. Its furnishings are very chic, boasting a variety of comfortable seating arrangements and a mahogany dining room providing sandwiches, sweets, and soft drinks for the mourners.

As we sit in the back, a series of photographs are projected upon an overhead screen.

"She really looks good there." My sister is reviewing each slide, trying to remember the woman who left the city so long ago.

"Why would she do that?" I had lost touch with Denise when she went to Howard Law School, but all the rumors I heard described a woman achieving every goal she had set for herself and enjoying all of life's finer things.

"Who knows why anybody does anything?" My sister's attention was split between my questions and viewing the slideshow. "I remember him. That's the football player she used to date. Remember him?" Another slide. "Oh my God, look at that outfit. It screams 1970." Another slide. "Remember when everyone used to wear hats? Like I said, who knows? All I know is what Claire told me. Do you think we should go view the body and see if we can locate the spot where the bullet punctured her skull?"

"No, not now. So what did Claire say?"

Claire was a pretty reliable source. Denise and I were friends, although I always felt I liked her more than she did me. Claire, on the other hand, was Denise's bestie. They had their own cache of secrets and experiences. Others of us passed in and out of her circle, but none of us were confidants.

"So girl, why is Claire telling you Denise's business? I mean, you know how they were."

"That, my sister, is the operative word. 'Were.' Based on what Claire told me, Denise felt like Kansas City wasn't big enough for her. That the people here were little more than barbecue, bone-sucking hicks. Denise had moved out and up, and I don't think Claire was in, if you know what I mean. Once Claire began to feel like that, I think she decided to unload all of Denise's dirt, especially now that Denise is dead. Claire said she feels no sense of obligation because Denise would always put her friends in DC before her."

I inched closer to my sister's ear. "What kind of dirt?"

The Dance

Overcoming

I felt sheepish and embarrassed. How could I tell Mary Cecelia, after expressing such a fervent commitment to my Benedictine vocation, that I had second thoughts and had joined the NAACP instead? I responded in a very adult fashion. I simply said nothing and slinked away.

My dad was convinced I was experiencing an identity crisis. I did need to be part of a crusade, he reasoned, but it wasn't a Christian movement. It was a social one aimed at justice and equality. A ground swell was brewing and not just in the Negro communities. The entire country felt the tremors. In my father's world view it was imperative that we, as a family, become totally involved. Everyone had to lift, he preached, if everyone was to rise. So much had been sacrificed, for so long, by so many to tilt the arc of the country toward justice. It was essential now that no Negro family be found lacking in the lifting.

My parents were in the adult council of the National Association for the Advancement of Colored People. My membership was with the youth council. At the first meeting I attended, I knew no one. Most of the members of the youth council knew someone. They had either attended one of the two predominately Negro high schools in the city or belonged to the prominent Negro churches. They were overwhelmingly college students or recently returning Vietnam War veterans. Those who attended historically Black colleges had already been involved in movements and demonstrations on their campuses, and understood how protesting worked. These were smart, savvy kids. Some were promoting acts of civil disobedience modeled after Gandhi. Others chomped for revolution. Some spoke of integration, others, total separation. I wasn't sure what to make of it all. College had taught these young people to stand and deliver. They were vocal, with impressive vocabularies to support their rhetoric. They were bold and seemingly without fear. They were attractive and knew it. This was their time, and they would not be denied.

When I attended my first meeting, I was terrified. The adult moderators and proctors tried, unsuccessfully, to impose Robert's Rules of Order on the group, but strong opinions combined with brazen youth often silenced sanity. However, even with the impetuous outbursts and over-the-top dialogue, the moderators succeed in reigning everyone in on a few goals to be achieved that summer. Those goals were that anyone in the community who needed it would be picked up and taken to be registered to vote that fall. Youth Council members, still in the city, would take anyone who needed a ride or a companion to walk with them to the polls to vote. Literature, posters, and yard signs promoting Negro candidates for offices would be carried house to house and business to business to be posted in windows and in yards within the Negro community. Above all else there would be demonstrations: marches, sit-ins, whatever the adult council deemed necessary to telegraph the message, "Ain't nobody gonna turn us around."

The next order of business was the introduction of new members. There were three of us who, after our names were called, were instructed to stand and tell the group something about ourselves. The first person to stand was a sophomore who attended Spelman College. She wore dark-rimmed glasses and had short cropped hair. She had graduated from Central High School, had several friends within the youth council, was an AKA, loved board games and charm bracelets, and collected stamps. Her wrist jingled as she described her involvement, through her college, with various civil rights organizations in Atlanta and what she believed she could bring that summer to this chapter. After she had spoken there was a rush of applause.

My self-introduction was next. I stood, recognizing no one. I said that I attended Mount Saint Scholastica College. I could see the frozen looks that almost shouted, "Where is that?" I could feel my voice quiver, my speech break. I said that I had been in the Sodality. More quizzical looks. I said I liked poetry. No one moved. I never stuttered, but my tongue was losing direction.

I was trying to say, "I want to make a difference and become part of the movement," but I was struggling to get the words to fall in the right sequence. I could see faces priming for laughter when I heard:

"What she is saying is that it is time for a change. We have waited long enough. Our parents have waited, our grandparents have waited, and their parents have waited, and nothing has happened. What she is saying is that if a change is going to come, it's up to us, every one of us, to come together and be that force that creates that change. What she is saying is, don't put off until tomorrow what you can do today. It's our time. That's what she's saying."

The speaker began to clap. Soon the entire room was applauding. I sat down, never really seeing who had spoken. When the meeting ended, several people came, introduced themselves, and welcomed me, but no one identified themselves as the speaker.

I was standing outside in a cluster of several girls, waiting to be picked up, when I asked, "Who was the girl who spoke while I was speaking?" The girl closest to me answered what everyone else seemed to know.

"We thought you knew her, that you were her friend. That was Denise. She's the vice president of this youth chapter. She just passed us a few minutes ago. She was wearing those cool blue shorts."

I saw Denise at all the meetings that summer. She was in charge of neighborhood canvassing. She would tell us the neighborhoods we would canvas, what we were to say, and the literature we were to leave behind. When she addressed the group, her speech was clear and purposeful. She did not preach to you. She just told you. Her manner exuded authority and birthright. There was an aloofness to her presence that made her hard to approach. She was extremely attractive, tall, and willowy with dark almond-shaped eyes. She had coffee-colored skin and hair too thick to blow in the wind. Denise was never rude but equally never inviting. She operated in her firmament of friends of which I was not a part.

Without trying to appear intrusive, I attempted to find out everything about her that I could. But by summer's end, all I had discovered was that she went to Howard. Whenever we had the Young Adult Council dances, I also knew she and a guy named Gregory could dance a spellbinding DC Bop.

I was enjoying the NAACP's activities and the sense of being part of a movement. The Civil Rights movement had birthed a smorgasbord of groups with so many acronyms it was hard to keep track of what was what. There were SNCC and CORE. Kansas City had its own upstart, Freedom Incorporated. New York had Malcolm X, Chicago, the Black Panthers, and we all had the ubiquitous Dr. Martin Luther King. There were pastors and preachers speaking in churches, stoking the movement. There were sayings and songs, gestures and anthems that served as oxygen to keep the movement burning. There was no containment of the oppressed people and those who supported them. The clarion call had been sounded.

Don't Need No Ticket

"People, get ready, there's a train a comin'! You don't need no baggage, just get on board!" Anyone who wanted to ride the freedom train and buck the Southern establishment could. All races were on board. All denominations were on board. Rich and poor were on board. Politicians and celebrities were on board. I was on board, empowered by the message that this was a new day. I no longer had to be accommodating to survive. Maybe my amphibian ways were drawing to a close and I could re-adapt. It wasn't a hard thing to believe. I had witnessed change and had been a part of it.

That summer the Youth Council had demonstrated through sit-ins and had marched for the right to eat at the restaurant in the Jones's Department Store, Howard Johnson's Restaurant, and Sidney's Drive-In. All three quickly capitulated. Victory belonged to the young. But Kansas City was not the deep South. There was jeering, name-calling, and the occasionally thrown rocks and bottles. The country, through the miracle of television, was already witnessing the horrific brutality occurring in Alabama and Mississippi. Most Kansas City merchants wanted the least amount of disruption, notoriety, and lost revenue. So they caved. When you are young and the establishment heels because of something you are a part of, you feel invincible.

Initially, I had missed Mary Cecelia, Sr. Patricia Ann, and the Mount. But as the summer waned, I sometimes wondered if they had ever existed at all. Dad had gotten me a part-time job at Milgram's Grocery Store working with stock. Some Sundays I would sleep in and miss ten o' clock Mass, a mortal sin, but not a mortal wound. When I did go, I would stand in the line during Mass, enter the confessional, seek my anonymous absolution, accept my penance, and receive a new infusion of satisfying grace. It was like a spiritual tune-up. Dad didn't seem to mind. To him, it was the movement that was paramount. What was essential was that my priorities were properly aligned. I was Negro first and then Catholic.

Matriculation

My first day at the University of Missouri at Kansas City, that old familiar feeling came creeping back to haunt me. The University of Missouri was a predominately White commuter school that had opened its doors that year as a branch of Missouri University in Columbia. I was now taking three buses each day: home to school, school to work, and work to home. When I entered my anthropology class, there were no other Negroes. When the professor arrived, out of habit, I stood.

"Sit down," the boy behind me insisted.

"Stretching," I justified. "Just stretching." I took my seat.

When class finished, I crossed the campus to the student union. I was trying so hard to fit in. I looked like the rest of the college community, rumpled and unkempt. Was I going to have to go through that whole gill-shedding transformation again? I was finding it a bit hard to breathe and felt confined. Inside the student union, things seemed more confusing. It was like an academic Ellis Island, full of all types and groups of people. I spotted the drama majors first. The hairstyles, colors, and exaggerated expressions made them a dead giveaway. The math and science group were all clustered around tables with dark-rimmed glasses and grave countenances as if they knew the exact date and time the world was coming to an end. The psych majors were all gazing into the middle distance as if they didn't care if it did. They hated their mothers anyway.

"Hey. Here. We are over here."

It was Denise, standing and beckoning. There they were, like a Rorschach test on white paper, three Black tables. I was never so glad to see her.

Everyone at the tables seemed to know everyone. I recognized some of the students from the NAACP Youth Council. Everyone was talking about something. Several card games were in progress. Denise was playing. I pulled a chair close to her.

"Don't say anything about what you see in my hand," she whispered. I nodded that I understood.

When she and her partner won, they cheered. It wasn't long before I was introduced to everyone. Denise's card partner was Claire.

"You play bid whist?" Claire asked.

"No." I felt exposed. It somehow felt that I should.

"Are you AKA or DELTA?" a girl I did not know probed.

"She's Catholic, and she's my friend," Denise decreed. That was that. We were all surprised. Everyone I didn't know began to introduce themselves. All had been at other schools the prior year: Lincoln University, Kansas University, Tuskegee.

"Rich here is a Morehouse man," one of the guys announced. "You can always tell a Morehouse man. You just can't tell them much." Everyone broke into laughter.

"Where did you say you went to school again?" someone inquired.

"I told you," Denise reaffirmed, "she is Catholic."

"That's right. That's right." That, again, was that.

I had been admitted to Denise's court. I now had a place at the table, and I would come to that table most class days for the next three years. Belonging to something, being a part of something, restores confidence and fills such a basic human need.

Being at court had its privileges. For one, I was always expected and accepted. No one derided my grunge look, even though I was the only Black person who looked that way. Denise always dressed as if she modeled for *Seventeen* magazine. Her skirts and sweaters matched. She always wore hose and sported an assortment of flats. A string of pearls was never out of place, and a gold Benrus watch band embraced her left wrist. The other girls looked similar. The guys were neat as well, with pressed slacks belted at the waist and trendy, colored sweaters. Occasionally they would strut, like peacocks, in their fraternity colors, doing a dance step to accent their attire. I don't know why I modeled the Colombo look. In part, it was because I didn't have the wardrobe, and in the White college world, grunge was in vogue. I also needed the money from my part-time job to help pay my tuition. No one said I had to, but with Mom still part-time with Miss Lottie, I felt that I should.

Stamped with Denise's approval, no one judged. I was considered eccentric, and that was enough. The tables were the flash point for lively conversations covering any number of topics. It was there that I eventually learned to play bid whist. Everyone at the tables had a common understanding of their destiny. We were to do better and achieve more than our parents. Being at court with Denise also meant that, depending on my class schedule, I could join her and three other girls in the midnight-blue Lincoln Continental her mother had let her drive. I loved pulling up to Milgram's Grocery Store in that big blue boat.

"You're in high cotton now, girl," the clerks would hoot when I sashayed inside.

I was the farthest point south and out of Denise's way, but she never complained.

When it was just the two of us, I would try and explain my circumstance. My parents had bought a new home, and my sister was a junior at St. Bernard's High School. Tuition had to be paid for the both of us. I needed to help out. I also proffered an explanation for why I looked so shabby. How could I possibly dress like a coed when, in the afternoons and evenings, I would be scrounging around in the back and basement of Milgram's, getting stock ready to load onto the shelves? Denise hadn't asked me to explain anything. I don't know why I felt compelled to comment. She just continued, each time, to go out of her way and drop me at the grocery store. I never understood my friendship with Denise. She seemed to enjoy my company more than my conversation.

Denise was more engaged with Claire, Madeleine, and Bootsy. When it was just the two of us, she didn't ask much, and she didn't say much. When it was just the two of us, I always felt there was a third, unseen friend. Loneliness kept her better company. I couldn't say if she preferred it, but she definitely knew it and was unafraid of its companionship. We always had the radio on when she dropped off her court. That was fun. The tunes of the day would make us pop. Everyone sang and knew every song. For most of the ride, the dial was tuned to KPRS so we could jam to the Temptations and the Coasters. When there was just the two of us, I could switch to KUDL for some Peter, Paul and Mary and Bob Dylan to broaden our repertoire.

It was November, our last class before Thanksgiving. I was searching for the dial when I heard the news. President Kennedy had been shot in Dallas. Denise turned the car east.

"Let's go to my house. We need to see this."

She pulled into the driveway of a bungalow on Cleveland. Low, neat evergreen hedges hugged the front yard. Denise rushed through the door into the living room and switched on the television. There were the indelible scenes. The motorcade, the shot, Mrs. Kennedy climbing toward the trunk, desperate for help, the motorcade speeding away, and the grief-stricken face of Walter Cronkite making the pronouncement that would stun the world. "President Kennedy died at one p.m. central standard time, two o'clock eastern standard time, some thirty-eight minutes ago."

It was too much for a country so optimistic, for a race so hopeful. I held my head in my hands and cried. I saw Denise sitting on the floor, bowing her head, and weeping. I can't say how long we were there—maybe a few minutes, maybe an hour. Denise was wiping her eyes as she rose from the floor.

"I guess I had better get you to Milgram's."

Work. I had forgotten about work.

"Yeah, I had better go."

For the first time, I took stock of the house. I guess I had expected something more regal. A castle with a moat, a chateau. This was just a two-bedroom house all on one level. The furniture was white French provincial encased in plastic. You could see the two bedroom doors off the living room. The kitchen, in the rear of the house, was silhouetted in the dim daylight pushing through its window.

No one was in the house but the two of us. It was evident from the deliberate arranging that everything had a place in this home and was in it. It almost looked staged. As we retreated toward the kitchen, I saw two pictures hinged together on the mantel. A lovely looking, clear-eyed woman and a handsome man in uniform were staring from gold-trimmed frames.

I stopped. "Who are they?"

Denise looked at me, then picked up the frame.

"These are my parents. Of course they were younger here. They met in college. They were so in love, like the movies. Daddy was actually a Tuskegee Airman."

"A what?"

"You know, a Tuskegee Airman. You don't know, do you? Anyway, when you're in the military, it's a pretty big deal. He's someplace in Asia now, part of a special advisory group or something like that. Momma doesn't tell me everything. I don't think he can always even tell her."

"You mean like James Bond?"

"Maybe."

My sophomore year wasn't stellar. I got two Ds and ended up on probation. I wasn't sure why I wasn't achieving better academically. I think I was having difficulty adjusting to the large classes. Maybe it was the commuting. Maybe it was the feeling of disconnect from the institution. Had it not been for the three tables in the student union and the common mission they constantly conveyed, I'm not sure if I would have graduated.

The summer before my junior year was bustling with activity. It was expected that the NAACP's Young Adult Council would cross pollenate with other organizations to help advance the movement. Many of us were involved in several organizations.

Dad said I didn't have to work. The winds of change had revved up to a cyclone. I was to volunteer in the offices of Freedom Incorporated, canvasing the neighborhoods to which I was assigned. Freedom Incorporated wanted to shatter the city's established patronage system and was promoting a slate of candidates it wanted the people who populated the Black wards to elect. Between Freedom Incorporated and the NAACP, I was pretty busy.

Then there were the fun events intended to cement a sense of esprit de corps among the young. The primary activity was the sponsored dances. I loved the dances. The music pulsated, and the dances screamed freedom. Couples still did the coordinated bops, swings, and provocative slow dances, but the most fun was when you danced by yourself. On the dance floor, you were the artist with your own canvas. Paint what you will. Dance as you please. Shake, shimmy, and gyrate to your heart's content. It was all about you, so do the jerk, the monkey, the hitchhike, the bus stop, or just do you.

Where was Denise? She would come to the occasional meeting but had stepped down from her leadership position and never came to the dances. I was Denise's friend, but I did not call her. She was not Peggy, who wrote each month and phoned when she returned home from college to say she thought she might get engaged that summer. With Denise, I did not visit, did not phone and gossip. With Denise, I was like a salad fork, not critical to the meal, but things were nice when I was there.

When my junior year began, I was wearing an afro and large hoop earrings à la Angela Davis. The hairstyle suited my ongoing grunge look. I now had a better part-time job at Hallmark Cards working in the warehouse. I had grown accustomed to having money of my own. I wasn't immersed in campus life, so why not work?

The first day of class, I made my way to the student union. There, like the phoenix rising from the ashes for another academic year, were the Black tables. It was a family reunion for the fifteen or so of us. A few new kids were at the tables. They had seemed lost at first; their faces reflected a certain refugee look. But the tables were our island signaling, "You belong here. You are safe now."

Denise was there. Where had she been during last summer? Her court was now in session. The regulars were playing bid whist, but she was not. She was in a huddle with Claire.

I sat by Bootsy, an elementary-ed major, who was finishing her card game. "I'm done." Putting her cards down, Bootsy began backing her chair away from the table. I tugged at the hem of her jacket.

"Hey, baby cakes." She spun and gave me a hug. "Love the hair thing."

"Thanks. How's your class schedule?"

"It sucks."

"Mine too. I have an eight o'clock with Dr. Silverman."

"Why'd you take that?"

"Had to. Needed it to graduate. So what's going on with Denise and Claire? If they get any closer, they'll become a cyclops."

"I guess you haven't heard."

"I guess not."

"Well, the rumor last year was that she didn't go back to Howard because of Tornado."

We had to move around so another player could play.

"What's Tornado?"

"The Kansas City Chief. Terrance the Tornado."

"What? You mean that Tornado?"

"I do, the linebacker. Denise is dating him."

My eyes were saucers. I watched the Chiefs on television, but I didn't know anyone who knew one.

"Grapevine says it could be getting serious. What I'm going to tell you now, girl, is in the vault. You dig me?"

"Deep." I pounded my chest.

Her voice sank an octave. "They went to Jamaica this past summer."

"Who goes to Jamaica in the summer?"

"Tornado and Denise. Grapevine said things got hot, hot, hot. We girls think—those of us in the know, that is—that she could get engaged as early as Christmas and at the latest in the summer. Can you imagine that wedding? It'll be the talk of the summer. With the money her dad has and Terrance being a Chief! You know they are just gonna show out, girl, not to mention that Denise will be set for life. I wouldn't be surprised if she and Claire aren't discussing the bridal party right now. I think I'm in it. As you can see, this is super serious. Like you said, who goes to Jamaica in the summer?"

Christmas came and went. There was no announcement. When the summer came, Denise went on another trip with Terrance to another island. Her circle of confidants had broadened. Four of us knew. Her mom had traded the Continental in for a Buick Electra 225. We called it a deuce and a quarter. But Denise was not doing the drop-offs anymore. She seemed to have other commitments.

By our senior year, Denise was smoking. When we sat at the table, she would brazenly display her set of Prince Gardner accessories. She had a cigarette case, a wallet, and an eyeglass case, all given to her by Terrance, but no ring.

Summer was pretty uneventful. The high points of that year were Nina Simone's performance at the university where the crowd went wild as she belted out "Mississippi Goddam." Nina sang another song, "To Be Young, Gifted and Black," which I adopted as my personal anthem. Denise had a song as well. Nancy Wilson sang it. "Miss Otis Regrets." Some days when the court had dispersed to attend class and only a few of us were left to study or muse about our future, I could hear Denise quietly sing, "And from under her velvet gown, she drew a gun and shot her lover down, madam. Miss Otis regrets she's unable to lunch today." I liked the song but not enough to sing it over my pizza.

The other grand event of our senior year was an announcement by Michael Pendleton, a pharmacy major. One day when all three tables were full, Michael described a miracle pill that would be on the market soon. He said if women took the pill every day, for twenty-eight days each month, they could have as much sex as they wanted and they would never get pregnant. Several at the table decried the pill as a placebo that would never work. Bootsy laughed, "That's just not possible." Claire swore she wouldn't trust it.

"But what do you think?" She turned to Denise.

Staring at no one, Denise simply replied, "I hope it's true."

What's love got to do with it?

As my graduation date approached, I felt exhilarated. There was a rush of expectation inside of me. No one in my immediate family had finished college. My parents saw the door opening. I could slip into the middle class. Proudest of all was my dad. This was the point of the struggle, the marches, the arrests, the sit-ins, the abuse. It had been necessary to build the staircase to upward mobility. It was never just about me. The struggle was ours.

"Make it happen, baby!" he enjoined me, pinning the mortar board to my hair. "You were never meant to be a nun."

I wanted to have my name called and stride across the stage, but that wasn't to be. There were too many graduates for that. We stood in blocks and were graduated by departments. It was nothing exceptional, but I was a college graduate. As I was changing out of my gown, Bootsy came up.

"Did you see him?"

"Who?"

"The Tornado, Terrance Newman."

"No."

"Well, he's out there. He sat with her momma. Her dad couldn't get away. He's in Vietnam or something. Terrance drove them to the graduation in his Jaguar."

"The football player did?"

"Yep. The rumor is they may go to Vegas and elope. Me, myself, and I prefer a wedding, but you know how that goes. Probably don't want the publicity and all that attention."

They did take a trip—somewhere. I know because when Denise came back, she did something extraordinary. She called to see if I would go to dinner. I was flattered and immediately said yes. Why I still wanted to be part of her deep inner circle, I couldn't say, but I did. We went to Stephenson's Apple Orchard, a great place, perfect for sharing confidences. All the major restaurants in Kansas City were opened to the public. With the passing of its Public Accommodations Act in 1964, spurred by Freedom Incorporated and others, Kansas City preceded the nation in this civil rights action. Everything we had done had mattered. But seemingly, to Denise, not very much. She was toying with something else.

The apple cider, relish plate, and apple fritter had been a part of the initial small talk. The main course was coming.

"I'm not your traditional woman."

"No, I don't think you are."

"I'm actually pretty progressive."

"I think you are."

"I'm not sure if I want that entire marriage and children scene." She paused. Her mind seemed caught in a terrible storm. "No. That's not me. Too boring. Too passive. What about you?"

"Me?" I was startled. Denise never asked about me.

"You, yes. What about you?"

"You mean do I want to get married?"

"Yes, do you? I mean I never see you date. You never talk about anyone."

It was all true. The hurt went deeper when the words hit the air. What was her point?

"You just never seemed like everyone else. I thought you might want to be a nun or something, since you're Catholic and all."

"Well, not exactly."

"Really? Do you mean you would want to get married?"

Was she kidding? Of course. I was twenty-two years old. I definitely wanted to become part of the legions of women who, following college graduation, called themselves wives. Wasn't that the natural order of things? People at church and from the old neighborhood had inquired thirty seconds after graduation about my marriage plans. But I could tell this was a loaded question, so I had to be coy.

"I think I can say—well, I definitely can say that I have considered it."

"Why?" She seemed stunned. "You of all people. What could you possibly get out of it?"

Could I say sex? That's what I really wanted to say, what every fiber of my being was screaming, but I shifted gears, and answered instead, "Well, it is a sacred institution."

It was as if my answer made her point.

"See? I knew you would say something like that. Your answer is so conventional, so safe. I thought you might be thinking like me. Work a few years and then go to Howard Law School. I had thought we could go together."

Denise wanted me to go with her to law school? At that moment her invitation erased all sense of carnal desire. Denise wanted me to go with her to law school.

Denise and law school would make me one of the coolest persons ever. We could become another Leona Pouncey-Therman, a super bad legal duo. It was an intoxicating proposition. My answer was yes. Together we would and did apply to Howard Law School.

I think my parents thought, following college graduation, I would be pursued by a talent scout offering me a cornucopia of job opportunities. That did not happen. My anthropology minor was only eclipsed by my sociology major. When the college had asked me to declare a major, I was torn between following Margaret Mead to the Trobriand Islands and saving the world. No one told me I could do neither. What kind of academic advising was that?

After I trooped through a variety of federal and state agencies, leaving futile applications, my career was finally jump-started by one of President Johnson's Great Society programs. I would counsel high school dropouts. Denise landed a better job opportunity. Her major had been history. After a number of attempts, she was hired as an intake counselor for the Missouri State Employment Office. The tables at the Student Union, for those of us who graduated, were no more. The philosophical debates were no more. Bid whist was gone. The court was gone. Life was no longer a what if. It was an it is.

What a time of contrasts. In some ways, things were glorious. In others, they were ever so frightening. We were wage earners and tax payers. For the first time, we had disposable incomes. For most of us, the first thing we bought were cars. I bought a Mustang. Denise bought a Camaro. The engineering graduate bought a Volkswagen Beetle, the pharmacy grad an Oldsmobile Tornado.

That first year no one could afford a new car and a new apartment. So we all stayed home. Still there was so much to experience. Terrance gave Denise a Playboy key, admitting her and her friends to the private club whenever she chose. Denise gave Terrance a *Playboy* subscription so he could read the articles. Denise spent a lot of time on Terrance's arm. I had to admit, she looked pretty good there. It was just the trips, those brief interludes when she would leave for a day or two and return. Sometimes she would miss work and call in sick.

"Did you take a trip with Terrance?"

She would shake her head in the affirmative but did not seem invigorated by the adventure. I would have asked more, but the storm was always rising. I could see the clouds forming in her eyes. By the end of July, Tornado was in training camp with the Washington Redskins. I was shocked; Denise was not. The truth was I was relieved that Tornado was gone. His notoriety was a weighted burden. That entire football crowd was a burden: pompous, presumptuous, and rude. Denise, through Terrance, had set me up with two players from competing teams. We went out when they played the Chiefs. Both dates were obnoxious. They were self-absorbed buffoons who were convinced that a date was synonymous with a sexual touchdown. By the end of each of those dates, I had perfected a pretty skillful onside kick.

I preferred the second-string crowd: the guys who had to make it happen, every day, in smaller, less flamboyant ways and who did not take for granted the success their efforts produced. I had met one sweet guy my second year at work. He had come into the office to sell us IBM Selectric typewriters. He looked smart and neat in his dark suit and tie. I was still saving what money I could for law school and trying to curb excesses. So when he asked me out to dinner at the swank Uncle Johnny's River Boat, I gleefully obliged.

With Tornado gone, I had suggested to Denise, who I now considered one of my best friends, that she entertain the notion of dating someone else. She glared at me as if I had asked her to commit hara-kiri.

"Someone else like who?" she sneered.

"I don't know like who, just someone else. I mean Terrance is in DC, and that limits when you can see him. Consider the possibility that you might meet someone else you like."

I knew such things were possible. It was happening to me.

She fixed her gaze as if teaching me a fundamental lesson.

"Time is precious. I do not have time to meet someone else. I do not have time to help make someone else. Frankly, I despise the term helpmate.

Any man I am with won't need any help. I am going to law school to make myself an exceeding expensive commodity, and any man that I am with will have a net worth far greater than mine. In my world, it's the only way. The relationship between a man and a woman isn't about love. It's about power. That's it, and that's all."

Our law school acceptance letters came on the same day in April. We met, again, at Stephenson's for dinner. We had ordered apple martinis. It was then that things really got interesting. One sip and Denise had embarked on an unfettered diatribe.

"No one will ever tell us we're not this or we're not that. No one will ever tell us, sit or wait, I'll be back for you. No one will tell us shit. We're playing this game on our own terms, and we will win." She had not even consumed the martini.

"Denise, what are you talking about?"

"Power, honey—raw, unharnessed power. It is the greatest aphrodisiac. Men know it, fight and kill for it, and love it. It's not us that they love. It's their power over us. They drug us with those sappy love songs and stupid movies that always suggest love is the answer. That love is the be-all and end-all. But they know better. They know all that love nonsense is just dope in our veins weakening our wills and blinding us to the truth. The truth, honey, is that men view us as weak, weeping wimps who they have to subdue and control. When they make love to us, it's not love. It's domination. Well, we've got news for them, honey: we're not those kinds of women."

I had something to tell Denise, but her mounting rage was making what I had to say all the more difficult.

"Listen, Denise, I have something to tell you!"

"What is it?"

"I'm not going to law school."

"What?" The anger in her voice soared to two hundred and fifty degrees Fahrenheit.

"I know. I was hoping I would just get rejected and I wouldn't have to tell you this, but I'm getting married."

"To that IBM typewriter salesman?"

How dare she denigrate the man I loved?

"Try and understand this, that is, if you can. I love him and he loves me. It is not about power or whatever the hell is currently possessing you. Frankly, the way you're behaving, I think you need an exorcist."

Denise sat back in her chair, took a drag on her cigarette, and exhaled the smoke through her nostrils.

"How could I have ever thought you were sophisticated enough to understand? It must have been the Catholic school, prophet-looking peasant outfits that had me fooled. I see now; I'm talking power to a peasant. Somehow I thought maybe you were more aware, enlightened. But no. You're in a state of arrested development. You're in love."

Denise was right. I did not understand what she was talking about. Everything with her was about power and who held it. Her parents had been in love. She had told me so. What was it about love that flung her into such a rage? By mid-May I had healed the wounds she inflicted while in her tempestuous mental state and asked her to be a bridesmaid in my wedding. She coolly accepted, was a passive participant, and two days later flew to Washington to attend Howard Law School.

From time to time I thought about trying to contact her, but with Denise, everything always felt forced. With her I could never clear the bar. The burden of the friendship was always mine. If a friend can move and not provide you a forwarding address, you conclude that the friend doesn't care. The handmaiden does not summon the queen.

Who Was Denise Scott?

"Did you hear what I just said?" My sister began a slow head oscillation, scanning the room to make certain no one was in earshot. Her voice had jarred me back. This was Denise Scott's wake.

"Did you hear what I said about the obituary? See, right here where they say her father was Major Melvin Scott."

I followed her finger to the obituary. "Yeah, I remember that."

"But do you also remember how we never saw him? How he was always in some place like Japan or Germany or Vietnam?"

"Right, right."

"According to Claire, there was no Major Scott. According to Claire, Denise never knew who her daddy was."

"Oh my Lord! What about all the things she had…things from Germany? Remember that mug and the kimono from Japan? And she had pictures. Who was that man?"

"How would I know? But according to Claire, Mrs. Scott, her momma, had a sugar daddy who would travel to places with his wife and bring things back to Mrs. Scott for Denise."

"Do you know who he was?"

My sister affirmatively shook her head. "It was Mr. Felder."

"The Mr. Felder who had the liquor store."

"Exactly. The Mr. Felder who owned the liquor store across from Parkview."

"But he was so nice."

My sister glared at me as if I had a sudden brain freeze.

"This has nothing to do with being nice! It's about creating your own narrative. See that man sitting up there beside Mrs. Scott? They say that's Denise's brother. Did we ever hear about any brother?"

"So where did he come from?"

"It makes you question everything, doesn't it? You can't help but wonder, did she really go to Howard for her freshman year and then bounce around Europe before she came to UMKC? Now, if this is a lie, I didn't tell it, but Claire swore Denise did go to Howard but lost her scholarship. She didn't have any money, so she got a job for a year in DC at Dairy Queen."

This was all too incredible. I took the obituary and began to fan. Was it hot flashes or this story?

"What I am about to tell you, according to Claire, is the killing part. Remember that Chief's player she was dating, Terrence Newman, the guy we just saw in the slide? Claire says that's why she went to DC. It wasn't for law school. It was that Terrence got traded to the Washington Redskins. Denise went there because she thought they were going to get married."

"So tell me, did she go to law school?"

"Claire's not sure about any of that. Maybe she did, maybe she didn't, but she does know that she never married Terrence."

"Why not?"

"It seems he got the daughter of a prominent DC doctor pregnant and was pressured by everyone—his parents, the team, his lawyers, everyone—to marry her, so he did. Now this next part is 'shame on Denise.' Our girl fell for the oldest male trick in the world. Terrence, Claire says, told Denise he was only going to stay with the pregnant princess long enough to placate all concerned, give the baby his name, and vamoose, he's gone. Guess what happens next?"

"I'm afraid to."

"Don't be. It's all so perfectly predictable, at least it is to sane people. Terrance marries the pregnant woman, and they go on to have three kids. He tells dumb Denise he is going to leave the wife as soon as the kids get through high school, and then it's college. So the last kid finishes college, and the bastard tells her the wife is terminally ill. Can you imagine? Denise, according to Claire, goes berserk, takes a gun, and shoots herself. Someone needs to recall her Black membership card. Any fool knows we kill other people. We don't kill ourselves."

For days following the wake I asked myself the question, "Who was Denise Scott?" Even though I never saw her again, I admired her. She was visually stunning, inscrutable, and determined. How could I reconcile the Denise Scott I had known with the woman Claire had revealed? Ultimately, I determined I didn't have to. Denise was a projectionist. She had shown me the person she wanted me to know. I was entitled to no more. Denise Scott owned her image.

The dance ends.

DANCE NUMBER FIVE: THE TANGO

The Song: "Private Dancer"
The Dancer: Bethany Harper

The Observance

I love chamber music: a violin, a cello, a piano. I love it, especially when it is played in soft, undulating melodies. The room is in the Waldorf Astoria Hotel. There is her pedestaled picture. It is striking by any measure. The face is elegant, and the colors, muted. Just the way she would want us to view her.

The guests are hushed. A laugh floats here and there, but no one's crying. Wait staff waft through the small gathering, passing hors d'oeuvres. The scene is so Beth. It's an intimate time with people telling intimate stories. The kind perfected for occasions such as this. Beth would have appreciated this memorial service. It's classy with the best wine, crystal, and linens. Of course it is. She had planned it.

Long before Beth donated her body to science, before she embraced that continuum of care concept, before she realized that Alzheimer's disease was clipping away pieces of her mind, Beth had planned this.

"How do you know Beth?" someone asked me.

"I worked with her."

"She was so brilliant and tough," swore another. We were forming a nucleus of commentators.

"She knew how to mark her turf," a woman recalled.

"You knew when she was in the room." Heads were shaking.

"She owned the room," testified yet another. A chorus of uh-huhs ensued and then a swath of silence.

The silence was finally broken by a nondescript corporate type: "You either loved her or hated her."

That comment elicited a vociferous refrain. "Oh yeah! Oh yeah!"

The Dance
Find a Way or Make One

Her name was Bethany Harper. She told me that wasn't her real name but never told me what her real name was. Bethany Harper could have been a name she gave herself to avoid any connection to her parents and family, from whom she was estranged. It may have been a stage name. Beth was an East Coast girl who had taken an unsuccessful stab at the New York stage. If her family taught her one thing, it was that life is neither fair nor fun. Beth sent herself through college, but it was her degree from the school of hard knocks that primed her for the life she would lead. The woman's movement would program her, but nothing could prepare her for what it meant to be a professional woman creating precedent in a man's world.

That's the way with conquistadors, pioneers, and astronauts. You enter the unknown, the uncharted. In time there would be laws, standards, and policies, but not when Beth began. There was only survive or suffer the abyss. I know because, in the beginning, I was there with her.

It was 1973, and we were hired to meet the affirmative action quota at International Telephone and Telegraph Corporation, a multinational conglomerate with business interests around the world. The company had made its mark in telecommunications but had diversified into a multitude of enterprises. These jobs were our second affirmative action opportunity. We had both failed at our first, she at Allstate for appearing too aggressive and me at Xerox for appearing too timid. With ITT, we had both vowed to try harder.

I had moved to Chicago, relocating with my husband, who had been promoted to work at IBM's mecca in the windy city. Beth was the referral of a friend in ITT's legal department. I had arrived nine months earlier. I found the job through a placement agency. I was being handled by a head hunter who was well acquainted with the EEOC implications for corporations with federal contracts. Xerox had been my first job placement. I had been hired as a sales assistant. I approached every call as if it were a speech meet. I talked about many things and never closed the sale. I went down in flames.

The newly formed ITT Educational Services was looking for school directors for their two schools in Chicago. Both were facing shifting demographics as their student populations migrated from White to Black. My resume, which listed my work with disadvantaged youth in Kansas City, signaled to the headhunter that I just might fill the bill.

"This may be the right time for us to get our foot in the door. I have you scheduled for tomorrow at nine thirty for the position of school director. Read up on this company and give them all that you got. You're not a sheep. You're a ram. Knock it out of the park."

I tried to be a ram that day. I arrived fifteen minutes early for the interview, wore a conservative navy-blue suit and white blouse, presented a firm handshake, smiled, and made eye contact. I did not take a seat until directed. When the interview began, there was only one man in the room. When it ended, there were three. I had done my homework about the ITT conglomerate and this subsidiary. I sprinkled my comments and responses with that information. I was poised but not relaxed and had confident, can-do responses to such questions as what are your greatest strengths and what could you do for our company?

I felt that I was holding my own in the interview. I had dress protectors under my armpits so no one could see me sweat. In a way, I felt gender ambushed surrounded by the three men, but their faces betrayed nothing. When the interview ended, all three men and I stood. We did a round of handshakes accompanied by long smiles, and I left the room.

I was on pins and needles for three days. When the headhunter contacted me, my heart was in my mouth.

"Oh my God, how did I do?"

"It seems that they want to hire you."

I could not believe my ears.

"They want to hire me? Really? They want to hire me?"

"Yes, but here's the catch."

"Catch, what catch?"

"They are hiring an internal candidate for the position," the employment counselor continued to explain.

"That happens a lot. You know many of these big companies are required to advertise job openings, through a variety of channels, to show they are reaching out and interviewing a strong cross section of candidates. All the time they have someone in their company they know they are going to hire. You see what I mean?"

I understood what he meant, but I did not see how that benefited me.

"Well, the short-short of this story is, they knew coming into the interview that you weren't going to get the position. I mean, how could you? You had no accounting experience, no significant supervisory experience, no marketing experience…"

My armpits were starting to boil.

"So how is this working for me?"

"It is working for you, sweetheart, because you took the game to them. You rammed it to them. You impressed the hell out of them. You closed the deal."

"OK, so what does all that mean?"

"It means this. They want to create an assistant's position to the director. Someone they think they can train and bring along."

The recruiter's voice was brimming over with delight. "And with you, they got a twofer."

My introduction to the corporate world was as a statistic. I had been in my position for several months. It was clearly awkward. I did not know enough about what I was doing and often felt more like a house pet than anyone's assistant. The man who assumed the position of director was accessible and knowledgeable. He had held several other positions in the corporation and was described as a company man who had transferred in from Detroit. He also had an established network of friends at Educational Services' headquarters and was welcomed by a bevy of employees who sought his favor.

His name was Peter Spencer. I would accompany him to meetings but never to lunch. He took that meal with several cronies who had accompanied him when he relocated. I was in most of his meetings but was not a part of them. Each month the school participated in a monthly operations review, a management oversight and accountability exercise employed throughout the entire ITT system. This meeting was always conducted by a regional manager, along with his support staff. All the major managers of the school attended as well. I was in these meetings but sat slightly back and to the side of the director. It was sort of like being the royal food taster. You had no real function but felt you would be the first to go if things didn't go well. I was trying to learn all I could and took copious notes. But the notes didn't always make sense to me, as these men spoke their own brand of jargon.

It was all about PBT and PAT, ROI and Cost-Benefit analysis. It was the cost per lead and cost per enrollment. It was budgets and balance sheets, forecasts, and reforecasts. It was about what was hard and what was soft, about MBOs and SWOTs. Did cash run ahead of accruals, or were accruals ahead of cash? I needed a translator. I was deep into one of those operation reviews, sitting in my assigned recessed seat with my head doing triple axels when I heard the regional manager address me.

"Bethany Harper will be in to meet with you next week. HR has interviewed her. The VP in DC interviewed her, and our marketing guys at both headquarters and in New York have interviewed her. The bottom line is, everyone thinks she can do the job. She delivers a great sales presentation, appears to think on her feet, and doesn't rattle under pressure. I mean, she's no bimbo. But it's not her feet that messed up their minds. Man, they say this one has a rack on her that makes your eyes pop." The room rocked with laughter. The regional manager continued. "No, seriously, HQ wants to make sure she can do the job. It's a new marketing initiative with a significant amount of revenue and profit forecast to come from this effort in the fourth quarter. Our guys think cutie pie has the moxie to do it, but they also want to make sure they aren't being blinded by the halo effect. What they want to know is, is it brains or boobs driving this hire? We need an objective interviewer."

Pete, as we all called him, gave me his office for the interview. When the receptionist phoned to say Ms. Harper was there, I sucked in my stomach, pushed back my shoulders, and went out to meet Bethany. It was only when I took her to the office and she removed her coat that I began to form a deeper appreciation of the men's dilemma. Her face alone was a photographer's dream: flawless skin that caught the light, especially when it brushed the rims of her cheeks and the tips of her perfectly sculpted nose. Her eyes were like liquid emeralds that could turn in the light to smoldering amber. They were not soft eyes that seduced you. They were strong eyes that dared you. Her mouth was held in a permanent pout, which I later learned was her cocked and ready position to fire when needed. Bethany's hair, dark and straight, was worn too long for the workplace.

Then there were the breasts. It was not that they were so large. It was more that her Scarlett O'Hara waistline made them jut forward with unmistakable promise. A nice blazer might have helped defrost her appearance, but Bethany was not the blazer type. Her total image telegraphed this is me, and I'm not changing to fit some cookie-cutter corporate mode. After she had taken a seat, I looked at the prepared outline of key talking points I had been given and began my address.

"Welcome to Chicago. Corporate invited you here to give you the opportunity to speak with people in the field. Your job is new, and everyone wants you to succeed, because when you succeed, the company succeeds. If it's all right with you, I have a prepared list of questions that those of us who work in the field would like to have you answer. When we finish I would like to take you to the Black Hawk for lunch. How does that sound?"

"Sounds like a deal."

Her innocuous smile left much to the imagination. What did she really think about all of this? I read each question. She answered. I recorded her responses. Some of the questions were so odd I felt awkward asking them. There were such questions as, "People in the field often describe people from headquarters as seagulls. They fly in, eat the food, shit over everything, and fly back. What does that metaphor suggest to you?"

As promised, I took her to lunch. As we settled in at our table and placed our order, I could tell Bethany was sizing me up. "So tell me, what was that Q and A really all about?" The ruse apparently hadn't worked. Why did they think it would? Only men would concoct a scheme so preposterous. I smiled, stalling for an answer. I wanted to quip, "Oh, it was just a breast analyzer test." But Bethany was too serious and would not appreciate the humor.

"From what I have been told, this new group that you are a part of is going to be a critical revenue generator for our division. Our people are convinced that you have the external contacts to bring federal, state, and city monies to the table. We also, however, recognize that you can't do it alone. If we are going to realize that bottom-line increase, my people believe it can only happen through what we call a collective impact. What that means is, all of us—New York, your division, ES headquarters, the field—we all have to meld as a team. That's why it became imperative to get you into the field, so we could gauge how you relate." I had no clue about what I was saying.

Bethany began to laugh. "Do you have any idea of what you just said?"

I returned the laugh. "Not a word." We relaxed and laughed together.

"How long have you been with this company?"

"Less than a year."

"Do you like it?"

"Enough. I consider it a real opportunity. So I want to do well."

"You need to do well. Do you know why? Because if you don't, you simply reinforce the preexisting male mindset that you couldn't do the job in the first place. They believe in the core of their psyche that women aren't capable of thinking logically."

Bethany began making circles in the air with her hands.

"We don't have the capacity for clear thinking and discernment. All they see when they look at us are emotionally ramped-up sex objects. I want you to know I understand what was going on in that interview. You were the pawn sent out to camouflage the real question, which is, 'Can that big-breasted cunt really do this job?'"

Bethany was doing a slow burn.

"Believe me, I know this scenario. I can't tell you the number of times I've been in the room when they are making their tart little wisecracks. I know what they're doing with those subtle moves when they accidently brush up against you and that not-so-subtle shit when they just reach out and grope you and you can't say a word…not a peep…not a sound because you know in some weird mangled twist of fate you're one of the fortunate few. You were selected to endure this bullshit. What is it we are? Oh yeah, we're the first. Do you know what I'm saying here?"

Beth was ramping up for a four-alarm fire. The men in the next booth had stopped talking to listen. I put my hands in the air and began slowly lowering them as if to say, "Take it down a notch."

She understood, decompressed, and began to sip her kir. The time had now come for me to reveal that I felt her pain, agreed we were in a league of our own, and recognized us as comrades in arms. We were a movement. I wanted her to know I loved movements and was ready for this one. Lowering my voice, I began to articulate our mutual struggle.

"We are like facial hair."

"Facial hair?"

"Yes, you really don't want it, but you have it. You would love to get a lip wax, but you can't. So you have to try to find a way to neutralize that which you are required to keep. So what do you do? You bleach it. It stays but is rendered invisible. It's neutered."

Bethany starred at me a few seconds before she spoke.

"I like that. It really is an apt analogy. That's their goal to professionally spay us. Keep us because they must, but limit our growth trajectory."

"Exactly."

"Have you ever noticed the jobs we're hired into? I call them princess turrets, places where we have no impact, can be seen but not heard. They're sterile positions like human resources, quality assurance, customer relations, corporate training, compliance. It's not marketing, finance, or R&D. We're the support staff. They're line managers. What's your title?"

"Assistant director."

"Yes. See how they contain you? You're not the director. You're the assistant. You're in the castrated position. I'm in one too. I do all the work. Make all these sales calls that the guys don't want to make, in places they don't want to go, and talk to people they don't want to pitch. They pay me less and placate me with a less-than expense account, and I have to be grateful because I'm the first. What I am saying is, it's a game. It's not real. It will only become real if we make it real."

"How do we do that?"

Tactic #1

I could tell Bethany and I were on the brink of a conspiracy, devising a strategy to make us relevant and visible within the company, and I loved it. She was right. Why was I the only one sitting in the recessed chair?

The plan was simple. Collapse all the male preconceptions and stereotypes and claim our rightful spoils. We would take the fight to the enemy. Confound and conquer.

Bethany believed the expectation both divisions held regarding our career prospects was that we would fail. She contended we had been affirmative-action hires, necessary to achieve corporate quotas. When the time was right, we would be released, another statistic to document the self-fulfilling White male prophecy that women and minorities were timid, intellectually inferior, and unprepared. The fact that the men underestimated us was our best weapon. They would be more transparent with us because in their minds our bar was already set. We weren't going any place. We were not their competition.

We were to create alter egos, disguises to hide our true identities. My disguise would be that of the asexual sidekick: Tonto to the Lone Ranger, Pancho to Cisco. My costume would be pantsuits with pastel-colored blouses. I would wear my hair in a smooth page boy. The total image shouted, "I'm Buster Brown, and I'm here to help you." My presence was totally nonthreatening and sycophantic. My goal was to advance from assistant director to director.

Bethany would play the vamp: tempting but never tasted, overpromising and under delivering. She was a siren, dangerously luring the enchanted superior to support her hidden agenda. She was a praying mantis, primed to devour her boss once she achieved her goal. If things got too complicated, she would seek refuge behind her protected female EEOC status. Image was everything. Beth clipped her hair into a chic over-the-eye bob and wore dresses made from materials that dropped slightly in the front and suggestively lingered at the right curves as she walked. Her shoes were in-vogue straps with heels that jetted her into the stratosphere.

Bethany's first goal was to become the director of her Government Enterprises Division, with continued advancement targets to follow.

We sealed the scheme with a promise to talk by phone each week and to meet each quarter. The call was to (1) share insights, (2) reconstitute our will to win, (3) review the prior week's successes and failures, and (4) plan the attack strategy for the upcoming week.

Bethany identified our first attack tactic to be "inserting ourselves into the action." She defined this to mean moving out of our comfort zone and finding ways to make our bosses need and appreciate us. We had to be observant, find a shortcoming, and then carpe diem.

"Listen to them in any meeting," she tutored. "They only talk about three things: the numbers, sports, and women, in that order. These men are a real fraternity and don't think the young turks aren't lying in wait to overtake the old guard. They do the same things we are going to do, just differently. They are playing the same game. The only difference is that they are in pants and have been playing longer. Believe me when I tell you, they are far better brownnosers than you or I will ever be. It's all a game. So look for your opportunity."

I watched Pete and noticed he grew anxious when the clock struck 4:30, and so I pounced.

"Pete, is that the employee full-time equivalency report?"

"Yeah, I need to get this finished and in the mail to HQ tonight."

I stepped forward. "I've been studying that report for some time. Look at this. Am I doing it right?"

I could tell Pete was pleasantly surprised. He took the report and examined it.

"Well, I'll be. You did the entire report? Yeah, this is right."

"Wow. I'm just glad it's OK. Then if it's all right, you can sign it, and I'll get it to headquarters in the five-thirty mail." Pete smiled again, relieved.

"Thanks, really thanks." Grabbing his trench coat, Pete rushed to catch his 5:10 p.m. commuter train.

Several days later I approached Pete again. This time it was the monthly manger's report. This was a narrative written by the director each month that put flesh on the budgets and described the rhythm of the school. It highlighted successes and downplayed challenges. It always addressed the four major areas of the school: recruiting and admissions, education, financial, and job placement. The expectation was that the document would highlight the goals achieved, identify the problems perceived, and provide the solutions planned.

Pete despised writing. He was a numbers guy. I could tell he was struggling. I had watched him over the months with the dictionary at his side, talking to himself as he wrote a sentence, crossed it out, and tried again. This monthly task, for Pete, was pure agony. It would take him at least two grueling days out of each month to produce the two-page report.

I had volunteered to proofread several of the reports to understand better the themes covered and the format used. Most of what Pete wrote was good but professionally paltry for a director capturing the lifeblood of his institution.

"Pete, would it be OK if I took a stab at this? If you like, I can take notes on your thoughts for the month and then write up the rough draft, which you can edit. If you're OK with it, then I'll type up the finished report. I don't know how to explain it, but I love to write."

Pete's face became a neon sign.

"You do? You love to write?"

"I know it's crazy, but I really do."

"Well I have to tell you that I hate this. I mean, I could give you some notes, and we could see how it goes."

Pete never wrote another monthly managers report.

Then there was the day Pete was squirming to get to his son's baseball game.

"Pete, if you like, I'll stay later and mind the store until six thirty each night. That way you can take the early train so you can be with your family."

Pete gave me a stiff upper lip and raised fist that I translated to mean "team player." He never asked, "What about your family?"

In time Pete began to trust me. He anointed me the avenging angel. I became the bad cop, the person who would say, "You're going to have to cancel your vacation. We're having an internal audit" or "I'm sorry, Susan, but someone else got the position" or "You will need to work overtime. I know this interferes with your daughter's birthday party" or "Your last week's pay was docked."

The crème de la crème came when I volunteered to help prepare the monthly flash. This was a financial exercise that compared the budget projections for each month to the operating actual revenue and expenses for that month along with the remaining months projected through the end of the year. It was a tedious, numbers-driven nightmare, requiring one to manually add columns of numbers by departments, by months, by quarters, and by year. All columns had to tie. The finance manager captained the exercise, but the school director or assistant cosigned as to the flash's authenticity and was therefore equally involved.

The exercise gave me a headache. I hated numbers unless they were attached to a shoe sale. But numbers were the lifeblood of the company. This was where you earned your stripes. When you knew where and how to generate revenue, cut expenses, and improve a bottom line, you were no longer in the wimp category. You were considered a player. My calculus was to subtly offer suggestions that Pete could act on as his. If those suggestions produced measureable results, then I would become more and more indispensable. Little by little, I was inching my way to the table.

My goal was to demonstrate, in every way possible, that I was there for Pete, that I was his wingman. Could I ingratiate myself anymore? The answer was yes. I knew I had descended to my lowest depth when Pete was taking his male managers and me to a Cubs game, but Corporate required that some management presence remain.

"Fellas, listen. You can go to Wrigley. It's fine. Have a great time."

For a few seconds the guys paused, looking at me, and then shook their heads, signaling genuine affection.

"What a girl!" I heard Pete remark as they left for the park.

What did I get for all of this? The employee of the month for three months running, the employee of the year for our unit, and a promotion that January to school director as Pete ascended the ladder to regional manager.

Beth and I were sipping kirs at Chez Paul's. It was one of our quarterly luncheon meetings, and we both had something to celebrate. Beth had been assigned an expanded Midwest territory to direct, and Chicago was a part of it. Money was pouring into the cities and states from the federal coffers and into a number of programs whose names were alphabets or acronyms. Their intent was to help uplift and train the disadvantaged. Most of these programs had been born during the Johnson administration and were designed to provide access to skills training. The Nixon administration expanded the Pell Grant and Federal Student Loan programs to include for-profit schools. Much of this was done in the spirit of the GI Bill, which was viewed as successful in integrating and upgrading returning World War II veterans, through training and education, into the workforce. If it had worked for them, why wouldn't it work for underserved populations, many of whom were returning Vietnam Veterans? Following this logic, such programs as CETA, CEP, and MDTA took flight.

Beth's new division was intended to market the variety of training programs in the ITT stable of schools to these various organizations and harvest a percentage of the federal dollars for the corporation. For many corporations, schools and colleges of all stripes, federal financial aid was emerging as a new frontier of opportunity.

"How's it going?" Beth smiled a devilish smile.

"My alter ego is becoming so strong, I'm beginning to wonder if I might be schizophrenic. If I saw myself in the mirror, I'm not sure I would know it was me."

"Oh, I know. Crazy, isn't it? But hey, it's paid off."

"That it has. As I told you last week, headquarters sent out the Blue Sheet naming me director of the Chicago School."

Beth began a laugh that emanated in her gut and rolled out her throat.

"Amazing! We're getting there."

Indeed we were. It was now time for Beth to be exalted.

"I saw the Blue Sheet on you last month, sales manager for the Midwest Division. Tell me if that's not music to your ears."

"It took us two years, hard work, and a lot of obsequious fawning and foolishness, but here we are."

"Man, talk about hard work. I almost killed myself! Do you know what Cynthia said?"

Cynthia was the African American receptionist, the "Spook Who Sat by the Door," signaling to all who entered that our workplace was diverse.

"Cynthia said Pete's posse was totally pissed when they found out I got the promotion. Those were his boys, his amigos. Each one of them thought, for sure, that they had the job. Bill, because he's the finance manager, and you know how finance issues drive this company. He told Cynthia the only way I could have possibly gotten the position was because I was sleeping with Pete. Jesse, the marketing manager, is so sour, swearing to everyone that without his efforts over the last two years driving up enrollments, the school would never have exceeded its revenue budget or attain the impressive profit hike that carried Pete to his promotion. Jesse told Cynthia he hoped he didn't offend, but affirmative action was the only plausible explanation for my promotion. Tony, that's the education director, believes he's the only intelligent member of the team and is convinced he knows how to communicate with Black people and was therefore too important to the school in his current position to be promoted. He told Cynthia he's the glue that holds everything together. Mark, our placement director, is out of his mind with anger. He let Cynthia know this is the third time he has been passed over for a promotion. Cynthia said he's really taking it personally and is going to ask for a transfer to another school."

Bethany did not seem in the least bit surprised. "Well, there you have it, grown men behaving badly. It could never be that you worked your ass off. These guys feel that a successful woman is an oxymoron. To acknowledge the idea of a competent woman somehow makes them feel inferior. And we're supposed to be the weaker sex! Oh my God, such fragile egos! I'll tell you one thing, men are not the tough, macho machines we've been reared to think they are. Let me tell you about my boss. The last time you and I talked, I told you he was suffering a major crisis of confidence. Remember, his dad was the president of that national ITT insurance company, and Tim was never able to match his dad's career pinnacle. He tried, but it just hasn't happened. You know the story. Everyone compared Tim to his father, and he can't measure up. He got into the corporate system because of his dad. He's better educated than his dad, but he can't get the traction he needs to make it to the mountaintop. When he was assigned to head this start-up division, he felt it was a demotion. He said, who wants to be assigned to a no-name unit like Educational Services to head up a marketing effort to get poor people into training programs?"

We were putting olive oil on our French bread.

"No prestige, my darling, no respect. For Tim it was the equivalent of a graveyard assignment. That's when I became his grief counselor."

"Yeah, you told me."

"You see, I was the eunuch, going-nowhere female, outside of the good ole boys' network. Tim didn't need to impress me. Who could he tell this pathetic story to? Not the wife—she thinks he's a loser as it is. Nope, it's me."

"It's you."

"It's me, and I smile. I listen. I console, but most importantly I tell him how great he is. I tell him that his friends, family, and the company are not recognizing his true genius. And then I go out and bust my ass and bring in the sales. We've been over quota the last five quarters."

I lifted my glass.

"And that makes you the new sales manager of the Midwest region."

"Exactly."

Tactic #2

Beth and I concluded that our most pressing strategic move would be establishing ourselves as competent leaders.

"Leadership that produces results—that's our challenge. We must demonstrate that above all else our objective is to achieve our business plan's goals. That has to be our first commandment," Beth decreed. I accepted her charge, as I was understanding the essence of leadership and its vital impact on employee performance more and more.

Leadership, as I attempted to execute the skill, became the art of bending the free will of others to yours and making them like the experience. Sometimes I could do it, and sometimes I couldn't. I couldn't do it with Tony. He ultimately relocated to another region.

Leadership is also about stepping up and doing the hard thing. I didn't know how long it had been going on, but I was growing suspicious of how Bill was handling the cash receipts for tuition payments coming into the school. He was doing things like taking cash and writing double receipts for different amounts. He didn't do it frequently, making the practice difficult to detect. Bill would have never attempted this ploy with Pete, but he knew I was new. He was experienced, and it would be an arduous task for me to detect the receipt duplications. I should have known something was wrong when Bill began to be so accommodating. I had convinced myself that my leadership skills had made him a convert. Had it not been for the watchful eye of Mattie, a student worker in his office, the deception might have never been discovered. Based on her "intel," I confided my concerns to HQ. They sent in the director of internal security, who conducted an audit of Bill's cash receipts and deposit practice. My suspicions were confirmed. Now I had to fire Bill.

Bill wasn't exactly a prince, but I didn't want to fire him. I had witnessed corporate firings as Pete had executed them, and the thought of executing one myself was unnerving. One would never describe Bill as warm or approachable. He had been my least favorite member of Pete's management team. He had never done anything to me that was particularly offensive, but his being totally lacked all humanness. What kind of person never smiles? I always felt it would take vice grips to peel back his lips to make him grin.

But I knew he was the only wage earner in his family, a single parent raising two children, and desperately needed job security. None of that could matter now.

Beth had pronounced the first commandment. "We must demonstrate that above all else our allegiance is to this company and its stockholders."

Bill knew the drill. He had been with ITT for a decade, from the moment he got his bachelor's in accounting.

"Don't give me the spiel. Just give me the check," he scoffed as he entered my office.

"Would you like to take a seat?"

"Hell no. I can't wait to get out of this hellhole. I see what's happening. The last place that I want to be is here with you and all these jungle bunnies."

I remained calm.

"I'm sorry you feel that way. However, if you know as much as you say you do, then you also know I am required to do an exit interview. You can do it standing up, or you can take a seat. That's up to you."

Bill's stare was a torch. Then we both took our seats. He answered the obligatory questions. I requested his keys, issued him his paycheck, informed him of the status of his benefits, and told him we would pack up and forward him his personal effects. I then asked security, who was waiting outside of my office, to accompany him to his office, to gather his coat and briefcase and escort him out of the building. As a final gesture, I perfunctorily wished him well.

Firing a person is nothing anyone ever feels good about, but that's how it's done: surgically, efficiently, and void of emotion. You can't change the outcome, so don't prolong the agony. Whether it's downsizing, rightsizing, group, or individual terminations, you learn to block your feelings and execute.

Mark, the placement guy, had a problem, but it was not with me. It was the company. Being passed over three times was three times too many. He gracefully tendered his resignation.

I had to admit I was thrilled when Jesse stayed. In my opinion, it's the marketing position that is critical to a director's longevity. College-trained educators were at the ready to fill the director of education position. All that was required was to take the raw material and form it to the educational program's specifications. In a multinational corporation such as International Telephone and Telegraph, with its top-down administrative controls and a separate reporting line in its financial and accounting infrastructure, the finance manager was not a direct report. The school director was usually only a sign-off manager to this designated corporate hire. The placement director typically was a position pirated from other HR or staffing companies. Successful marketing managers, however, were unique, instinctive, resourceful, and scarce animals. Jesse was one of those, and he stayed. I had worked the last two years with Jesse and knew it would be my leadership task to convince him that I held this job because I was competent and not because I was an affirmative-action hire. Regardless of what he may have thought, I knew Jesse's skill set could make me a superstar.

I studied various marketing plans used by my colleagues at other schools and compared them to ours. I digested all sorts of media material and the type of leads they generated. I learned that a referral was the strongest type of lead and that television was one of the weakest. Newspaper leads were good; high school leads were cheaper. Testimonials were one of the best forms of advertising.

Jesse was a past master at all of this and could recognize the cost per lead and cost per enrollment within seconds of seeing the numbers. He could build budgets based on historical experiences and deliver on them in the future. To be able to work with him, I had to learn more. This meant putting myself through admissions representatives training. It wasn't easy but necessary. I had understood some of this working for Pete, but I now had to go for the deeper dive. When Jesse was gone, or any of our admissions representatives were ill, I would do the sales presentation with the inquiring applicant. I probed for the dominate buying motive, presented the benefits, overcame any objections and closed the sale. Not immediately, but in time, I gained Jesse's respect and ultimately his friendship. Together we would make the Chicago school one of the best in the ITT Educational Services firmament. Affirmative action now had a friend.

Tactic #3

Beth and I were in the Pump Room, sipping our kirs. Another two years had passed. Things had changed. Beth and I no longer called each other each week. Our professional lives had become too hectic. She now only came to Chicago occasionally. Beth was no longer in Educational Services. She had ascended to another division, as its director, promoting agricultural products.

The waiter had just prepared and tossed our Caesar salad tableside and was leaving as she began explaining, "Believe me; I would never have gotten this position if any of the guys thought they could successfully do it. It was just that this division's sales had torpedoed. Things were so bad, the guys felt taking the sales manager job would doom their careers. So I stepped up and took it. You know how it is with us firsts; we have to strike when the iron is hot."

"Here! Here!" I saluted her in a toast.

"It's a tough job, baby, but somebody had to do it." I smirked.

"I guess I am that somebody," she confirmed. "And I am turning this puppy around. The guys think I am a miracle worker. The truth is, I am just a hard worker. You can't quit when you're a first."

"Amen. Amen to that."

"Here's the other trick, my darling. To really be successful you have to build a network. You've got to have people in the right places to help you step up when the moment comes. Even if it's something that nobody else wants, somebody has to tell you it's there. Most people don't get the opportunity because they don't even know it's there."

"That's true."

"Of course it's true. You're from Chicago. If there is one place that exemplifies it's not what you know but who you know, this town is it. All that scientific research about objectivity and finding the best qualified is crap. In the end, it's who you know. As the saying goes, your net worth is your network."

I realized the point she was making and responded, "You are so right. Kennedy would never have made it to the White House without Daley."

"I'm telling you, it's the only way."

"So who did you know?" I playfully inquired.

Bethany smiled a sly smile. "Someone" was all she volunteered.

I knew not to press further.

"So how are things with you?"

"Great. Jesse and I were named director and sales manager of the year."

"Congratulations! Since I am no longer associated with that division, I don't get the Blue Sheets anymore. So what happens with you now?" I hadn't thought that far. I was still euphoric having been named the first woman and minority to be director of the year.

"Oh, I don't know. Things are pretty good now. I think I have found my stride. For the first time in a long time, my life seems to be balanced. I mean I'm going home earlier now, and the kids are all in school. I only hope Jesse doesn't leave. There's talk about him getting a big promotion into headquarters. If he goes, I'm toast."

"Oh, screw Jesse. Let me tell you something about this balance nonsense. Nothing is ever balanced. Nothing! It doesn't work like that. You're either slaying the dragon, or the dragon is slaying you. That is how it is if you plan to survive in the corporate world. If you want balance, you work for the government. So get over this home-life issue and Jesse. I will bet you, now that he's named director of the year, Jesse is not trying to stay in Chicago with all those students with all those problems. You have to know when it's over, and it's over. You guys have had a great run, and it got you one step higher up the ladder. I have been scanning your market area, and things will only go downhill from here. Look at the handwriting on the wall. There are too many new schools now competing for your demographic. Your market is saturated, your media plan is going to start to fail, and all your percentages will start to decline. Nothing lasts forever. It's time to plan your exit. Both of you should leave at the height of your best game. Start sending up those smoke signals, darling, and tap into your network. If you want, I'll try and help you, but it may mean relocation. As Paul Simon once said, "Make a new plan, Stan." I smiled but did not respond to her offer.

Beth had been right. Jesse accepted a plum of a position in headquarters. The Chicago for-profit education market was saturated. Advertising and recruitment costs were rising, and enrollments were falling. Over the next three years, I slipped from my perch as the darling of our division. Beth continued to rise.

I was in Pete's region. It had been the highest-producing region for the past three years, despite my school's decline. I loved my school, and over the prior six years had surrounded myself with competent people who were committed to quality and who cared about our students. I could trust these people. It was the external environment that was suffocating the business. Under Pete's direction, we had flexed expenses, downsized, and moved to a smaller, more efficient facility.

For the overall company, things were good. ITT Educational Services had embarked on expansion with new schools blossoming across the country. Pete's star continued its ascent. He relocated to the Indianapolis headquarters as the vice president of operations. As a school director, I interacted with any number of people at headquarters and had a cadre of good contacts. Bethany's admonition about developing a network had not fallen on deaf ears. I now had two well-placed colleagues at HQ, Pete and Jesse.

It had not been lost on me that since I joined the company, there had been only two other women elevated to the position of school director, and one of those had left. Twice a year ITT held major manager's meetings. These were usually held at exotic destinations like Cancun, Bermuda, or Martha's Vineyard. These meetings were designed to build and reinforce teamwork, to disseminate corporate policies and propaganda, to roll out new initiatives, and to reward the overall management group. It was at the second meeting of that year when I buttonholed Pete.

"Pete, don't you think it's time this company had a female regional manager?"

"Maybe. Did you have anybody in mind?"

"Maybe." We both smiled.

Next, I cornered Jesse.

"I hope you never forget, Jesse, my friend, that you would not be here today if it weren't for me."

"I think about it every day," he jovially responded.

"One good turn deserves another."

"I feel the screws being put to me now."

"I hope so."

"Listen, anything you're probably thinking about would be outside of my jurisdiction and in somebody else's wheelhouse."

"I know, that may be true in the direct sense, but in the indirect world of influence, you'll have a vote. So if my name ever comes up, think about all I've done for you."

"My God, it's a bribe."

"No, no. Just a thought."

It would be another major manager's meeting and three months after that when Pete would summon me to headquarters. I was getting nervous. Pete was ecstatic.

"Come on in. Right here, sit down. Don't look like I'm going to kill you. So I've been talking with HR. We're creating a new region. It's going to be comprised of California, Nevada, Arizona, maybe some other states. Hell, I don't know. I'm recommending you for regional manager. It'll be perfect for you. We only have four schools in California now, but we're growing. Should have ten in two years. But you could grow as the region grows. I know you. You're a workhorse. When we get it all worked out, we'll run the customary announcements, but Jesse and I have the hook-ups in HR. They'll call you in for the pro forma interviews, but baby, this is a done deal."

Pete could tell he was more excited than me. "Are you OK?"

"I don't know what to say."

"It's a lot to take in, I admit. So go think about it. Anyway, it will be a few months before this hits daylight."

Be careful what you pray for. California? What had I been thinking? My husband worked for IBM, and IBM was starting to have hiccups. It had been set back on its heels as Wang and Microsoft began to overtake the computer market. I had two children. One was ready for high school, and both were ensconced in an array of friends and activities. California? There was nothing I really liked about the Golden State. I loved seasons and hated the Beach Boys. Varnished, perfect people were turnoffs. I preferred the unfinished people of the Midwest. They gave you hope that you could look better. What was I to do? Tell my husband, "Leave your job and pack up. We're moving to California." That would be way too emasculating. Was I to tell the kids, "Mommy and Daddy are plucking you from your schools, cliques, and clubs to take you to Hollywood"? The thought of it all was too overwhelming. When I was rational, I knew it was impossible. I could buy bacon and fry it up in a pan, but I couldn't risk a divorce or uproot my children. It was time to face a hard fact about the women's movement. I couldn't have it all.

Friendship Realignment

This was not going well. Beth and I were sitting in Le Parakeet. She had just ordered an escargot appetizer. You know things are not going well when you are about to eat snails. Over the years Bethany had grown more and more accomplished, achieving heights I could never have imagined. She was now the vice president over one of the corporation's hotel chains. Beth was in town for the National Restaurant Association's annual show. Beth was not smiling. I was staring at the snails.

"So you told them no?" I felt like the wayward daughter who had just confessed to her mother that she was pregnant."

"Beth, we can't have it all."

"No, we can't."

"It's complicated for me."

"Yes, it is."

"My life isn't just my life," I pleaded.

"No, it's not."

"I have to think about other people."

"Yes, you do."

Why didn't she just shoot me and get it over with? The prolonged punishment was excruciating.

"Beth, I'm not you."

She did not dignify that comment with a response. The silence began screaming around the room. The snails were gone, and so was Beth. Her parting words were, "I wish you all the best in the world. I have to run. Put your lunch on my tab." Beth extended a limp hand, and I shook it.

How could Beth understand? Who even knew anything about this woman? What was her real name? Who was her family? God knows I had tried several times to broach the subject of her personal life, but Beth wasn't having it. Her liquid eyes always flashed caution, caution, and I stepped back.

Rumors always ran rampant about Beth at HQ. To the guys at headquarters, she was a real ballbuster: a woman who negotiated like a man to include deals, promotions, and lovers. "Everything she did was business," they said, "everything." To them Beth was ruthless and frightening.

In the ensuing years, Beth and I exchanged the obligatory Christmas and Birthday cards. When rumors of takeover attempts at ITT began to swirl, the hotel chain Beth managed was divested and sold to a European group. She was a part of that sale.

Beth did not contact me again until the summer of 2009. She found me at work.

"Still in the school business, I see."

"Seems so."

"I have to give you credit for perseverance."

"It's not perseverance. It's survival. After college tuitions, grad school, weddings, and the collapse of IBM Selectric sales, it is all about survival, sweetheart."

We both laughed.

Beth told me she had retired four years ago in the south of France and had recently been diagnosed with the early onset of Alzheimer's. She had moved back to Upstate New York and had taken up residence in a place called Shady Grove. If ever I had the time, she suggested, I might come and visit her. That was Beth's way of asking if I could come, and so I did.

Shady Grove was a euphemism for a senior care facility built on the continuum-of-care model. A continuum-of-care facility is like checking into "Hotel California" with room upgrades. First, you're a resident in senior living. As you age or grow more infirmed, you advance to assisted living. If you then have major health challenges, you advance to skilled nursing care. Shady Grove was a senior care facility with panache.

It was like entering a five-star hotel replete with a doorman, front desk staff, luxury apartments, full-service restaurant, and guest residences. When I was cleared to go to Beth's apartment, I found her protected in a sleek, mid-century modern, two-bedroom unit. The help answered the door, but I could not determine if the personnel was medical or domestic. Beth was sitting in her living room in a burgundy cowl-neck sweater and navy-blue Katherine Hepburn slacks. Her face had more creases than I remembered, but she was still breathtaking. Her perfectly arched eyebrows touched the dipping wave of her gunmetal-gray hair.

I had been apprehensive about this visit, but I shouldn't have been. Beth's smile was inviting and relaxed. Her hand patted the cushion beside her.

"Come sit here." I did. She grabbed both of my hands.

"It seems we've both become old women."

"I think so."

"But it was fun. Wasn't it?"

"I've missed you, crazy lady."

"Me too. Listen, I have reservations in the dining room. Shall we go?"

So there we sat in the dining room of Shady Grove, sipping kirs and reminiscing through all the strategies, the failures, and the triumphs. At long last, we both felt released from the need to be first. As we finished a chocolate soufflé, Beth looked across the table and for the first time asked, "By the way, how are your children?"

After that day, I called Beth once a month. She always seemed upbeat but increasingly scattered. The last time I spoke with Beth, she began singing a few bars of something in French and then put down the receiver. I could hear the song trailing off into the distance. Seconds later a woman came to the phone.

"Hello," she said.

"Hello, I was talking to Beth."

"I'm so sorry, ma'am, but Miss Harper has left."

When I returned from Beth's memorial service, I felt diminished. The service was precisely as Beth had arranged. As she always said, "Prior planning prevents piss-poor performance."

Beth had entered an unchartered world in an untested time. She overcame and achieved through personal sacrifice, keen intellect, and fierce determination. Because of Beth, my professional performance was better, but hers was perfect. The dance ends.

DANCE NUMBER SIX: INTERPRETATIVE DANCE

The Song: "I've Gotta Be Me"
The Dancer: Mattie Davis

The Observance

The receptionist announced that a Ms. Anderson was there to see me. I was baffled to be interrupted and in no mood for strangers.

"I don't know a Ms. Anderson. What does she want?"

"She says she's a friend of Mattie Davis."

"Mattie Davis? Give me a minute. I'll be right there." Mattie Davis. Talk about a blast from the past. I couldn't begin to say when I saw Mattie last. As I made my way to the lobby, I saw an elderly, semi-blond, strong-boned lady clutching several Marshall Field's bags. I extended a hand, but instead of clasping mine, she just smiled.

"Thank you for seeing me."

"No problem at all. I see you have been shopping at one of my favorite stores. I love Field's."

Marshall Field & Company, the venerable Grand Dame of State Street, had lived in better times.

She had come a long way from her glory days of "Give the lady what she wants." Time had not been kind. The store had been handed off from one owner to the next. There had been face-lifts and makeovers but none surgically effective enough to keep her from looking worn and bent like *Cat's* Grizabella. She was the last survivor of State Street's golden retail age and was now in the grip of a final transition from Marshall Field's to Macy's. Yet, even as she was listing, the store retained an air of elegance, a refinement that no other store could touch. For many, myself among them, the thought that this great lady could become a Macy's was too much to bear. Macy's would make her a New York rag barn: a sight too painful to watch. It was the spring of

2005; the lady, as we knew her, was drawing her last breath. Mourners from far and wide were coming to get that last souvenir, collect some memorabilia of a bygone era.

Green mesh bags with the distinctive white cursive logo that spelled Marshall Field's were selling like hotcakes, and Ms. Anderson had one of them.

"I love that bag. It's great. I bought two. Anyway, come with me. I want you to tell me everything that's going on with Mattie."

Ms. Anderson followed me to my office.

"Please have a seat." She sat, and so did I.

"So you know Mattie."

"Yes, I do."

"Do you know I haven't seen her in years? Where in the world is she?"

"She's here," came Ms. Anderson's definitive response.

"Here? You mean in Chicago? I thought she had moved to Minnesota. When did she come back here?"

"No." Ms. Anderson wanted to make clear. "I mean she's here." Ms. Anderson was pointing to the bag in her lap.

"You mean the Marshall Field's bag?"

"Yes."

"Mattie's in the Marshall Field's bag?"

"Yes."

"I'm sorry, Ms. Anderson. I'm afraid I don't understand."

Ms. Anderson opened the bag, removed a wood box, and slid back a lid.

"This is Mattie."

I rose to my feet, horrified.

"This is Mattie," she repeated.

"That's Mattie?"

"Yes, it is. We were married." Ms. Anderson's shoulders began to shake. She started to weep, her tears falling into the box.

"Oh, I'm so sorry."

This was getting too bizarre. "Maybe you should close the lid." Things were already strange enough without Mattie turning to mud. "Why don't you put the box back in the bag? I'll just put the bag on my desk, and you can tell me what happened." Ms. Anderson agreed.

I gave her a Kleenex. She dabbed her eyes and began.

"Mattie and I met at a club. I couldn't keep my eyes off her. She was so striking. I mean, you know how tall she was."

I stared at the Marshall Field's bag.

"She was tall all right."

"It was simpatico, inexplicable. We just knew right then and there."

"Then and there" was all I could say.

"Our life forces just merged into one. We were never apart again. There was never anyone else for us. Just each other. When Canada allowed gay marriages, we went to Toronto and tied the knot. It was the most beautiful day of our lives. We were married. Then last year, she got sick. You remember, Mattie smoked."

I shook my head. I did remember that.

"When they told her she had six months, she came right back at 'em. Called them lying bastards."

"She was a fighter, that Mattie." I remembered that as well.

"She gave it all she had. I knew she didn't want to leave, but last week she couldn't fight anymore. And here I am."

"And here you are."

There was a piece of the story I seemed to be missing.

"Ms. Anderson?"

"Yes."

"I'm so sorry. Your love story is so beautiful, and I am sorry for your loss, but why are you here?"

"Why? To do what we are supposed to do. Mattie said she had told you many times where she wanted to be buried. She said you would know and that I could count on you to make it happen."

Ms. Anderson's glare was shifting to skepticism. "Don't you know?"

Did I know? Did I know? I remembered a person who had liked me more than I had liked her. A woman who had been there when I needed a friend, someone who was always willing to step into the furnace on my behalf.

"Don't you know?" Ms. Anderson demanded again.

The years, the years, quickly turn back the years. Time raced backward, and there was Mattie. The woman was a study in contrasts: part cast-iron and part autumn-leaf.

"You couldn't make it in my neighborhood, looking like I did, if you weren't hard as nails and tough as last month's meat," she once told me. "Could you see me as some delicate little darling and surviving on Sixty-Third Street?"

No, I could not. Mattie was rough and at least six feet tall. In another time and place and of another race, she could have been a runway model. But born and reared in Chicago's badlands in the 1950s and '60s, she was a gang member, a Blackstone Ranger. But that was another lifetime ago, before finding her way to Minnesota and true love. Now here she was on my desk, and I was struggling to remember.

"Do you know what she wanted or not?" Ms. Anderson was becoming agitated.

"Yes, I know," I finally answered. Ms. Anderson was gleeful.

"Oh my God, thank you! Thank you! Thank you! What is it she wants us to do?"

138

At that moment I felt like Tonto addressing the lone ranger: "What 'we,' White man?" But in honor of my departed friend, I bit my tongue and replied, "She wants us to take her to the Museum of Science and Industry."

Ms. Anderson was more confounded now than ever. "To a museum. Are you sure?"

"Yes I am sure. You see, there's a park that borders the west side of the museum. Four women stand in a row there. They are called the Maidens of Caryatid. Mattie went to that museum when she was a child on a school field trip. She said it was the happiest day of her life."

"When I die," she would tell me, "I want to be buried there. I want those beautiful ladies watching over me. They won't be like my momma. They'll never leave."

"That's what she wants?"

I patted the Marshall Field's bag. "That's what she wants."

"Then that's what we have to do." Ms. Anderson popped up, military straight. "Let's go do it."

"Wait, Ms. Anderson, I'm at work. I just can't leave and go to Jackson Park with you and Mattie here." I reverently patted the bag again.

"Then when can we go? My train leaves tomorrow afternoon."

"OK, then why don't we do it first thing in the morning?"

"What time?" I couldn't believe I had been drawn into this.

"Say around nine thirty."

"Is that a firm nine thirty?" What? I had said "around." I didn't want to be a part of any of this. I don't do burials. Was this Heidi-looking senior citizen actually challenging my arrival time?

"Ms. Anderson, I live far south and commute during rush hour. So for me, around nine thirty is as close as I can get. So why don't you take Mattie here with you, leave your phone number and an address, and I will pick you both up tomorrow around nine thirty, and together we will go to the museum."

That morning I put a long-handled heavy-duty barbeque fork and spatula in my car and went for Ms. Anderson and Mattie. We made our way to a spot in the park—a place where I thought one caught the best perspective of the four handmaidens. There I began digging in the dirt with the barbeque fork. The grass was damp, but the ground was still solid.

"Listen, Ms. Anderson, we're not going to be able to put the box in here. The ground is too hard. I think we should maybe pour the ashes into this hole I just made. I can't get much deeper."

Ms. Anderson understood. With respect and solemnity, Ms. Anderson kneeled, withdrew the box from the bag, slid back the lid, and oh-so-carefully emptied its contents into the fresh hole. She took her hands and covered over the hole. A slight mound remained, which I patted as flat as I could with the spatula. Ms. Anderson and I stood. We both appeared a little uneasy.

"I think maybe we should say something," I offered.

"Yes, I think we should."

"You go first."

Ms. Anderson stared at the pancake-size spot.

"Mattie, when you left you took the part of me that was light and happiness. My world will be forever dark until I see you again."

I followed. "Mattie, be at peace. The Maidens of Caryatid have you now, and they will always attend to you. Artemis will protect you."

The Dance

The Me I Want to Be

Beth had been in Chicago several times talking with a host of state and federally funded agencies. The Welfare Rehabilitation Services (WRS) program came first. This agency wanted to contract with the school to train fifteen women. All were on welfare, and all were mothers. The goal was to prepare them to be clerk typists. The program was for six months and taught receptionist skills, typing, customer service, business English, and math. At the program's end, the school was to place a high percentage of the women in jobs throughout the loop.

One of my duties as assistant director was to provide the orientation whenever we got group contracts from the various agencies. It was a very stimulating time. For its first eight years, the school had primarily catered to young White women, fresh out of high school, whose families had the capacity to pay their tuition. The school taught them secretarial skills: typing, speed-writing, business English, math, and social etiquette. The goal of the training was to produce graduates who were technically proficient, socially adroit, and outfitted in personalities calibrated to please. No young woman went to an interview without a hat and gloves, and every graduate's raison d'être was to make her boss look good and support his agenda. These were the Stepford wives of the office. That is until the dawn of the social programs. These programs offered core urban dwellers, through federal and state funding, access to private education at such business schools as Catherine Gibbs and Patricia Stevens.

The dilemma for the schools' management was that most of the students admitted to these programs were poor and minorities. As they came through the doors and took their seats, the White middle-class students, at least in Chicago, got up and walked away. Within three years of participation in the various social programs, our school's 98 percent White census had flipped to 98 percent Black. In my position as assistant director, I was the conduit, the person assigned to manage the transition and help assimilate these unexposed clients, as the agencies termed them, into the workforce. As the person in charge of orientation, mine was the first face they saw. Mine was the first voice they heard talking about another way to be and what it meant to work in the canyons of downtown Chicago.

I had already conducted several small group orientations. Usually, they were in clusters of five or eight. Beth was beginning to bring in groups two to three times that size, but I had planned that this orientation would be the same as all the others. With every orientation, I would bound into the room with a beaming smile and chant like a cheerleader, "Welcome, everyone, welcome. We are so glad that you are here. Now I know you've had to go through a lot to get here—paperwork, interviews, tests—but give yourselves a big hand. You made it."

I began a vigorous clap. Several stale claps followed.

"OK, people, can we try that again? You're about to begin a program that will change your life. This is good news. You are saying yes to change, yes to self-improvement, yes to becoming employable, yes to a new day. Let's congratulate ourselves. Can we give ourselves a big hand?"

I commenced another round of vigorous clapping only to receive the wimpy slapping of a few sluggish hands. That was when I heard, "What's wrong with you all? Who here didn't get what the lady said? Can we give ourselves a big hand?" With that, a person started clapping, and another and another. Soon the entire room was clapping, and people were smiling. Energy flooded the room. I had conducted an excellent orientation.

When it concluded, and the women were filing out of the room, I pulled over the woman who had initiated the clapping. "Thank you. You were a game changer."

"It wasn't that. You just didn't know how to get 'em going. Half of the chicks in this room don't even want to be here. Their case workers are making them do it. Some of them have been in so many of these kinds of programs, heard so many speeches and promises that don't go anywhere. To them this is just one more thing they have to do so they can keep gettin' their checks."

"Is that how you feel about being here? That it's just one more thing you have to do to keep getting your check?"

"Not me. When I see you standing up there, and you look like me, I think, this time it's real, and I'm ready for a life change. I'm glad to be here."

Mattie was the mother of an eight-year-old son, Deon. They still were living in the neighborhood where she grew up. Deon's father was a gangbanger. He was currently in prison. She called him Duke. When Mattie talked about Duke, she said she had been with him since she was fifteen. She was not his only woman, not even his main squeeze, but that was fine with her. He was better to her than her momma and still maintained sufficient street equity, so nobody bothered her and her boy. His prominence in the gang, even from behind the wall, afforded her and her son both protection and some modicum of prestige. If the truth were told, Mattie wasn't into her baby daddy or any other man. Her relationship with Duke had been a simple matter of survival. From it had come her son, whom she loved more than life. Deon enhanced Mattie's life in other ways. He afforded her access to a monthly welfare check and public housing, which she shared with her mother and younger sister, who also had a son.

Mattie knew and understood the world she inhabited and wanted a better one for Deon. Things were already getting difficult. Her son had to repeat second grade and was reaching an age where the gang was sure to suction him in. When I conducted her entrance interview, she stated that this WRS program might be her ticket out. Mattie had never worked a real job. That was her mother's legacy. Her mother had been a Mississippi sharecropper eking out a going-nowhere life under the yoke of an abusive husband. She had fled north, taking her two baby girls with her. Chicago and the Robert Taylor Homes were as far as she got. The projects hadn't been so bad at first, and the welfare checks were much more money than her mother had seen in her life. Over time, the Robert Taylor Homes and its occupants sank under the weight of shattered families, joblessness, drugs, and crime into an inescapable, dysfunctional circus.

Mattie knew the Robert Taylor life all too well and did not want her son to inherit it.

"I'm willing to do what it takes," she vowed in the interview. "Just show me what I have to do."

There were motivational examples Mattie could also name. Her girl-friend, Donnette, had finished a program like ours and had gotten a job as a clerk for the city. If Mattie finished this clerk typist program and got a job, she reasoned, then she and Donnette could get an apartment in South Shore or maybe even Chatham.

I liked Mattie. Her presence gave me the aura of having a bodyguard. I gave her a part-time, college work-study job assisting me with scheduling, filing, and running errands. Her presence at my side sent silent messages like, "Don't fuck with me!" à la Grace Jones. Mattie moved with machismo. Her imposing stature was that of an immovable six-foot cinder block. Her face was pretty but incongruous for that of a ghetto warrior. Her afro cap of hair, enormous hoop earrings, laced-up combat boots, and bell-bottom pants all combined to telegraph the message, "I am not the one."

Mattie could smile, but she had to practice lip flexes several times before it happened. Her favorite gesture was to roll her eyes high in their sockets and expel a sigh that bellowed the whole world is for shit.

A Rose by Any Other Name

I never informed Mattie that I thought of her as my bodyguard. The roles just developed naturally between us. It wasn't that I was in any real danger. The WRS students I had in my care to mentor and counsel were probably more afraid of their surroundings than I was of them.

Coming daily to Chicago's loop, for these women, was daunting. Being educated in a downtown office building was new. Interacting in a predom-inately White environment was new. But that was, in part, the point. To remove the "clients" from their natural environment, their comfort zone, and help them assimilate into the broader mainstream.

My job was to create a safety net of support, to sensitize the teaching faculty, and to provide a cultural context for the administration. Above all else, my job was to reassure all parties involved that this training goal could be achieved: to prove that in twenty-six weeks, our school could train, graduate, and place fifteen unprepared women as clerk typists.

Mattie was excited about having a real part-time job and shadowed me constantly. Each day, when her classes were over and her work-study job had ended, she would head for the L train and home.

"Can't wait to tell Deon and Donnette about today" would be her parting line.

I remember when I truly understood who Donnette was. Mattie had brought the attendance forms for me to review. Students with five absences were to be flagged for a counseling session. Mattie was waiting for me to complete the list so she could notify the students of their appointment times.

"You really like this Donnette. Is she your best friend?" It was just small talk meant to fill the vacuum.

"She's my girlfriend."

"Is she your best friend?"

"She's my only girlfriend."

Mattie was saying more than her words, but I decided to let sleeping dogs lie. The next day Mattie felt compelled to explain. "I need to tell you something."

"What is it, Mattie?" Mattie was visibly nervous and clumsy with her words.

"Well, I'm not sure if you really get me. You know what I mean? I'm not sure you understand who I am. I've thought about this a lot. I talked to Donnette about it, and she said that I just have to be straight with you. I sure hope what I'm about to tell you doesn't change things, but you see, I'm a lesbian."

My mind was momentarily jostled.

"Are you saying you're gay?"

"Yes, I'm gay."

Gay. Mattie was gay. I had never met a gay woman. The school employed an effeminate, male typing teacher who used a lot of exaggerated hand gestures, wore pinched-waist pants, and polished his words with prissy pronunciation, but no one said he was gay.

Once when I was in eighth grade, my mother and I were on the bus, and a person boarded wearing beautifully tailored slacks. The hair was styled in deep, molded waves. It was the face, though, that I still remember. It was perfectly smooth with arched brows, buffed cheeks, and painted lips. The person walked down the aisle and sat in the seat in front of us. "Momma," I whispered, "is that a man or a woman?" My mother turned, cupped a hand over my ear, and whispered, "That's a queer." Nothing more. I never saw one again.

Mattie was definitely not an androgynous-appearing person. You knew she was a female. It was just that everything about her seemed angry and ready to engage in some type of survival combat. Whenever you met her, the greeting more appropriate than hello would have been stand down. When class was over and no one was around, Mattie's expression would soften. Her essence contained a sort of hidden wonder that she guarded like a host in the tabernacle of her soul. Being vulnerable was her fear. She must never be vulnerable. So here she stood, staring at me, hungry for me to affirm her, but afraid that I would not. The thing she feared most was happening. Mattie was vulnerable. I saw her eyes begin to sink. She should never have trusted me.

"Mattie, I don't care what you are. All I know is you're the best student in this class, and I'm glad you're here." I wanted to say more, but I didn't have to. Mattie had me in a bear-hug that was squeezing out my life force.

"Let me go, Mattie. Let me go."

"I'm sorry, I shouldn't have done that. I didn't mean anything."

"I know that. Now can we get on with this scheduling?"

"Sure. Sure. Tomorrow I'm gonna bring you some banana pudding."

I had delivered my response to Mattie with more sophistication than I actually possessed. There were so many questions I wanted to ask. How do you become a lesbian? What do lesbians do when they make love? What do you tell your son? So many questions, but I never gave voice to any of them. These questions were a salve for my curiosity and had nothing to do with trust or friendship, just nosiness. Mattie mistakenly believed, because I bore all the accoutrements of a professional, that I really was one. Mattie was wrong.

During the last six weeks of class, students were seen by the placement director, Mark, for their exit interviews. Placement was a big component of the WRS contract. We were required to place, at a minimum, 70 percent of the graduates if we were to have a shot at renewing the contract. Mattie was the top performer in the class. She could type seventy words per minute, spell like a prodigy, and had greatly improved in the area of public speaking, but she hadn't been selected for an interview. Mark had placed over 60 percent of the students, but not Mattie. He was also coming to the end of his rope, as those graduates remaining were either uncooperative, underprepared, or pregnant. When I approached him about Mattie, Mark offered me some tepid explanation that sounded like he could give less than a damn. After the fourth week and no interviews for Mattie, I went to see Pete.

"I hope I'm not disturbing you," I apologized as I entered his office.

"No. Come in, come in. Have a seat."

"I wanted to talk with you about placement and retention for our WRS program. Retention on that program is eighty-five percent. We budgeted seventy-five. We are going to come out of this smelling like a rose. Bethany's got another contract twice this size for us coming down the pike. As you know, enrollments are also up in our core business. So programs like WRS are just value-added. Bethany told me, off the record, that our New York and DC schools aren't doing nearly as well with their numbers as we are."

"I've got to hand it to you, kid, it takes somebody like you to make this all work. You have to understand the nuances of this kind of market. It's not what we are used to dealing with. But you seem to understand it."

"Pete, could I talk with you about something?"

"Of course. Shoot."

"Well, I have to tell you, I have loved working with this pilot group. And you are so right, one does have to understand the nuances of this market. These adult, single moms have different needs from the traditional student this school has historically served."

"Now I realize that. But you tell me what you need, and I'll see that you get it."

"Well, now I'm concerned about one student. Can I confide in you about something?"

"Absolutely."

"It's about Mattie Davis. Do you know the student?"

"Yes, I know her."

"Did you know she's gay?"

"Does a bear shit in the woods? Does a cookie crumble? Is the Pope Catholic? Hell, everyone knows she's gay!"

"Everyone?"

"Ev-er-y-one. That woman is so butch. You could spot it a county mile. Look at those outfits. The boots, the leather jacket and pants, that haircut. Since she started working for you, she now carries a briefcase. The boys all think she has a whip in that thing. Didn't you know?"

"I do now. I learned a few months ago."

"Learned? What's to learn? You should be scared to death. Don't go into the locker room with her."

"Pete, I'm concerned about her."

"Concerned about her?" Pete sounded bewildered. "A dyke like that will cut you fifty ways from Sunday before you know what hit you. Why do you think all these other women give her so much real estate whenever she comes around?"

"I'm concerned because she hasn't been sent on any job interviews."

"No, and she won't be sent on any. Listen, we can't control who these agencies send us. She just becomes a part of that thirty percent placement statistic that we can't help. Mark said it's challenging enough placing this population. You know we're opening doors here. Mark spends days convincing employers that it's time to give your people a chance, and when he finally gets a nibble and that employer softens to yes, you can be damn sure we're not going to send out Betty Butch?" Pete paused and then underscored. "It's not going to happen."

The Eyes Have It

The last week of school we took the students for a picnic at Jackson Park to celebrate their graduation milestone. For several of the women this was their most significant achievement since high school. Many had never been to this point in the park or to the museum itself. The picnic spot was in the shadow of the Museum of Science and Industry, facing west. The Museum of Science and Industry is one of two surviving structures from the 1893 World's Columbian Exposition, when Chicago was the gleaming white city on the lake.

As we munched hot dogs and toasted with brightly colored cups filled with coke, Mattie confided to me that the Museum of Science and Industry was her favorite place. It was the first space where she felt happy and safe.

The memory reached back years, when she thought going to school was a good thing, even fun. Mattie had come to the museum as part of a field trip. Sitting on the school bus, her first awe-inspiring sight was the Maidens of Caryatid, frozen in time, for all to see. They were there now, standing fearlessly in the distance preparing to serve Artemis, the goddess and protector of young girls.

"Look at them. They didn't even have any real eyes. You don't want to mess with people who don't have eyes. It's hard for them to love what they can't see. So if they come at you, you got some hell to pay. When I first saw them staring at me with no eyes, I knew they were some tough sisters full of potion-making magic and hidden powers that we don't even understand. That quartet of bitches could cast a spell on you from which you could never recover. But if they cared for you, they gave you protection like I don't know what. That first time, when I looked at them from that bus window, they saw me. I tell you, something went through me from my head down to my legs, and I knew then that they loved me. I felt 'em say, 'Don't' be afraid anymore, little girl. We got you.' Imagine when women like that love you. Just look at them." Mattie gazed admiringly. "Them some mean motor scooters. They make me feel real safe. I have only been here one other time. I don't remember why. I do remember I was all grown up and had on a skirt. I walked up close and looked at them, and they looked back at me, just me. They said them same words, and I got that same feeling. When I'm here with them, it's like being in church. It's like this is a holy spot, a protected haven, or something. I'm getting that feeling now. Do you feel it?"

That's the magic of art. It's all about how it impacts the viewer.

"Not as much as you do, I'm afraid."

"Man, those chicks move me. When I die, I want to be buried right here with me looking at them, and them looking back at me."

Mattie had been graduated four months, and Mark had never scheduled her for a job interview. Pete had been summoned to HQ to interview for a regional manager slot, leaving Mark to marinate in despair. His natural personality was sour, but the company's recently announced decision to make its four schools, located in major urban centers, feeder institutions for training minority populations had set him against the whole world. It became the backdrop for a lot of repressed anger. Mark would mutter disparaging comments within ear shot of anyone, but especially me, about African Americans.

"If African Americans were as capable as everyone else," he proffered, "the company wouldn't have to change everything for these bubble brains; we wouldn't need all these special services."

By his account, the company had lost its rudder and was steering into a place of no return. This business model, he prophesized, would cost ITT more to deliver than it would ever make. Pete, he had determined, had blinders on and was only being considered for a promotion because he was posting phony numbers that would soon deflate when these pointless poverty programs became extinct. Mark grew even more outspoken about affirmative action, swearing it overlooked the competent and replaced them with the inferior to satisfy some insane Washington mandate. Further, how could anyone expect him to find jobs for all these jungle bunnies now seeking admission to the school? One or two candidates, maybe, but finding jobs for all these decadent descendants of the African diaspora was virtually impossible.

Pete became a regional manager. When I interviewed for the position of school director to replace him and was ultimately promoted, the camel's back was broken. Mark resigned amid a flurry of expletives and walked out the door. I was beyond overjoyed when Mark moved into unemployment. If he had remained, my life would have been a living hell. As I took the reins of the school, there was no doubt in my mind what my first executive action would be. I hired Mattie.

Mattie would call me each week after graduation and ask, was she ever going to get an interview? I had admonished her, telling her to be patient. Rome wasn't built in a day. But I knew she was losing hope, not just in me, but in herself.

The Zebra Who Changed Her Stripes

I had promised myself, if I got the director's job, I would find a way to hire Mattie, but I still had i's to dot and t's to cross before it could be a done deal. There were all the obligatory interviews required to establish that I had examined a pool of candidates and found her to be the best. There was all the paperwork to be completed and the supporting rationale that HR required before executing any hire, and then there was the requisite second level approval of your regional manager. That would be Pete. When the paperwork landed on his desk, I got the call.

"Can you please tell me why? What did I ever do to you but try and help? You want my career to end before it begins, is that it? Why are you doing this? Is there something I don't know about you and this dominatrix? I really want to understand."

"I know to you it seems strange."

"Strange? You say strange. I say career ending for both of us. I just got my job, and I like it. I really do. Please don't make me question your judgment. You already have me questioning mine. Couldn't you just see this? I show up in Chicago for an operations review meeting with people from Indy, maybe even someone from New York, and there sits the pervert princess at the front desk. We work for one of the most conservative corporations in the whole world. It can't happen. There is no way I can approve this hire." Pete was starting to overheat.

"Pete, Pete. Believe me; I get it. I know who these people are, and I know you stepped out on a limb when you pushed for me to get this position. I know I was a tough sell. I'm sure you called in a lot of favors to get it done, and I promise I won't let you down. Please don't misunderstand. My proposed hiring of Mattie Davis isn't personal. This is one hundred percent business."

I could tell Pete was experiencing a trust issue. "In what way?"

"Remember when Mark left? We thought the placement rate on the WRS contract had exceeded seventy percent. That turned out not to be the case."

"Why? What happened?"

"What happened was that Mark was fudging the numbers. Two of those students the WRS program supervisor could not be verified as placed. Mark had indicated on his reports to us that they were, but when the agency verified our placement numbers with the employers, it was only sixty-seven percent. As you know we need a minimum of seventy percent to get the contract renewed. I had Tina follow up on all unplaced graduates. The only one still available for placement was Mattie Davis, and the only job I knew we could verify for her would be ours. Placing her would take us just to seventy percent. That WRS contract renewal is fastened into our budget with a ten percent enrollment increase. If we don't get that contract, we will take a significant bottom line hit, and frankly I don't know if we would have enough time remaining in the year to recover. Neither one of us can afford a high-profile mess coming out of the gate." There was silence on the other end of the phone.

"Pete, are you still there?"

More silence, and then Pete spoke. "Put her in the back. Some place where no one can see her. We'll keep her long enough to seal the deal, and then we'll let her go."

"Makes sense. I've got just the spot."

Pete sighed in resignation.

"OK, that's the plan."

When I received all the appropriate clearances for the hire, I phoned Mattie to come see me. She arrived at my office registering an obvious irritation.

"You want to see me?" Her eyes were fixed in a punishing stare. Sometimes anger and hurt wear the same mask.

"Have a seat, please." Mattie flopped defiantly into the chair. Her expression said it all: So what the fuck do you want? I answered the silent question.

"I would like to offer you a job." Her cement face cracked. Her eyes grew moist.

"What's wrong with you?" I chided mockingly. "You don't cry; you murder people."

"I'm not crying, and I don't murder people." We were both smiling.

"Is this for real?"

"This is for real."

"I would work here with you?"

"Right here."

"Right here, you, me, and all these White people."

"Just you and me, kid." The tears had made her eyes glisten.

"I need to think about it."

"Go ahead. Think about it."

"I just did. I'll take it."

"But you don't know what the job is or how much you'll make."

"Don't matter; I'll take it."

"Doesn't matter?"

"That's what I said. It doesn't matter." We were still smiling.

"It's not that easy though. I have a few stipulations." Mattie frowned.

"What are stipulations?"

"Things you have to agree to do to get the job."

"Such as?"

"You can't do drugs."

"I don't do drugs."

"You have to be here every day on time."

"Not a problem."

"Work hard."

"Not a problem."

"Trash that attitude you came in here with."

"Do I have an attitude?" Mattie seemed shocked at the suggestion.

"As my boss, Pete, loves to say, 'Does a bear shit in the woods?'"

"OK, OK I'll work on it. Is that all?"

"Just one more thing."

"What is that?"

"It's your appearance." I could tell the words were pricking.

"What's wrong with my appearance?"

"On Sixty-Third Street, nothing maybe. But this is a very reserved company in downtown Chicago. You've got to come to work looking less like Genghis Khan and more like Mary Tyler Moore."

I could sense her feelings start to scorch.

"And that means what?"

"It means, first of all, those boots have to go."

"I don't wear high heels."

"That's fine. A nice flat will do, but these boots belong to your past, not your present. Consider wearing skirts."

"I don't wear skirts. My legs don't look right. Kids called my legs toothpicks, Olive Oil legs—can't wear skirts."

"Then pants are OK, but make them appropriate for the workplace and get some blouses, something soft, maybe some ruffles." Mattie's face contorted in disgust.

"And let's get more hair and less earrings." I punctuated my closing statement with a smile.

"Is that all?"

"That's all. You still want the job?"

Mattie reared back in her chair and then forward. She was wrestling with restraint.

"What I really want is to tell you…"

"What do you want to tell me, Mattie?"

"I really want to tell you…thank you."

"Does this mean that you agree with the stipulations?"

Mattie bared her even teeth. I could not tell if she was smiling or preparing to dismember me. She then stood, extended her hand, and asked, "Does a bear shit in the woods?"

I can't say when I crossed the line. When I stopped being curious about what Mattie did with her vagina and began to care more about what she did with her career.

Mattie could not have been more right. It was just the two of us. In response to my request, she discarded the combat look and, with her first check, bought three pairs of slacks: black, gray, and brown plaid and a pair of black flats. Over the course of the next two months, she bought several blouses in soft pastel colors with ties and ruffles.

The job I had assigned to her would put her back in her comfort zone. Mattie would be the payroll and cash receipt clerk. She would return to the business office, where she had been a student worker with Bill. All initial student contracts written by the admissions reps went to her to log and record the student application fees and any tuition payments. She would help prepare the payroll. I knew I could trust this woman from the ghetto in ways I could have never trusted Bill.

After Bill's double dipping discovery and subsequent firing, I had waited to request a replacement. I needed time to get Mattie ensconced in her position without negative feedback from an intimidated new hire. She had earned brownie points with Pete for sniffing out Bill's dirty deed and wanted nothing to tarnish the good will she was amassing. Pete had told me HQ's finance people were eyeballing a guy in Saint Louis for the position. I liked him well enough, but I wanted Mattie firmly in place before human resources announced the opening.

Mattie and I were joined at the hip. It wasn't a conspicuous coupling. She was rarely in my office during work hours. Our consort was mainly by phone or in the evenings when most of the staff were gone. To all appearances, Mattie stayed to herself. She wasn't a water cooler magnet and didn't engage in school gossip. She usually met Donnette outside of school for lunch. She could now deliver a perfectly practiced smile and a warm good morning and good evening. Her workplace was a cubicle outside of the finance manager's office. When George from Saint Louis was hired, they became the perfect couple. In any other time or place, one would think they were married. They never spoke or looked at each other. Each knew the other was there, but it didn't seem to matter.

George, like so many accountant types, preferred to exist in isolation. He was a master of detail and accuracy but a mute in expressing himself. If he had opinions, George held them within himself. He was the first with his monthly reports, and he drooled with excitement when we were preparing budgets, forecasts, and the monthly flash. In my opinion, he would go far in the company.

While it appeared that Mattie and I had very little overt interaction, she was my covert operative. We developed a system of eye signals that meant, "Girl, have I got something to tell you" and hand signals that meant, "Meet me in the fourteenth-floor bathroom," which was ten floors above our school space. There were the carefully choreographed phone calls, where I would pretend she was Mr. Snider from a contract agency, if someone was in my office when she called.

After 6:30, when most employees had raced to a bus, train station, or a parked car, Mattie and I would meet. Behind closed doors and alone, we would conspire.

"Did you hear what happened in Mr. Blake's business math class?"

I hadn't. "What happened?"

"I guess some of the students started mouthing off, and Mr. Blake, trying to regain control of his class, began calling them 'you people,' like 'You people need to learn some manners.' That just made them all go crazy. We really need to get more color up in here. These teachers can't handle these students. They're not used to them. They're good teachers, but they're not ready for this."

I knew Mattie was right. The students did need to see more teachers that looked like them. You didn't want every student-teacher incident to be distilled down to race, but I was aware of the swelling cultural divide. It was a situation the school began experiencing as the African American student census began to outweigh the White in our classrooms. It was also a delicate proposition. The instructors were company employees. You couldn't terminate them just because the classrooms had gone dark. Still, I had to address the element of race if our school was going to be successful with this student demographic. The students and their teachers were two groups of people, residing in the same city, who rarely encountered one another. The school may as well have been in China. The two groups could not communicate.

When I presented my dilemma in an operations review meeting, Pete gave me a budget to schedule sensitivity training. I held frequent employee meetings to inform and sensitize everyone to our changing demographic and to answer any questions no matter how awkward they might be. It was painful, but over time the employee either adjusted and stayed, requested transfers to the more traditional schools within the company, or sought other employment. In the end, there was enough employee movement for me to recruit and solidify my own team.

Mattie was the jack-in-the-box surprise. Six months into her hire, Mattie's coworkers voted her employee of the month. She was honored for her strong work ethic and reserved, professional demeanor. When an employee received that recognition, the HR Department at headquarters and the regional manager followed with congratulatory letters. I got a phone call from Pete.

"Are we talking about the same Mattie that I know?"

"One and the same."

"What happened? Did she get a boyfriend or something?"

"I can't say. I'm as shocked as you are."

"She clearly can't look like she used to."

"You saw her when you were here last month for the OR."

"Where was she?"

"Outside of George's office."

"That was her?"

"Yep!"

Pete was dumbfounded.

"She must be going both ways or something. Anyway, keep an eye on her, and keep her back there with George. I've got to hand it to you, that's the perfect slot for her. Because if it's not a number, George will never see it."

Mattie and I did not share a social relationship. We never discussed my life, only hers. She used me as a tape measure to gauge her progress. She had a goal in mind for herself, and I was her road marker.

A year after she took the job, Mattie and Donnette moved in together.

"It's a two-bedroom apartment in South Shore. Deon has his own bedroom. No more sleeping on that dilapidated living room sofa. Do you know sometimes he couldn't even get to sleep because my sister and her friends are there watching TV and doing whatever? Did I tell you I put Deon in Catholic school just like you? He's safe now. I don't go to the currency exchange anymore to pay my bills. Now I have a checking account. Donnette and I took Deon to Six Flags…" And so it went.

Mattie's life had become a present, and every day seemed like Christmas. When ability connects with opportunity, it creates a synergy that's amazing to behold. When combined, they birth the twins: confidence and success.

Give the Lady What She Wants

After eight years Mattie had grown with me and the school. She had received two promotions and was now accounts manager. George had moved up the ladder as finance manager at the company's flagship school in Indianapolis. The new finance manager was young, funny, and adored Mattie. Pete had moved on as well. He was VP of operations and had forgotten Mattie even existed. What is it in the human experience that insures at some point things will go wrong?

Things went wrong for Mattie on September 19, 1983. When the storm blew in Mike, the then sales manager, his face contracted in horror, bolted into my office.

"Call the police. Some crazy person is attacking Mattie." I followed him to the reception lobby just in time to see Mattie being chased from the school. We followed them onto Wabash Avenue, where Mattie and her assailant both got tangled and lost in the crowd.

Mike and I had raced for the elevator, but we didn't see them anywhere when we entered the street.

"Where did they go, Mike?"

"I don't know."

Poor Mike, he was only four weeks on the job and my second sales manager after Jesse. Mike had requested Chicago, as it was now considered a Type A school, which meant it paid the highest salaries. On the way back to my office, I questioned him.

"Well, what happened?"

"I really can't say. It was noon, so most people were out or in the lunch room. I was going down the hall when I heard these loud voices followed by a bit of commotion. So I started toward the finance office when out runs Mattie followed by this other person."

"Did you know the other person?"

"I don't think so."

"Was it a student?"

"No, I don't think so. I mean if it was a student, wouldn't Mattie call for help or something? She just raced for the stairwell, and the other person was behind her. They ran past Miss Compton in the bookstore. She saw it. I didn't know what to do. So that's why I ran and told everyone to call the police."

It was a surreal afternoon. The police did come. All we could report was the incident and give them Mattie's contact information. The police promised to investigate the situation and to follow up with us when they knew more. School gossip ran rampant with theories as to what had happened and why. Some said it was a disgruntled student angry over an account dispute. Others believed it was a homeless person, high on drugs, who had stumbled into the school and tried to attack her. One employee believed it was Mark, seeking revenge over the rise of Black people.

Late that afternoon, the police called. After all the hysteria, Mattie was home and safe. That news was all the more baffling. Home and safe? I phoned her. Deon answered. He reported she was not available. I phoned again. Again, the same reply. By eight that night, I had phoned five times. The next morning Mattie did not report for work, nor did she call. It would be three days before I would hear from Mattie.

"Could you please meet me?"

I could tell she had been crying. "Where should I meet you?"

"Under the Marshall Field's clock at State and Washington."

When I arrived, Mattie was already there. Her face appeared swollen and strained.

"God, you look awful."

"I feel awful. Can we go somewhere and talk?"

"Where would you like to go?"

"Some place dark."

Angelo's, a restaurant, was dark with high-back booths. I took her there.

"What the hell is going on, Mattie? I've tried to call you. You didn't come to work. We're all but worried sick."

"I know, I know. It's just been so unbelievable, so crazy."

"What's so unbelievable? What's going on?"

"It's Donnette."

"Donnette? What's going on with Donnette?"

Mattie looked at me and then dropped her eyes.

"This is going to really sound crazy to you, but Donnette wants to become a man."

"And I want to become Jacqueline Onassis, but you just can't become someone because you want to. So you're right. It does sound crazy. If you would, please help me understand what's going on here."

"No, it's not crazy. Today, a woman can become a man, and Donnette is doing it. She has had a hysterectomy and removed her titties."

"What?" The color drained from my face. I had met Donnette on several occasions when she visited the school. She didn't come a lot or stay long, but she was always pleasant in both her manner and appearance. I hadn't seen Donnette in some time.

"Why would she do that?"

"She said she had always felt that she was a man. She says she thinks like a man, and now the doctors can make her a man."

"The doctors can do that? How?"

"I don't know, but she keeps going back and forth to this doctor who gives her shots and stuff, and now she has a beard and a mustache."

"What?" Mattie had propelled me into shock.

"Her voice is deeper than any man's at the office, and when we go out to eat, she goes to the men's room."

"Oh my God."

"I'm telling you, this is some crazy shit."

"Well does she have a…"

"A dick? Not yet. All this shit cost money. And it is causing us mega problems. In almost every way now, we are totally incompatible. I began to notice over a year ago that we didn't have as much money as we used to, and we both had gotten good raises. Later, I found out she's saving for these surgeries. So listen to this, I want to save for a house, and she wants to save for a penis. What kind of shit is that?"

I could only shake an incredulous head.

"And my Deon, he is absolutely freaked out. You know how hard high school is. Kids can be cruel. I know that for a personal fact. It's important in high school to be like everyone else, to not stand out, and to be a part of the gang, whatever that means. Deon's having enough issues just trying to fit in. I've been working so hard so things won't be for him like they were for me. I just want him to finish high school, go to college like you did, and get a job where he can wear a suit. He can't cope with all this, watching his auntie become his uncle. Then there is me. Look, I'm a lesbian. If I wanted to be with a man, I'd be with a real one. I'm not trying to have one made." It was at this juncture that Mattie emphasized her next point by punctuating the air with her finger. "What's so hard to understand? I don't want to be with a man."

"No, I understand."

"You do, but Donnette doesn't. So when I told her it wasn't gonna work, she went ape shit and came up to the job and said she was gonna kill me. Do you know that crazy bitch came up to the school, pulled out a piece, and asked, 'Do you have a prayer you want to say?' All I could think about was Deon. I jumped up and hit her so hard it hurt me. Then I started making tracks."

"Oh my God, Mattie!" My vocabulary was ice cubes. All I could do was repeat myself. "Oh my God!"

"I've tried to protect Deon and me, so I went to the police and put her under a restraining order, but I tell you that bitch is crazy."

"I'm so sorry."

"I tell you, it's them drugs. You can't have somebody cutting off your stuff and pumping you full of drugs and be OK." It took all of this for Mattie to arrive at her main point.

"Listen, I can't stay in this town anymore. I've got to leave. I've got to for me and my son. I tell you, with all the changes that bitch is going through, she could be walking beside me, and I wouldn't even know who she is. That's why I wanted to talk to you. Do you think you could help me?"

"Mattie, what do you want me to do?"

Resignation had weighed her into a forward slump. "I've got to leave Chicago. I've got to leave the school. I've got to leave you. You've been better to me than my blood, and I so hate to ask, but could you get me a transfer?"

Two months later, Mattie was gone. I was the only one who knew that Friday, Mattie would not be coming back. I gave her the end-of-the-month paycheck and a big hug.

"I'm going to miss you, 007."

"We really fooled them, didn't we? They never knew that I was *On Her Majesty's Secret Service*."

"They never did."

Mattie went to a new start-up school in Wisconsin. We talked frequently enough at first, but over the months, less and less. The following year she left the company. We never spoke again.

My husband and I were going for a holiday to Puerto Vallarta. He didn't like Mexico; I did. When he didn't like something, he would become stubborn and contrary. The security screening lines at O'Hare were a mile long. I was rushing, and he was lagging. As I was reassembling myself on the other side of the screening section, he came and sat down to put on his shoes.

"I saw you over there yakking with that TSA agent," my husband was scolding. "One would think you knew him."

"I do know him," I responded with a devilish grin. "That was Donnette."

Ms. Anderson was getting out of the car at the train station, gripping her Marshall Field's bags. She was heading back to Minneapolis.

"Take care. It was nice meeting you. Oh, by the way, whatever happened to Deon?"

To that question, Ms. Anderson beamed the broadest smile ever. "I'm sorry, I should have told you earlier. I'm a grandmother. Our son's married with two kids and is an executive for 3M. That Mattie, what an angel! I guess she left me something to live for."

That Mattie, what an angel! They are always among us. We just have to learn how to see.

The dance ends.

DANCE NUMBER SEVEN: THE BALLET

The Song: "Putting It Together"
The Dancer: Rebecca Silverman

The Observance

We are sitting shivah. I am glad my husband is with me, or I would have no one to talk with. I am in Rebecca's family room. This is the first time I was ever in her home. I have known her for years, but I was not in her house, and she was not in mine. We make too much out of houses. That is not where friendship resides.

This is just a family room, like so many from the tri-levels of this era. This is not Rebecca. The Rebecca I knew lived in soft grace and delicate nuance. Her existence was in balance, beauty, and things that soothed the ear. My Rebecca held a lease on words spoken that stirred the heart and soothed the mind.

I sit, so glad my husband is here. We both smile at faces we have never seen and sip hot coffee. I don't know Rebecca's friends. She didn't know mine. I am an outlier here. I am not inside the curve. We smile, answer the repeated questions, and sip hot coffee.

It's winter in Chicago, a place that becomes the operative definition of hell freezing over. It is an inescapable, all-consuming cold that seems to surge from the pit of the lake and sweep out with double-edge razor winds to the surrounding suburbs. I am on the North Side. It's Wilmette. The barber-cutting cold has found us. The coffee feels good. In a minute my husband and I will leave and head south where more people like us reside. It doesn't matter the cold; the news had already congealed my blood. Was it two days ago that it came? The call wasn't a surprise. Her doctors had predicted six months. They were wrong. It was eight, and Rebecca was glad. The two extra months gave her the holidays of Thanksgiving and Hanukkah. They gave her time with her family. Always gracious, Rebecca was grateful.

The two months gave her the fall, which some say is Chicago's most beautiful season. This one certainly had been spectacular. Every tree and bush were on fire. The leaves didn't fall; they danced to the ground for Rebecca. The breezes, at times soothing falsetto, at times deep baritones, serenaded her when she listened.

It had only been two days. Tomorrow they would put her into the ground. Burials would never happen this fast on the South Side. It would take forty-eight hours just to contact everyone and get new phone numbers replacing the disconnects. People would have to borrow money, make arrangements, and do any manner of things to get to the service. By the time the minister and everyone was in place, the deceased would be twelve shades darker than he was the day he died.

But not here. This was the North Side, and I am sitting shivah. Tomorrow Rebecca, as is this custom, will be prayerfully dispatched into a bed of dirt with only the brown ground to keep her warm.

The Dance

Déjà Vu

I loved Rebecca Silverman. I didn't know that I would, but how could I know? It was the mid-eighties, and things weren't going well. ITT was being assaulted by countless takeover attempts and began divesting itself of its core businesses. The huge multinational corporation, with all its many subsidiaries, was no longer a solid "Big Blue Marble." Harold Geneen, the creator of this corporate powerhouse, would retire in 1983. Its many holdings would be spun off. Every division was under scrutiny, and any part that comprised a division was being examined as well.

There were rumors that ITT Educational Services might leave the mothership, forming an independent entity that traded its educational shares on the stock exchange. If that were to happen, only the division's strongest schools would transition to the new company. Weak schools, dragging down the value of the nascent business, would have to be sold or closed.

Ours was now a weak school. The years of harvesting government contracts and reaping minority business had taken its toll. The desired urban student came with liabilities that drove up default rates and drove down persistence and graduation outcomes. That experience was making the recruitment of core city dwellers less and less attractive, sending the management racing for the suburbs. Education had become the pathway into the middle-class, replacing factories as the engine to drive people into the workforce. Every post-secondary school, college, or university—public, private and for-profit—either had branches or was creating them.

As a marketing strategy, branching was a lucrative maneuver, as there could be several institutions in the same market sharing advertising, management, and administrative costs. Major urban centers, with their collar suburbs, were a marketing paradise. New York, Los Angeles, Chicago: these were the marketing meccas. Every type of school system or person with means seemed to be starting and branching schools. White was in; Black was out.

Newspapers, radio, and television were drowning in sleek ads and testimonials baiting the public to attend this school or that one. Call centers were placed in many schools to handle the inquiries. In Chicago, the student minority demographic we attracted had become saturated. Our budgets were predicting declining revenue and profits year over year. In an effort to stop the bleeding, headquarters reached out to outside consulting groups to provide us better marketing and media strategists. The consulting group HQ selected for Chicago was Weinstein, LTD. They were to analyze the school's various media and its placement, calculate the conversion rates on those media buys from cost per lead to cost per enrollment, determine each media's efficacy, and as necessary, seek other available media or markets.

Rebecca was the school's contact person. At least ten years my senior, Rebecca was the essence of professionalism. She had cut her teeth at the Patricia Stevens Modeling and Finishing Schools and knew a thing or two about proprietary education, marketing, and media. Unlike most of the major marketing brands with their slick, fast-talking, data-dropping sales teams, Weinstein was chic, Chicago based, and understated.

Everything about Rebecca signaled class and refinement. She never raised her voice. Her demeanor generated a calming influence and projected a deep well of knowledge that was most reassuring. At our initial meeting was the new regional manager, Rebecca Silverman, David Weinstein, my sales manager, and myself.

Rebecca and I melded in that first meeting. I respected her knowledge so much that I invited her to my office, after our group lunch, just to pick her brain. In a short time our conversations had migrated from marketing to music. Rebecca's husband played with the world-renowned Chicago Symphony. He was a first violinist. I confessed that I knew very little, if anything, about classical music. I should be her guest, she insisted, that next Sunday when the symphony would be playing at the Symphony Center. I accepted. My husband and I arrived to find two box seats reserved in our name. During the playing of Stravinsky's *The Firebird*, my husband's eyes bulged, silently petitioning that I perform the Heimlich maneuver. He seemed to be choking.

At intermission, I reminded him that this was business. I also resurrected the countless boring dinners I had smiled and suffered through plying his IBM customers. When Rebecca inquired as to how we were enjoying the performance, I assured her we were having the best time ever and thanked her profusely. Following the intermission, my husband relaxed, unfolded himself, and fell asleep. To my surprise, I really was enjoying it.

Several months later, Rebecca invited me to another performance. It was in the afternoon with just the two of us. As the symphony played, I caught the porcelain glow of Rebecca's profile. It was Greek sculpture. Sitting beside her, I too began to feel elegant. I straightened my back, thrust out my chin, and enjoyed the symphony. Rebecca was someone to emulate. I hoped she liked me, because I liked her. She seemed to know so much and do so much. When she asked if I would like a season ticket to the Goodman Theatre as her partner, my yes was immediate. Rebecca loved the arts. She believed the arts were pain management for being human. They were the sandpaper that soothed the soul. The words she spoke were art. The way she walked was art. What she loved most in the world was art. Every invitation she extended to me, to experience the things she loved, I accepted.

To see *Sunday in the Park with George.* "Yes."

To hear Handel's *Messiah.* "Yes."

For tea at the Drake. "Yes."

To watch the Hubbard Street Dancers. "Yes."

To the Lyric. "Yes."

To the Art Institute. "Yes."

There were the holidays with Rebecca: lunch beneath the Christmas tree, with my children in the Walnut Room, at Marshall Field's, *The Nutcracker*, and *A Christmas Carol.* Rebecca wove these experiences into traditions. For my children, these were all times to see Aunt Rebecca. If our relationship had been nothing more than an admiring interlude, that would have been enough, but the truth was it traveled deeper, into places hard to define. Rebecca was the first to try.

"I feel as if I have known you before, met you before," she said, but we both knew that was not the case.

"You're from New York. I'm from Missouri."

"Yet I know I have known you before."

"I think it's because we get along so well together."

"Perhaps. Do you believe in prior lives?"

"I'm not sure if I know what you mean."

"I mean that you may have lived before at another place, at another time."

"Why would anyone want to do that?" I could not imagine that.

"For any of a variety of reasons. To correct prior mistakes, to reconnect with those we love and may have lost, to build on things learned, or to finish unfinished business."

"But you're Jewish. I didn't think Jews believed in an afterlife."

"Well, our Torah is relatively silent on that issue, but there are some of us who do. Kabbalists embrace it. What we believe is that life is not necessarily a one-time event, but an ongoing one. It helps explain life events that are otherwise inexplicable, such as why children must suffer."

In the summer the Chicago Symphony would travel and play abroad. Chicago's Symphony conductor, Georg Solti, was considered one of the best in the world and was invited to play in the world's greatest symphony halls. When the symphony traveled, the wives accompanied them. That summer, the symphony headed east to the subcontinent. When Rebecca returned, we met in the courtyard of the Art Institute for lunch.

"I couldn't wait to see you. I've so much to tell, but first here." Rebecca placed a box on the table. I opened the box. To my delight, I found a chain made of gold that sparkled like diamonds.

"This is so beautiful." I lifted the chain from the box into the sunlight, where the color dazzled with even more intensity.

"Exquisite, isn't it? Indian gold is so much purer than our gold. That's why it shines like that." There was another bag. "This is for the kids. Hope they like it." I didn't open that bag but slid it under my chair.

I loved this courtyard with its umbrella-covered tables and center fountain. It was an envelope of a world that sealed off the hustle and bustle outside. Rebecca leaned forward on the table, her hands folded to prop up her chin.

"Well." Her voice was a tease. "I have some very exciting and interesting information to share with you." Her eyes were dancing more than the chain. I was being taunted.

"What is it?"

"Well," she repeated. "When I was in India, I saw many things: the Taj Mahal, Goa, Leh, Mehrangarh Fort, and the Sun Temple.

"You know I'm jealous."

"And I saw a seer."

"What is that?"

"It's a person who can look at your past and your future. He did a reading for me."

"What did he read?" I was almost scared to ask, but knew I had to. Rebecca was mesmerizing.

"Remember, when I told you I felt as if I knew you…perhaps from another life?"

"Y-E-S." Where was this going?

"It turns out that I do know you. Very well in fact." I could only nod in her direction.

"I know you because you are my younger sister."

"I am?"

"Yes, yes!" Rebecca was effervescent.

"It's amazing, isn't it?"

"I'm trying to get my mind around it."

"It's a lot." She patted my hand. "It's a lot."

"Yes, it is. I'm your sister?" I stared into her blue eyes. We certainly didn't look alike.

"According to the seer, there was some sort of political upheaval. Our parents died in the struggle. Our brother tried in vain to save us, but he too became a victim."

"We had a brother?"

Rebecca was ecstatic. "Yes. Yes, we did. The seer could see things only so clearly but it seemed to him as if there was some type of pogrom."

"A pogrom? What's a pogrom?"

"In our history, it's often a mob-like assault where Christians attack Jews. The Christians would get riled up accusing us of killing Christ, and they would seek retribution. Pogroms were horrible."

"Are you saying I was Jewish?"

"It seems so."

What in the world had happened? I didn't even own a small business.

Rebecca continued. "I fought fiercely to protect you, but apparently I couldn't. We were separated." Rebecca stretched her hands across the table. I joined mine to hers. Rebecca's face was a broad smile.

"Don't you see? We're here now, in this time. Together again with a chance to get it right."

I pondered this possibility for a moment and then dismissed it. If I had been here before, I surely would have learned enough to know not to come back penniless and powerless. I would be Nefertiti.

Deserting the Sinking Ship

No matter how Rebecca reasoned to our relationship, it was fine with me. I seldom had, if ever, met anyone kinder or more generous. It was an honor to be thought of as her sister. From that moment forward Rebecca set out to protect me. It would be several months after the revelation. It was a stormy Monday and another operations review. The regional manager and his marketing team arrived at the school wearing dark suits and bearing coffin-shaped briefcases. They had summoned the Weinstein Consulting Group, Rebecca and her boss David, to the meeting. The conference room was wallpapered in pressure.

Everyone knew something had to be done. We were hunkered down over the conference room table in a frantic effort to find a tourniquet to stop the bleeding. Every new initiative had failed. Every metric was going south. The gossip vine was rife with rumors and speculations. Then the Blue

Sheets arrived. I had been handed the morning mail envelopes minutes earlier. During a lull in the planning session, I opened them. When I gasped, everyone turned.

"What is it?" Rebecca asked. I handed the Blue Sheets to my regional manager.

"I can't believe this" came his dumbfounded response. "Hey, everyone, let's take a break." All the men left the room.

That is how it is done. There are often no warnings, no lead time. The corporate ninja stealthily descends, destroying the present. The old order passes. The new one begins. The president of ITT Educational Services and the vice president of operations had vanished. My friend in high places was now someplace else. Farewell Pete. Rebecca saw my visible distress. She bounded to the ready to administer her brand of office triage.

"Your hand is shaking." She took the Blue Sheets from me and read them.

"What does it mean?"

"It means I've stayed too long at the fair. Rebecca, I think my ship has sailed or maybe is sinking. The Blue Sheets say New York has just replaced two men; one of them was the only friend I really could depend on in this corporation."

"What does this mean?" Rebecca then read, "ITT Educational Services is spinning off from its corporate parent and moving to the stock exchange. Rebranding the company and implementing the appropriate infrastructure will follow."

"I think it means ITT Educational Services will be separating from the mothership, taking on a new identity with new managers at the helm, and that any school unit that's not returning the required minimum profit to the bottom line is toast." I paused, folded my lips inward, and then admitted, "I am toast."

Rebecca was sitting beside me. "It's not that your ship sailed. You are on the *Lusitania*. You saw those bozos in here. They don't know what to do. If they did, they would have done it. But I'll tell you what you've got to do. You've got to get out of here. This marketing plan is not going to work. The ones we developed before didn't work, and this one won't work either. We can put the numbers together any way we want, but you will not hit these targets. David knows it too. He told me so. These media numbers we use showing your school capable of penetrating thirty percent of the market, these numbers mean nothing. They are based on generic populations and not your demographic. These guys keep looking at the history of the media buys and how they performed. None of that matters in this current environment. The truth is, there are already too many schools dipping into the same well. You're going to spend more and get less. I've told you this before, but those trouser-wearing mega-men want to believe what they want to believe, and David just lets them. I mean, he proposes, but it's their dollars to buy what they will. But David said they couldn't buy enough media to achieve your sales targets, and your reps will not be able to close at their historical levels. The net-net, my darling, is you have got to get out of here because when it's all said and done, they will never say your media market is saturated. They will say it's you. Crap rolls downhill, and someone has to be sacrificed. You're in charge. So it will be you."

"I know. I know how it works." I felt a lump rising in my throat. "You want to hear something funny? This is the best job I've ever had. It really is. To be honest, I'm not sure how to get another. I've known for some time this day would come. My only firewall was Pete. I guess I had better begin applying for jobs." I was beginning to feel sorry for myself.

"Are you crying?"

"I could be."

"Well stop it if you are. Here." Rebecca went for her purse and removed a neatly folded embroidered handkerchief. "Here, wipe your eyes. I never want these macho managers to see you cry."

"My God, what is that?"

"What? It's a handkerchief."

"I haven't seen one of those since my grandmother died." I dabbed my eyes.

"Listen to me. For one thing, one rarely, if ever, gets a god job when applying for it. You only get a really good job if you know someone. You can have an even better job if you own something." Rebecca had taken the handkerchief and was wiping my eyes and straightening out my hair and clothes.

"The best of all worlds is when you know someone and you own some thing. You look OK now. I want to explore an idea with you. Let's finish this meeting so we can talk. So look alive; here they come."

Act Two

Rebecca and I were season ticket holders at the Goodman Theatre. It was Thursday, and we had great seats: dead center and dress circle. The Goodman is a regional theater that makes an effort to introduce the works of little-known or local playwrights. That was the case with this performance.

"Do you want to stay for the discussion segment following the play?" Rebecca inquired at intermission.

"Not for this play. I'm not a critic, but I really can't follow the plot."

"It's not working for me either. I'll tell you what, let's just ditch the second half and go down for coffee. I have something I want to discuss with you."

We talked a bit more about the play and what the playwright intended, and then Rebecca abruptly changed the subject.

"You said yesterday that things in the company are getting crazier and crazier."

"Not just crazy, insane. Did I tell you the new president came to the school? He was very stoic, no humor. I could tell he did not like the student demographic we are serving. I couldn't tell what he was thinking, but it wasn't good."

Rebecca bit her lower lip.

"I have a friend who is part of a group that is starting a new type of school. It's called online training. It deals with education using computers. The students don't go into a school. My husband and I are going to invest in the start-up. This friend is a lawyer. They don't know much about curriculum, but you do. I told him about you. He wants to interview you."

"When?"

"Next week."

Ray Goldstein was an affable, ample man with a Van Gough beard. His approach to our meeting was unusually casual. I could tell his aim was to prepare the environment by relaxing me through socially engaging small talk. But Rebecca, who had accompanied me to the meeting, wasn't having it. She had set this stage and would direct the cast.

"Ray, Ray, don't ask me how I am. I just spoke with you yesterday." Gesturing toward me she added, "And she's fine as well. Now, I have already briefed you about my friend. As I told you, she is smart, organized, and has been trained by one of the best corporations in the world. Most important to your purpose, she knows how to run schools. So tell her what you've been telling me."

Ray, taken slightly aback, shrugged his shoulders in resignation and responded, "See, we are a group of investors, and this is a start-up business. Our product is distance learning, no brick-and-mortar schools, all online. We have the IT people, we have the curriculum, though right now we only have a handful of programs that have been converted to be delivered online. We have much of the infrastructure in place, but not all of it. That's where you come in. You would handle all the approvals and compliance issues with the states in which we plan to operate. You would also handle accreditations and recognitions by the Department of Education. Of course we would need to staff the operation for the appropriate teaching faculty, financial aid, and student support functions. You should look at the other administrative functions we may need as well."

"She's got it. She can do this." Rebecca's confident close forced Ray to concur.

"I know she can. Brad will get you an offer letter and a start date in the mail next week."

"Great!" Rebecca was done. With that, we stood up, shook hands, and left. As we headed for the elevator, Rebecca patted me approvingly on the shoulder.

"Great interview."

"Indeed" was all I could say. Rebecca scored Bethany's point in high relief. It's not your net worth; it's your network.

We had left the opera. It was *Carmen*, sung in French. I had finally mastered the eye coordination required to synchronize the acting and singing with the libretto. Rebecca, after the symphony, definitely preferred operas. It was a hard acceptance for me, especially since we only went once a year, but still I could not deny that the voices, costumes, music, and moving gestures all combined to make the experience magical.

Rebecca, on the other hand, seemed instantly familiar with every opera ever written, making me speculate that in her other lives she may have spoken the Italian, German, French, or Russian used to tell the stories. Music was an elixir for Rebecca. It relaxed her, made her easy to smile. After every performance we attended, she would leave humming some part of the score. As we headed for the parking lot for our cars that evening, she was humming. We were saying goodbye in the lobby when something occurred to her.

"Did you get that offer letter yet?"

"Yes, today."

"Wonderful, but I don't want you to sign it for at least three more days." She could tell I was questioning the warning tone in her voice.

"It's because," she explained, "Mercury's in retrograde. We need to wait."

"Of course."

We started our engines and went home.

Rebecca had oversold me. This was not a simple start-up, and I had to hit the ground running. I was facing a steep learning curve. At this point in my life, I had learned one of life's greatest lessons—when in doubt, fake it. That was exactly what I did. Because Ray's schools were online, the company could house their headquarters anyplace. His were in Marina City. This is the corn-cobb-shaped building that Steve McQueen drove his car from in the movie, *The Hunter*. The building, while unique, was aging. There were newer buildings stretching for the skyline. But this iconic structure had an address that was its name, a floor plate that worked for a start-up with growth aspirations, and a space that could be sublet at below market rates. When I threw the name out to the group as a possible location for our headquarters, my intent was merely to appear engaged, as I was really out of my depth when discussing real estate.

When the group responded that the suggestion was brilliant, I smiled, all the while hoping my armpit shields would not fail me. As time went on, I found myself learning a lot about what people thought I knew. My chief asset was, that when it came to schools, I knew more than any of the others. I also had learned a critical lesson when working for ITT: hire people to work for you who knew more than you did. Rebecca would remind me many times to remember that I was the conductor and not the violinist.

It was fascinating and fun putting a new business together.

ITT had an infrastructure overlaid by another infrastructure. It was a top-down, line-reporting, report-driven management. Tech-Ed Inc., the start-up, was none of that. This was teamwork personified. Decisions were made by a phone call on the fly. Everyone did some of everything. I realized, as I became a part of Tech-Ed, why Ray hadn't said more. Distance education was still a novel training concept, like so many concepts birthed by the Internet. Distance education was just plain new. Tech-Ed lawyers were creating language to protect it. Bankers groped to finance it. The hardware side of IT sought to erect it, and the software side endeavored to display it. My job was to ensure that our product did what we said it would do.

Words were still being formed to describe distance education. But no matter how amorphous the concept, everyone agreed it was coming, and when it finally arrived, it would be big. We weren't exactly sure what we had, but the trend lines showed personal computers arriving in everyone's homes at light speed. Personal computers, in concert with the Internet, did astonishing things. Mary and her little lamb didn't have to go to school anymore. School could come to her.

When Ray planted his feet in the office and assumed his Moses pose, he would prophesize. "This technology, this mode of education delivery signals the beginning of the end of ivy-covered walls. Colleges, as we have come to know them, will become as obsolete as the horse, stage coach, and train. So people, let's stay focused here. It's gonna be big. I promise you. Distance education is gonna be big."

We never knew when Ray was going to prophesize. Most of us had offices or cubicles placed around the perimeter of the office. The center of the room was filled with computers. When Ray was moved to deliver a message, he would stand in the center, touch a computer as if it transmitted a code only he understood, and proclaim his news.

"Listen to me, everyone. No one can imagine what is happening here. No one can possibly conceive the way distance education will work. You won't need to see the teacher, the classroom, or your classmates. It's all here. Right here." Ray patted the computer. "Imagine, it's just this machine and the student. The fact is the student could be anywhere. For that matter, so could the teacher. One could be in Atlanta and the other in Philadelphia. This baby here,"—another love stroke to the computer—"means anyone could be anyplace."

We would all emerge from our offices or cubicles and listen, caught up in his rapture. When Ray finished his message, we would applaud and return more committed than ever before to make it happen. This atmosphere was less formal than the highly structured ITT. We were charting new territory. What worked today didn't work tomorrow. What was true today wasn't true tomorrow. David Weinstein's company headed up the marketing effort for Tech-Ed, producing television and radio spots to captivate the viewer. The ads essentially promoted education with comfort. Rebecca headed up the team that developed the website. New words were on our tongues like homepage, hyperlinks, and landing pages. I wasn't involved in the advertising initiative and only participated as a part of the test group used to view and rate the proposed ads and ideas. I had more than enough to do contacting various states to get approvals to operate. There was considerable travel at first, but it was manageable now. The kids were older.

IBM seemed to be having an identity crisis and had recommitted to mainframes. The once pervasive IBM Selectric was deposed and replaced by the up-and-coming Wheelwriter. There were convulsions in the corporation, and my husband was coughed out in the downsizing. He accepted a severance package and walked away dismayed. He returned home to figure out what he would do next. It was only by the grace of God and Rebecca that my husband and I weren't experiencing the same fate. Truth be told, I was energized. I had liked ITT, but I loved Tech-Ed. No one felt like they were the head honcho or the big kahuna. Many evenings, with pizza, soda, and beer, we would gather and review where we were, where we had to go, and what if any corrections would be required to get us there.

Two days before we launched the website, Rebecca and I paid a visit to the Art Institute. We hadn't been there in quite a while. They were featuring the paintings of John Singer Sargent. I had never seen anything like this. His canvases were enormous. On some the people posed, literally, as large as life. At any second I imagined Margaret Stuyvesant Rutherfurd White or Madame X could walk from the frame and say hello. It wasn't just the immensity of his work; it was the artist's ability to reflect reality. Singer's portraits were so real. A photograph was not as precise or as beautiful. I couldn't explain why, but my feet tethered to the floor at each canvas. I could only stare, transfixed.

"You're under his spell, aren't you?" Rebecca had not missed my taking root at each masterpiece.

"I've never seen anything like this" was my awestruck reply.

"You see their souls. That's what you see. What you are experiencing is the power of a magnificent artist. You don't know these people, and yet somehow you do."

Life at Tech-Ed was getting better and better. The company was getting bigger and bigger. Weinstein's ad campaign had worked. Why travel to the little red schoolhouse when you could get all you needed to know in the comfort of your pajamas sitting at your dining table?

I recruited the best teachers that I could find to deliver lectures on each topic in the courses' syllabi. The teachers themselves were everywhere. We did some actual on-ground lectures in the study centers, situated throughout the country, for those students suffering from wall separation anxiety and wanted a classroom environment and instructor interaction. We developed test banks with questions and chat rooms for students to study together and exchange ideas.

Ray's prophecy was correct. We were on to something. Nothing is more fun than seeing an idea, where everyone's minds have merged, come to fruition. I marked time now with the summers. Each summer Ray threw a huge Tech-Ed outing for all employees and their families. It was a Wisconsin weekend. Tech-Ed rented a lodge. There was swimming, golfing, tennis, and horseback riding. There were all types of meets, sports activities, and games. Friday evening was the cookout, and Saturday evening was the grand banquet with bonus checks for all employees.

As always, in the summer, the symphony traveled abroad. With the exception of one year, Rebecca traveled with them. Like a child at Christmas, I would wait for Rebecca to return bearing gifts. There were opals from Australia, silk scarves and jade from China, Seiko watches from Japan, and rosaries from the Vatican, blessed by the Pope. More than gifts, Rebecca returned with stories. She was my personal Marco Polo bringing back personal accounts and histories from the places she had visited. Places her feet had touched that my eyes would never see. I savored her stories like fairytales.

"Don't be so entranced," Rebecca would caution. "These are just places, no more beautiful than here. Every country, like ours, has its warts. History always has warts. Among all their amazing achievements, there are always warts."

"I think I could enjoy the warts."

World travel, for me, was a fool's dream. Travel meant money. My husband and I had a mortgage to pay, car loans, and children to send to college. My travel was pretty much confined to business trips for Tech-Ed, the Wisconsin getaways, and those unforgettable pressure-cooker family road trips.

"If I could visit the Great Wall of China, St Peter's Basilica, or the pyramids, I think I could handle the warts that went with them," I assured her.

Rebecca smiled. "Maybe."

Living in the present was getting better and better. That fall, Ray announced that we were moving to new digs. Our address would be 311 South Wacker Drive. You know you have arrived when your building is crowned in white lights and called a castle. It's strange how employees take ownership of and self-identify with things they just use. I suppose it's an unavoidable by-product of trying to belong. We always take possession of things that are not actually ours. It was only seconds after moving into our new space that everyone was claiming, "My new office, our lounge, my computer." My new office was amazingly large with mahogany paneled walls, and a window that looked east to the lake. The only thing that would have made my chest buttons pop more would be to have one of the offices in the corners.

Ray was so confident in the upward trajectory of the business, he hosted an elaborate open house, decked out with several bars, carving stations, and buffet tables. Acrobats performed spellbinding stunts from brightly colored drapes that dropped from the ceiling. A jazz combo played in our lobby. Ray began making other organizational changes as well. Eight months following the move, he strutted into my office, planted his feet, and delivered a personal pronouncement.

"We can't be all things to all people, darling, so I'm naming you vice president of compliance." I chafed a bit at the news, as Beth, years earlier, had told me these were neutered positions without clout. Girl stuff! It also meant my support staff would be cut to three people: an executive assistant and two compliance assistants. Still, there would be very little travel, and I liked the title of vice president. Frankly, it was more sound than power. Ray handed out titles like M&Ms. Everyone was director or vice president of something. But you had to be in Tech-Ed to know that. To the uninitiated, vice president sounded powerful.

When I told Beth I was vice president of compliance, she sent congratulations and a plant. She had never heard of Tech-Ed, and I'm sure was not that impressed.

I took Rebecca out to celebrate my new title. After dinner she asked the question that strips one's soul.

"Did you get more money?"

My response was sheepish. "Well, not yet."

"Is that a no?"

"Well, just not yet."

"So what do you think is going to happen next, Ray's going to come sauntering up to you on Mother's Day and give you a raise for having kids?"

"Listen, it was awkward."

"What was awkward?"

"You know how it is. We had just moved. I've got this gorgeous new office, and then Ray comes in and gives me a prestigious new title."

"Sweetheart, that's when you say, keep the title; give me a raise."

"I know, but we're growing so fast, and everything is so expensive. Jesus, I saw the budget for the new space. It's over a million dollars a year."

"That's not your problem," Rebecca was scolding.

"You have got to stop always feeling so grateful, so glad to be there. I can assure you, no one else is thinking about the lease cost. Those guys in that office, I know who they are. I admit they work hard, but no harder than you. And they don't go home and make dinner, do homework, read to kids, and please a husband. So, for God's sake, stop feeling so grateful. Repeat after me; it's a mantra: 'I am not grateful. I work hard. I want a raise. I am not grateful. I work hard. I want a raise.' Can you say that?"

I nodded my head.

"Now say it."

"I am not grateful. I work hard. I want a raise."

"Again."

I said it again.

"Now can you say it tomorrow to Ray?"

Again I shook my head in the affirmative, but my heart was beating base drum pounds. I secretly doubted if I really could.

"Good. So now go do it."

We were sipping after-dinner coffee. Her mood grew pensive. "You know, I'm not sure, but I think something is going on with Ray. Do you think he's behaving strangely?"

"I hadn't noticed."

"I've known him a long time. He's normally a pretty transparent guy, but not lately. Yes, something is definitely going on."

It was two days later. Rebecca was at Tech-Ed. "Did you ask him?"

I had not. But I did not have the courage to tell my friend the truth. Instead I told her yes, but that he would have to look into it and get back with me. She seemed unconvinced by my reply. Perhaps it was the way my tongue tied on so few words. I really had wanted to ask, had even approached him a few times. But my desire to ask kept giving way to the terrifying feeling that I might be going too far, and I was not prepared for his response. Rebecca searched my eyes but didn't press the point. She seemed more preoccupied by her earlier Ray suspicions.

"Something's going on, I tell you. He's up to something."

Rebecca was oh so right. Something was going on. One month following that conversation, Ray called all the major managers into the conference room to announce that Tech-Ed had been sold. Some company that knew nothing about education was acquiring it and taking it public. He told us how the sale was good for Tech-Ed and good for us. It sounded like Humana selling a healthcare plan to hospice patients. The presentation fell flat.

Following the IPO, nothing at Tech-Ed was the same. I knew this drill, had seen it before. The death star prepares to annihilate the company. The storm troopers march in, destroying and dismantling all that you had made, all that your ideas and team had built. Ray received an unspeakable buyout check and stock in the new company and absconded to Florida. The other minor partners took the money and left for parts unknown. Within the year "our" space was cut by 75 percent. "Our" IT support was shipped to India. "Our" computers were theirs. What was left was later merged with another school group acquisition that offered both online and on-ground campuses. Headquarters was moved to California. Duplicate functions and positions were eliminated. With a six-month severance package, my position was erased. Nuclear, totally nuclear! All that we had built was gone in a routine IPO, and I was too timid to ask for a raise.

Encore

It was summer. Rebecca and I were lunching, again, in the courtyard of the Art Institute. Another summer trip had folded for the Chicago Symphony. I wasn't as excited this time about the destination or the gifts. I had collected three things since meeting Rebecca: more age, more experience, and more scar tissue.

"I knew that bastard was up to something. I knew it." Rebecca's face was flushed. Her blood pressure was rising. Even Picasso's blue period could not bring it down. Weinstein's marketing contract had been terminated. The new owners contracted with the renowned Leo Burnett Advertising Agency. David was too small.

"Business is ruthless, just ruthless. Who said, 'We don't have permanent friends, just permanent interests?' When those interests diverge, watch out. Still, it's not the end of the world. We have options. I've been thinking. I have saved some money, and I got money from that investment in Tech-Ed. Maybe we can open a women's boutique in the South loop? Somewhere near Printer's Row. Rent's cheaper there. I was thinking of something where we get high-end used clothes, maybe on consignment. Many of the women who travel with the symphony buy those designer outfits to go abroad. They would gladly loan theirs to us for a price, and we could rent them out to people who need that 'special' outfit for that 'special' occasion but can't afford to buy the label."

The twinkle was reigniting in her eyes.

"If we did that we wouldn't have to spend a lot of money on inventory. Of course, I would give you a percentage of the ownership. I don't know, say twenty percent, and you could pay me back with sweat equity. What do you think?"

Darling Rebecca, still trying to save us. How could I tell her what she had to know? I tilted my head. Staring into her azure-blue eyes, I wondered again how we were related. If nothing else from all of this upheaval, I had at last excavated some courage, which translated meant, "to get to it, you have to go through it."

"Rebecca." My tone came so direct it startled her.

"Yes, what is it?"

"I have a job."

"You have a job?"

"I do."

"Where?" She began to look around as if it might be at the Art Institute.

"It's with a school chain. It's not as big as ITT, but it's coming. While you were traveling, I started to reach out to people I knew to see who they knew. Here's the irony. My first sales manager, Jesse from ITT, remember I told you about him? Well he's a regional manager now with this school group. When I went for the interview, I didn't know what to expect. I always felt we had a good rapport, but you never know what these guys think. I mean, imagine, I had been his boss once upon a time, and now he could be mine. So I'm sitting there, nervous as a cat on a hot tin roof, and Jesse walks in, gives me this big bear hug, and says, 'So when can you start?' That was it. I had a job. The title's not so great. It's school director, not vice president. But if I grow the school, the pay increases, and the benefits are good. It's not a big school. We're going to get new programs to try and kick-start the growth. A year ago this was a family-owned school group, and then this company acquired it. That's how they plan to grow their stable of schools, through acquisitions. Pete always said, 'Be good to them going up; you might meet them again coming down.'"

"I'm really happy for you. I really am." But Rebecca wasn't smiling.

"One more thing."

"What's that?"

"The company is introducing a high school presenter position. The person holding this position only works during the time when school is in session. They don't work during the summer. This schedule leaves that person free to travel with the symphony." I saw the shadow of a smile beginning to crease Rebecca's lips. I continued.

"This person only has to come into the office every afternoon after her high school visits to drop off her leads for the admissions reps. There is an incentive compensation bonus that kicks in after the school receives a certain number of leads. Since this is a new position, I've asked Jesse to let this person report to me so I can help direct and evaluate the position's effectiveness."

Rebecca was now in a full-blown smile.

"And once a week the person who has this position will have to meet with the school director for a program review lunch. Might you be interested?"

"You have really come a long way. And you're trying to take care of your big sister. I'm so proud of you."

"I'll take that as a yes!"

For a few moments we didn't say anything. All you could hear was the ice clinking as we stirred our tea.

"Can I tell you something?" I asked.

"Of course," she replied.

"Life really sucks."

Rebecca threw her head back and laughed.

"See, you can laugh about it all because the way you view things, you'll get to do this again sometime."

"No. No. That's not why I'm laughing. I'm laughing because life is doing exactly what it's supposed to do. I think that's how we learn, how we grow strong."

"Well, speaking just for me, once is enough."

Rebecca's mouth formed a chiding smirk.

"No, I mean it. For me, once and done."

"Oh, I knew what you meant. Life can be harsh and ugly and then surprisingly beautiful. I definitely know that to be true. You see, I've already had two lives in just this one lifetime."

How was that covert comment meant to be interpreted? "Are you talking about those pogroms when you grew up in New York?"

"No, before that, I had another life."

"Come on, Rebecca. How many lives have you had? So where was this one?"

"Remember that lunch when I said there are times children must suffer?"

"Vaguely."

"I know for a fact that children suffer. I lived that life as a child in the Juden Ghetto."

The nose of the car split the dark heading south. My husband was taking me home. I had sat shiva.

"Honey," I called to my husband across the night. "Would you be my theater partner this season at the Goodman?" I patted my right coat pocket. There it was: the envelope Rebecca had given me the last time we were together. It was the balance of her Goodman season tickets. I knew exactly why I had them. Art was not for whiners. It was emotional medicine to help humanity understand and endure the hurts and pains of life. For all those years, all those times, the arts had reassured and fortified her, working their way into her bloodstream like enzymes breaking down iron and converting it to steel. I sure hoped Rebecca knew what she was talking about when she said we were sisters. Maybe next time we could get it right and come back as identical twins.

The dance ends.

DANCE NUMBER EIGHT: THE SHOTGUN

The Song: "Shotgun"

The Dancer: Wanda Robinson

The Observance

My choices are a roller set or a flat iron. I am at my hair salon, where I go each week. Age brings thinning hair and gray strands. For these two reasons, I am hell bent on conditioning and coloring. I am also concerned about the amount of heat on my hair, and so I consider: do I roller-set today or flat-iron?

My high priestess of hair is Catalina. She tells me she holds an assortment of certificates and credentials authenticating her ability to do all manner of things to one's hair, but I have never seen them, so I take her at her word.

Catalina is in her early sixties, but she looks younger and is very stylish. It is in her best business interest to look this way. It reaffirms the proposition that if she can look this good, so can her clientele. There is another trait that she has in common with most other beauty practitioners, and that is a proclivity for secrecy. Most hair stylists know more about their clients' lives than their life partners, parents, children, pastors, or best friends combined. They are willing and engaged listeners. If requested, they can dispense sage advice and if not will stand above your head and silently empathize. If all you need is an hour or two of free-range ranting, they'll permit you that as well. The miracle of it all is that you leave looking and feeling better than when you arrived.

Catalina maintains an intriguing roster of clients who would probably self-identify in every way imaginable. Her stature at the salon is well established and validated by the precinct in which she practices. Catalina operates in a private room, one of five, with a shampoo bowl and a closed door. This privileged perch of privacy provides support for the premise that "only your hairdresser knows for sure."

The dryers are in an open space where the client sits under a hot dome, alone, to come to terms with all that she has just divulged. But it isn't just a one-way relationship. There are times when Catalina, unprompted, provides critical information that she feels her client should know. Today is such a day.

"I'm going to put the deep conditioner on your hair and clip your ends. They're starting to split."

"That's fine."

"I need to figure out what's causing this breakage. It could be the weather though. It's been so dry."

"It certainly has. Catalina, just do what you have to do."

"Is that audit over at your work?"

"Thank God, it is. It about drove me crazy."

"Speaking of crazy, what did you do with that teacher who was getting it on with the other teacher in the library?"

"Now that was insane. Can you imagine a student looking through the stacks trying to find a logic and critical thinking book and coming up on that? Then things really got confusing, because some of these students have vocabulary and comprehension challenges. When the student filed a complaint against the two teachers, he accused them first of plagiarism. We had to dig deeper to find out what the student really meant. The student thought plagiarism was some deviant sex act like adultery because his English teacher had told the class plagiarism meant taking something that wasn't yours. When we finally sorted out what the student meant, I had to fire them both; they were good teachers, but I had no choice."

"Stupid is what you call that. What's a student supposed to think when he sees his teachers behaving like dogs in heat?"

We both shook agreeing heads. Catalina was clipping when she remembered.

"Girl, did I tell you about Wanda?"

"Wanda?"

"Wanda. You know Wanda Robinson."

"What about her?"

"What about her? She's dead. That's what's about her."

"Dead!" My shoulders drooped. "When's the service?"

"There isn't a service, at least not in Chicago. Her oldest son, I heard, sent the body to Tennessee. I think that's where she's from. You know I did her hair for years. Remember you referred her to me. Then after that thing with her son, she stopped coming."

The Dance

Mother First

Wanda wanted to be the best mother ever. She had seen the formula first-hand and knew that it worked. The scion of a God-fearing family with a hard-working father and a devoted stay-at-home mother, Wanda and her siblings had been reared respectful, obedient children. What was the refrain neighbors used to refer to their clan? Salt of the earth. That was it: foundational, fundamental salt of the earth. When Wanda's parents instructed her to go to college, she went. When they directed her to become a teacher, she did. When they insisted it was time to get married, she did. For her husband she selected more salt, Sterling Robinson.

Sterling understood the value of not making waves. The son of a single mom, he had lived the hard-knock life and didn't want any part of it. His mother's determination and a caring high school counselor's recommendation landed him at Eastern, where he earned a bachelor's degree. The late '60s and early '70s were a time for firsts. It was a barrier-breaking moment when Sterling was hired by the Chicago Police Department. He knew his life was about to change. He was now breathing rare air and would make the most of it. People liked Sterling. His can-do attitude drew people to him. He made himself one of the boys. Sterling could take a joke even if it was at his expense. Sterling believed himself a man on a mission. Determined to overturn the stereotype that African Americans were shiftless, lazy, and licentious animals, Sterling offered up his family as a testament to how a Black middle-class family looked.

When Wanda and Sterling met, they were of one accord, evenly yoked, willing to be that model. They had the church wedding and week-long honeymoon. After she had become pregnant, Wanda left her position as a high school business and commerce teacher. As her mother had done before, Wanda stayed home, content in her South Side gray stone. Wanda cooked breakfast and set the dinner table. After the birth of her two sons, she put the boys and the dog in their fenced backyard to play. Wanda volunteered as a room mother at the boys' school. Every Sunday the family went to church. The boys recited Bible verses before meals and always addressed adults as Mr. or Mrs. Every summer the family took a two-week vacation.

When I met Wanda, Sterling had ascended to the rank of detective. The oldest son was a freshman at Cornell, and the youngest was a sophomore at De La Salle High School. Wanda was silently giving herself props for having been a very good mother and felt assured enough in her parenting to return to work. She applied as a typing instructor at our school. I conducted her second interview.

"You haven't been in the workforce for some time."

"I was home raising my sons." Her voice was both proud and defiant.

"That's commendable. It's great when a woman wants to do that."

"We could afford it." That smarted.

"Of course, you know this is a full-time, year-round position. It's not high school, where you get the summers off."

"I know that. To be frank, I would never want to teach in high school again. The children are too undisciplined, the parents have too much to say, the community runs the schools, the administration's hands are tied, and the teachers are at the mercy of it all. Most of your students are older, I believe?"

"That is correct."

"They seem to have more personal obligations as well."

"That is correct."

"It seems, based on my interview with your education director, they want to learn."

"They really do."

Wanda patted both hands on her lap.

"So you see, that's why I want to be here. I have no patience for sassy brats who think they should tell me a thing or two. What I teach, as I assume you know, requires discipline. I cannot abide a smart-aleck kid who doesn't respect me or my craft. No, I cannot." She looked around the room. "This school will work just fine."

Wanda was a little presumptuous. "I trust you can manage a classroom."

"But of course. I have already told you that I'm a stickler for discipline."

"This perhaps sounds foolish to ask, but this is primarily a typing instructor position. Can you type?"

Wanda shoved two sheets of paper in my face. I took them to look while she informed me, "I just took these three five-minute timings for your education director."

I quickly reviewed her scores: eighty-five, seventy-five, eighty—all three with no more than two errors.

"I'm a little rusty," she amended, "but not that much."

"Not that much at all," I admitted, impressed.

"I'll get better with practice."

"I'm sure you will."

"I think it's only fair to tell you that I am a hard-driving instructor. I don't have a lot of patience for excuses and pity parties, and if these students are who you say they are, that's the last thing that they need."

"I agree."

Now Wanda was pointing at me. "I will be here every day on time and ready, but if I am on time and ready, I expect my students to be as well. Does that make sense?"

"Yes, it does."

"And another thing, I don't coddle. These are adults. Adults need to act like adults. We don't help people when we tolerate a climate of excuses. Do you agree?"

"Yes, I do."

"Good. I think we see eye to eye. Now, I can start Monday morning. I know you have night classes. If you need me, I can work Tuesday and Thursday evenings, but never Monday or Wednesday evenings. I don't need any insurance; my husband covers me. I will need two weeks in the summer for our family vacation. If I haven't earned the time, it's OK that you dock me. And one last thing, I teach shorthand. I can do both Gregg and Pitman. I am better at Gregg, but I do both. What else do you need?"

I paused and thought, who just interviewed whom?

"Do you need something else from me?"

"I don't think so. I'll just see you Monday at eight fifteen."

Typing Teachers

In case you have never had one, typing teachers are control freaks. They are like drill sergeants with a timer. Wanda marched into her classroom and all too soon was christened with the epithet Warden Robinson. Her credo was, "No one rises to low expectations." She enforced that premise in all that she did. That target was nonnegotiable. Wanda's prime directive was to lecture and demonstrate proper typing protocol. Every student's fingers were to be properly curved on the home row. This would be followed by practice and more practice. Then the drills would begin. Wanda would stride through the typewriter aisles after setting a target of achievement. Like a general bolstering the troops at the D-Day landing, Wanda spouted her pep talk. "We will strive to be the best, right?"

"Right," the class would echo.

"All things are possible, right?"

"Right."

"Are you saying yes?"

"Yes."

"Are you saying yes?"

"Yes."

"Then let's make your yes mean yes. Hands in position on home row. Eyes on the copy. Begin."

Students in Wanda's advanced typing class had a better time of it. Following her demonstrations, explanations, and timings, there would be a fifteen-minute music period when Wanda would pull out her portable forty-five record player and have the class type to the beat of the music.

Most of Wanda's students loved her classes, but some withered under the pressure. They would often resort to the school's complaint procedure, landing both Wanda and the student in my office for a conference. These encounters were never pleasant, as Wanda tended to view the student as a noncommittal, excuse-riddled quitter, and the student conversely viewed Wanda as an insufferable, overbearing tyrant.

In time and resorting to the most benign language I had in my arsenal, I could generally talk both parties back from the ledge and persuade them to try again. I did not have a lot of interaction with Wanda. She didn't brownnose or try and buy me gifts. She was polite but not friendly. She arrived on time and left punctually when her day ended. Her coworkers respected her but did not fraternize with her. She took her two-week vacation as scheduled each year and produced the best typing students of all the business instructors.

It was during the drama following Pete's corporate eraser and my planned departure that Wanda scheduled an appointment to see me. An employee with Wanda's profile, when requesting to see me, usually planned to resign and either ask for a letter of reference or tell me what was wrong with everything or everyone.

"Wanda, please come in. This is such a pleasant surprise. Please have a seat."

She took a chair and responded, "Thank you for seeing me." There was a trace of appreciation and tenderness in her voice. I sat in a chair beside her.

"I have left my husband."

"Oh no! I am so sorry to hear that."

"Yes. Well, he doesn't know it yet."

"OK." She sensed my confusion.

"My things are still at the house. I only have what I wore to work, and I'm not going back."

I was stunned. "Oh my goodness!"

"I know, but you see, I can't. It's a long story. I needed to let you know that I will require the rest of the week off to find a place to stay and buy a few things." What composure. I was shattered.

"Please tell me, is there anything I can do?"

"Yes, there is. If Sterling calls, I would appreciate it if the receptionist could say that I no longer work here."

"I can do that, and since you won't be here for a few days, you aren't working." My attempt at a little comic relief fell flat. "So take as many days as you need. Do you maybe need me to take you around?"

"No. I'm fine. When I left, I did take my car."

"Just let me know if there is anything that I can do."

Wanda clasped my hands with both of hers. "Thank you so very much."

Wanda and I did not talk again about leaving her husband. I wondered how one so private and self-contained felt about sharing something so personal and hurtful with me. For sure no one at the school knew, or it would have circulated in some form or other on the school's grapevine, but there was nothing. I varnished my ego with a little self-praise, saying Wanda told me because I was someone she could trust. But another small voice came to contradict my inflated ego. "She told you," it said, "because she had to."

When it became clear that ITT was spinning off our school, Wanda and I fell in league with Rebecca and joined Tech-Ed. I needed an assistant. I had an administrative assistant at the ITT school, but she was a lifer who liked ITT more than me. She had transferred into the Chicago school from a sister school and was now transferring to one of ITT's start-up locations in the suburbs. But Tech-Ed was also a start-up, and to achieve the goals Ray had articulated, I would need an assistant. When I thought of the people I knew who I felt I could work with and trust, I wanted Wanda. She had never done anything like this before and was packed with self-doubt during the interview.

"All I have ever done is teach," she explained. "Of course I know the elements that comprise a good assistant, but I have to warn you, I have never done it."

When I described the fluid nature of the position without set hours or days, Wanda surprisingly responded.

"Yes, I can do that. The more you talk, the more excited I become. It sounds as if it would be a challenge for both of us. I think I'm up for it."

Neither of us said much more. I was frankly curious as to what had happened after that day in my office, but I didn't pry, and she didn't volunteer. There was a silent, secretive quality that enveloped Wanda. Several of my prior administrative assistants had been what I called flip-flops, telling me how much they adored me, while each month they were flopping and fawning before the regional manager and HQ staff at every operations review. There would be no flip-flopping with Wanda.

We both tendered our resignations on the same day and stepped together into the unknown. Tech-Ed seemed at times like a think tank. Everyone was always floating ideas to Ray about how to do this or that. The place was filled with kinetic energy. Every major manager was an idea machine. I had a ton of ideas to bring to Ray, but before I did, I wanted to audition them first with Wanda. At times I could get so excited about an idea, I had a hard time containing myself. When I found myself percolating, I would step to my office door and call Wanda.

"Come here. Come in here."

Wanda had come to know the signs, the panting petition, and the movement of the feet. Wanda would enter the office, take a seat facing me, and utter, "I know where this is going. It's happening, isn't it? Another bright idea." After that, she would sit patiently while I blurted out my latest brainchild. Wanda would listen carefully, sometimes even take notes. When I finished, she would ask insightful questions and offer constructive criticism.

Instinctively, I knew I could trust her. In time I could sense she was trusting me. Her stern visage began to soften. She would tell a joke or two. They were usually extremely corny, but Wanda would laugh with such gusto that I found myself laughing along. When it wasn't Rebecca, Wanda was my frequent lunch date. When we didn't eat at the Little Corporal, Wanda would run to the lower-level deli and get us lunch.

Wanda, in many ways, was a mother hen. She would screen my calls and find an excuse to expel a super-social coworker who wanted to stop by and chat. She kept a tight leash on my schedule and screened out superficial issues she could resolve herself. When I told her my daughter was applying to colleges, Wanda chaperoned me through the application process. She had gotten a son into Cornell. I knew Wanda and I had become friends the day she requested, "Do you think it would be possible for me to use the conference room maybe two evenings a month? The earliest I would need them would be six thirty in the evening."

"Oh." I had to admit I was surprised.

Wanda explained. "I have a few groups I meet with each month. Most of the people work downtown, and we need a meeting place. Would meeting here be all right?"

We held each other's gaze in an awkward silence, and then I broke. "Sure, why not? Tell me the dates you want it, and I will have Leslie book it."

As close as we were, there was still so much about this woman I did not know.

The Son Who Got Away

"Auntie, Auntie." It was Faith on the phone.

"Hi, honey, what's up?" Faith had finished Northwestern undergrad and was now a second year at the Northwestern University Pritzker School of Law.

"I have something to tell you. It is so confidential. You never need to ever repeat it, but I think you know this woman."

"What woman?"

"Can I come to see you?" Her voice was steeped in urgency.

"Yes, of course you can."

Faith and Wanda were still making small talk when Wanda ushered her into my office. They had met at the beginning of the school term when I took us all to lunch. When the door shut, Faith popped out of her seat like a jack-in-the-box.

"That's her, Auntie. That's her. I knew it."

"Faith, calm down. Who is it?"

"Mrs. Robinson. It's her."

"Wanda?"

"Yes, her."

"What about her?"

"Our law school is involved in research dealing with persons who have been wrongfully convicted and are on death row. I am involved in research on one of these inmates who our professor feels have been wrongfully convicted. I've seen the press releases and court papers." Faith stopped short and held her breath. Her next words kicked me in the stomach. "It's her son. I am researching Mrs. Robinson's son." The weight of that declaration forced me down. I sat.

"Are you saying Wanda's son is on death row?"

"Yes. Yes, I am." Faith cautiously slipped a manila folder from her book bag and extended it toward me. The phone rang. Faith yanked the folder back. I jumped. Seconds later, I heard a knock, and Wanda opened the door.

"I'm sorry, is everything OK? You didn't answer your phone."

"Yes, yes, it is. But Wanda, can you tell the receptionist that you will take my calls for the next thirty minutes?"

"Of course." Wanda was closing the door but then reopened it.

"Is everything all right?"

"Yes. Yes, it is."

"Can I get you anything?"

"No, I don't think so. How about you, Faith?" Faith's voice had ascended several octaves.

"No, I'm fine. Thank you."

"OK." Wanda complied and closed the door.

"Did we seem nervous?" I asked.

"I'm not sure." Faith extracted the folder again. I began to read about Gregory Robinson, the son of Wanda and Sterling Robinson.

According to the newspaper article, Gregory was a notorious member of a Chicago gang. On the evening of March 1, ten years ago, Gregory and two other gang members entered a neighborhood convenience store, where they robbed and brutally bludgeoned to death the eighty-two-year-old proprietor and his seventy-eight-year-old wife. In the trial that followed, the two accomplices testified that Gregory had been the leader who had single-handedly inflicted the brutal beating. Gregory was sentenced to death by lethal injection. Since the date of his sentencing, Gregory had resided on death row.

Gregory, however, voiced another story. He had told Northwestern professors and anyone else who would listen that, yes, while he was a gang member, he was nowhere near the convenience store on the night of those heinous murders. In fact, he did not believe the two named accomplices were there either. He contended that all three men were randomly rounded up by the Chicago police and brought in to be questioned by the Burge Gestapo.

Jon Burge, as almost anyone who lived on the south side in the 1970s through the 1990s knew, was the dreaded district commander who applied his own brand of interrogation in an effort to extract justice. Burge's torture techniques were legion, described as inhumane and sadistic.

In Jon Burge's distorted belief system, if you were a Black male, you may have not committed this crime, but you had committed some crime. If you were in a gang, Jon held that belief as gospel. Because he invoked this urban creed, Burge felt himself perfectly and professionally justified in apprehending, detaining, and torturing any African American male he perceived as afoul of the law.

Gregory Robinson fit Burge's capital crime's profile. He had a rap sheet, belonged to a gang, and was already on his radar. According to Gregory's statement to Northwestern's lawyers, students, and a host of others, he had been beaten, choked, and suffocated with plastic bags. Unable to withstand the torture and facing the written statements of the other two suspects, who had capitulated to a plea bargain naming Gregory as the perpetrator of the heinous crime, Gregory had confessed to the murders. Gregory Robinson was charged with first-degree murder and sentenced to death.

During his time in prison, Gregory had written, studied, and with his mother, Wanda, pursued numerous schools, organizations, and individuals who could help prove Gregory's innocence and overturn his conviction. Several powerful groups and organizations responded, providing research, advocacy, and enlightenment regarding Gregory's case. Northwestern would use its lawyers and its law school to help defend several inmates now on death row. One of them was Gregory.

When I finished reading the contents of the file, I handed it back to Faith.

"This explains so much."

"In what way?"

"Well for one, why Wanda never talks about her second son. It's always the first son. The Cornell graduate who went to USC and got his master's. It's only the first son who rises through the ranks on whatever he attempts. There's nothing but silence about the second son. It's like he was born and then appropriated by aliens."

"Wow," Faith whispered.

"You know what else? She never talks about her husband anymore. I have wondered what happened with them."

"She never talks about him?"

"She left him several years ago, but I don't know if they are back together or what. I just know she no longer takes her two-week summer vacations."

It was the day after Wanda had used the conference room. Leslie came to me that morning with a few papers and a note pad. That afternoon I asked Wanda into my office.

"I believe these are yours." I handed her the pad and papers. Her discomfort was palpable.

"Where did you get these?"

"They were left in the conference room." Wanda knew the handwriting.

"Seth. Seth. The meeting ran late. Everyone was in a hurry to leave. I usually clear the room and turn off the lights. He must have left it. Did you read the notes?"

"I'm sorry, but I did."

"Did anyone else?"

"I don't know. Leslie brought it to me."

"That's probably good if Leslie got this. She's a good kid and not very curious."

"Hopefully."

"So what do you think?"

I sought to lighten her obvious distress. "Just when I thought I was the most amazing person in your life and had all the great ideas. I had no idea you had contacts at Amnesty International and knew Sister Helen Prejean."

Wanda looked at me with pleading eyes. "I'm trying to save my son."

"I know. I really do."

"No you don't. How could you? Until it happens to you, you really don't know. Until you have lost everything, saw the life you were building dissolve like sugar in water, had the child your body birthed beaten like a dog and locked away in solitary for over ten years, witnessed him lose touch with his family, his faith, and all the things that you spent years trying to lay down to build him into a man, only to see what is standing before you, at times, not even seem human. He's not a name anymore; he's a number. It's not your son that you birthed and taught to walk and sing, to say his prayers and stay awake to see Santa. It's a creature. It's what's left after everything hateful and vile stripped your son away. And you wonder what happened? When did it begin to change? How did I miss it? You did the same thing for him that you did for the other one, the exact same thing. What happened? What made the difference? Was it the devil? I want to believe it was the devil. If it's the devil, then it can't be my fault. Everyone knows that I am not as strong as the devil. And then there is the convulsive, reoccurring guilt that grips your stomach and shreds it into fibers that catch and pull at one another, and no medicine you swallow takes the pain away. All you want is one thing. Only one, and you'll give up everything that you have for it: your husband, your home, your clothes, your friends. None of that matters if you can get just that one thing. You pray and you pray for just that one thing. You ask only for one favor, and it's the same favor for over ten years. You ask God to remove that creature with that number and give you back your boy, fun-loving and free. Tell me, do you know?"

The meeting in my office proved cathartic for the both of us. Wanda grew increasingly more transparent, allowing me to see a woman in pain. In return, I administered the only medicine I had, just listening.

"Remember the day I asked to meet with you in the office?" We were alone. The meeting in the conference room had just ended thirty minutes earlier. The Tech-Ed employees had joined the mass of humanity hours earlier, moving for the city's four major stations with their commuter trains. City dwellers rushed for the L trains or the CTA buses. A few brave hearts would wade into the parking lots to begin their slow drive home. Wanda and I were alone, drinking the dregs of the office coffee pot.

"I remember that day well. It was so strange."

"I was so relieved when you didn't ask questions. Things had really begun to unravel between Sterling and me. Burge had beaten our boy, and Sterling, who was in the police department, wouldn't do a thing about it. He wouldn't talk to anyone, wouldn't say anything. We were together when we talked to Greg. His face was swollen. His left eye was closed. He told us everything that had happened. How they had hit and tried to suffocate him. Both Sterling and I knew he didn't do it. Not that night. He couldn't have. You see, he was home with us. He had been asking me to make gumbo. So that night I told them both to be home by eight. He wasn't in a convenience store murdering those old people. He was home with us. Sterling knew it. That man had beaten our boy, and Sterling didn't say a word. He wouldn't tell our lawyer, and he wouldn't testify. I told them I would testify, but the lawyer said it wouldn't help Gregory's case. I would be just another mother giving her son a lame alibi.

"I asked Sterling to tell the police, the internal affairs division, his boss—anyone—what had happened and what we knew. He only said things didn't work that way. He said complaining would be dangerous. He said you don't rat on another police officer. And finally he said, he could lose his job and his pension. His pension? We were losing our son, and Sterling was trying to save his pension. Sterling always drank, but that morning he came home, he had been drinking a lot. He woke me up, screaming and shouting in a violent rage. He told me to stop talking to people. I had started to try to get help from pastors and organizations. Sterling said I was destroying his career. He told me how hard it had been to get where he was in the force, all the abuse he had tolerated, and how I was destroying him talking all the time about Gregory. He said Gregory had been a juvenile delinquent, and I was a derelict mother who didn't know her ass from a hole in the ground. He said if I didn't stop all my ranting and troublemaking, he would hurt me bad. I tell you I was terrified. He shook me like a rag doll until I told him I understood. Then I got dressed for work and never went back."

Wanda was indeed the perfect assistant. We both had secrets to keep. Mine were the moments of insanity that occasionally racked Tech-Ed: Ray's hair-brained ideas, the marketing team's inflated numbers and constant traveling, and my fear that the organization was growing too fast without the infrastructure to support the growth. Then there were my great ideas. I had a multitude of them, and Wanda, my supportive critic, listened to each one. In return, I always made sure the conference room was available for her clandestine meetings. I would fill the conference room with snacks and always had a ready explanation for anyone who asked what types of meetings they were. Wanda never asked me to, but I began making donations to Amnesty International.

Wanda burst into my office with boxes and bags.

"Ask me where I'm going."

"What is all of that?"

"You never answer a question with a question."

"OK. Where are you going?"

"Ireland." It was rare to see Wanda bubbly. In fact, I only saw the phenomenon one other time.

"What in the world are you going to do in Ireland? Is it a vacation?"

"It is a speaking engagement." She placed her bags and boxes on the floor.

"Amnesty International is sending me to the Catholic University of Ireland. I'm speaking on the death penalty in the United States, and the disproportionate number of incarcerated African Americans."

"Are you serious?"

The serious Wanda returned. She could only be ebullient for a short amount of time. "I am dead serious, and OK, I've never given a speech like this before and certainly not to an audience like this. I mean I've spoken in church, testified, and said prayers, but nothing like this. Seth wrote the speech. We went over it, and it is exactly how I feel and what I want to say. We're trying to draw attention to the problem by highlighting what happened to Greg. I'm taking handouts and statistics. Could I ask you for a favor?"

"Of course, Wanda, what is it?'

"This is going to sound crazy, but could you teach me how to give a real speech?"

Wanda was in my wheelhouse now. Those years with Sr. Patricia Ann weren't for naught. Stand, breathe, and let me hear those endings. The corporate presentations at key manager's meetings, the practices with Bethany were constant warm-ups. Could I help her? Does a bear shit in the woods?

Each evening we hijacked the conference room. There the teacher became the student. We practiced pausing for emphasis, eye contact, commanding the room, hand and body movements, execution, inflection, and when to use humor. Everything she did, I instructed her, had to be deliberate but seem unrehearsed. Leave nothing to chance. Memorizing her speech was critical. Key phrases had to be second nature. No matter what happened, if she memorized her key phrases, she could always recover.

Wanda bore traces of a Southern accent, but I let that be. This was not *My Fair Lady*. Furthermore, she was going to Ireland. Now that's an accent. Things were going well. Wanda had reduced her speech to several 5 x 7 cue cards, which contained her key points. The trip was next week.

"You know, I never knew he was in a gang."

"You mean Gregory?"

"Right. I never knew he was. He was doing what the oldest boy did. Went to the same schools, everything. Gregory was a happy child. Much more outgoing than Herbert. My Herb was more of an introvert. He had a few good friends, but not a lot. The house was always full of Greg's friends. He was a natural leader. People loved him. I never knew he was in a gang. Boys would come to my house, and he would take down my China cups and serve tea. What kind of gangbanger is serving tea? Sterling knew he had been in trouble. Knew he had been arrested. He said he had tried to help him get out of the gang, tried to protect him, he said, but nobody told me. I never knew anything until we saw him that day in the jail, and his face was all smashed. I swear to God, I never knew."

By Wanda's account, the trip to Ireland was met with critical acclaim. It must have been so because once she returned, she had become a bit of a sensation. She was slated for speaking engagements in Chicago and other select cities. She was speaking out about her son and others on death row who were put there, she said, by Burge for crimes they had not committed. Wanda began to request days and parts of days off to be on panels and committees regarding the death penalty. She was the darling of Amnesty International while the Northwestern Law School's drumbeat for justice grew louder and louder. A variety of coalitions supported her. Wanda spoke in churches and synagogues, at luncheons, and at demonstrations.

When the press began to take note, it became harder and harder for Wanda to remain anonymous. People in the office now recognized her in connection with church and community activities where she passionately told the story of the son she was trying to save. Wanda's notoriety was becoming a chink in Sterling's armor. Ray had taken the office for Tech-Ed's annual Wisconsin getaway weekend. It was a family thing. Wanda rarely went. It made her feel awkward she said, but this time she was there.

The nonstop pace was causing tread wear on her nerves. "I need a getaway. I never thought I could feel relaxed around a hundred people, but I need to get away." My husband knew her story and had called her insisting that she ride with us.

"I don't really know these people either; you can leave them if you like, and just talk to me," he had assured her.

Wanda and I were in the hot tub early that Saturday morning. We were the first people there. The late-night sing-alongs, the s'mores, drinks, and children pretty much guaranteed a late arrival for the others. The soaking was soothing. No need to open our eyes.

"He wants a divorce."

"Who?"

"Sterling."

"I thought you were divorced."

"No, I left, but I never divorced him."

"He's worried I am drawing too much attention to him and could cost him his job and pension."

"That's crazy. You can't cause another person to lose their job and pension."

"He is afraid that since I'm still his wife, I'm entitled to a part of his pension. He believes as long as we are married the union could contrive something that would make him lose it. He wants me off his pension, and he wants a divorce. In return he'll give me back the house. He says it's fully paid for and looks the same as it did the day I left, china and all. He just wants me off his pension."

"Are you OK with that?"

"I'm fine with it. I don't want any parts of that Judas money. Plus, when Gregory gets out, he can come back home to his house. He can invite his friends, and things will be fine again."

Free at Last

Things were escalating. More and more information was being released about the torturous practices of Jon Burge. Any number of groups were now circling the wrongfully convicted charges of several death row inmates. The major media news outlets had upped the ante, continually releasing stories of abuse and discoveries. In light of the torrent of new revelations, Illinois' embattled governor, George Ryan, was rethinking his position on the death penalty. An armada of various interest groups was dispatched to the prison for conferences, stories, and interviews with or about these men whom the governor might free.

And then there was the money. The millions of dollars the inmates would receive for the years of life they had lost behind bars. Wanda was swept up in all the brouhaha that was building.

As organizations and the media advanced aggressively upon her for interviews and speeches, Wanda attempted to retreat. On alternating weekends, Wanda would go to the prison to be with her son. She wanted to protect her boy, feeling all the attention and talk of money would prove damaging to someone who had been isolated from society for almost a dozen years.

"He was a kid when he went behind the wall. He's now an almost thirty-five-year-old man. I don't want Greg to get his hopes up too high, grow overconfident. You can't trust people. They will say one thing and do another. I can tell Greg is already smelling the fresh air. If all of this doesn't work, I'll lose him for sure. It seems no matter what I do, they're going to kill my son."

Justice isn't mercy; it's just justice. When the announcement came of the governor's pardon, everyone at Tech-Ed was elated. Wanda's plight in defense of her son was no longer a secret. Most of the employees admired the woman who would sacrifice all that she had to bring a buried story to life. Wanda's son would not be just a number; people would know his name.

In discreet ways, the staff tried to register their support. They would leave inspirational cards with money inside, pies, cakes, and stuffed animals. It was their way of saying, "More power to you, Wanda! We're with you." We all knew things were coming to a head. Then, there it was: Governor Ryan, delivering the riveting words at the DePaul University College of Law, saying for all to hear that he would pardon four men on Illinois' Death Row "who had suffered the manifest injustice of having a false confession tortured out of them by the Chicago Police."

Freedom was hours away. Wanda, in the divorce settlement agreement with her husband, had reclaimed her home. She had hired a service to come clean it for Gregory's arrival. Several support organizations had sent flowers. I had paid Catalina to give her a chic hairstyle. The perfect son, Herbert, would make the trip, along with an entourage of others, to the prison. The press was already in place. CNN sent Wanda morning coffee two hours before she crossed her threshold to greet the press.

The release of the wrongfully convicted men was being covered by all the local news outlets. It was now for certain, as recompense for the stolen years, Gregory Robinson would soon be a millionaire.

I was at the salon in Catalina's private styling room. She was doing a roller set. We were sharing a box of tissues. Her portable television captured the poignant scene. The mother reached for the son as he passed from incarceration into freedom. This was not the *Pietà*. Wanda's son was alive. She would have him, and she would hold him. Her exuberance was ubiquitous. Had it been bottled, it might have comforted her in the days yet to come. All that was saved were the tears.

Gregory's motorcade arrived at the spotless house. Friends and neighbors had brought food and spread a bacchanal feast. The prodigal son had returned. Gregory Robinson was a hot commodity. He was being offered college admission and scholarships to several of Chicago's universities and, should he complete college, almost certain admission into law school. Gregory was scheduled to describe his twelve-year ordeal at numerous speakers' forums. He was everyone's guest. He was prayed for in churches and exalted by civil rights and social justice groups. While Governor Ryan went to jail, Gregory Robinson was the toast of the town.

Be Careful What You Pray For

Wanda had returned to work. She was being contacted less and less for comments and appearances. She seemed to relish returning to her old routine. By now Tech Ed had moved its offices into the opulent 311 South Wacker Drive building. The only thing more intimidating in the neighborhood was the Sears Tower casting an even longer shadow across the street. Our building had its own green space where we could sit outside in the noonday sun. With such a bright day, why did I see clouds in Wanda's face?

"Is everything all right?"

"Sterling came to the house last night."

"The bastard! What did he want?"

"He wanted to talk to Gregory. He's retired now. He got his pension. He's remarried."

"He came by to say that. He's a sickening pig."

"He said more. He said he knew Gregory wouldn't understand, but he loved him and he was sorry."

"Yeah, right."

"He also said that he had come to warn him."

"About what?"

"He said that Gregory is making enemies in the wrong places. He said his sources told him Gregory needs to stop talking to the press, complaining about the system. He said that Gregory is starting to run with the wrong crowd. He needs to shut up, take the money, keep his nose clean, and let sleeping dogs lie. If he doesn't, Sterling said things won't go well for him."

"Was that it?"

"Yeah, it was. He told him to take care, shook his hand, and left."

We had turned away from the sun. That was the most cryptic comment I had ever heard.

"What do you think that means?"

"I'm scared" was her tense reply.

Her friends and associates had been advocating for intervention. "Gregory is going to need counseling. He is going to need help" was their incessant rallying cry. Friends who knew me but not Wanda insisted that I relay the plea. "Get him help. Gregory will need help."

I heard the concerns but proceeded with caution. How far does one dare travel into other people's affairs? Wanda and I were friends. We shared business secrets. I knew about her husband, sons, and all the suffering the family had endured. She had been to my home on several occasions. We had traveled for business together. We were indeed friends, but not best friends. Wanda's guard was too high for me to claim that designation. There were two women, one in Tennessee and one in Chicago, who I believed held those distinctions; I did not.

Feeling pressured and slightly responsible, I did attempt one day to advance the Gregory issue. Wanda seemed uncharacteristically relaxed. Things appeared to be going well. I wasn't sure what Wanda had expected when Gregory returned home, but one thing was certain: nothing would be the same. Adjusting to Gregory, the superstar, was something completely different from the quiet existence with her son I think Wanda had imagined. She became his scheduler and spent a considerable amount of office time planning his agenda and confirming his appointments. But Gregory, the money man, was on an over-the-top roller-coaster ride. Feeling overwhelmed and skeptical of Gregory's old neighborhood friends, Wanda wanted to move to the suburbs. But Gregory loved the house and the old neighborhood. Properties up and down Drexel Avenue, he pointed out, were being gentrified. He wanted them to stay put, upgrade, and remodel the house. He told her it could be their mother-son project. They would redo the house together. Gregory gave his mother the money, but Wanda soon found herself alone selecting countertops, hardwood flooring, and new kitchen appliances. Gregory's purchases, when he made them, seemed driven by impulse and were without explanation. More often than not, they simply made no sense.

Sometimes Wanda found Gregory's purchases ridiculous and showy. "Why would he buy a crystal chandelier that's larger than the dining room table? Gregory's adding decks now onto the back of the house at all three levels. Can you believe it? Yesterday Gregory had them deliver a baby grand piano, and no one we know plays."

Sometimes Wanda found Gregory's purchases endearing, giving her a glimpse of the boy she loved. "I came home today, and Gregory had bought me a poodle. This week is my birthday, and Gregory is sending me roses for seven days. Gregory took me to Mercedes-Benz of Chicago and bought me a Mercedes. I've always wanted a Mercedes. All the Black boujees either have a Mercedes or a BMW. Goodbye, broke-down Camry. Hello, sexy momma."

Where there is the scent of money, moochers are soon to follow. It's an easier hide if the amount you received isn't published in the *Sun Times*. But when it's there in black and white and read by a population that doesn't realize you have to subtract attorney fees, five million dollars makes you sound like the richest person on the South Side.

"These people. These people," Wanda complained. "You would think we are the Salvation Army or something. I swear Gregory is getting more and more like the Godfather. When he is home, there are people in the house all the time, and every one of them has a problem, needs a favor, and wants a loan. My Gregory is such a sweet boy. He sits, he listens, and he tries to help."

Despite her protestations, Wanda did enjoy some aspects of it all. She tried to remain her same old self, but money alters you. It imbues you with a sense of power and social magnetism you didn't before possess. For Wanda the return of this new Gregory, and the introduction of more money than she had ever seen in her life, had created a tightrope she was trying hard to walk.

As with her other friends and concerned colleagues, I, too, was seeing the signs of fraying and decided that day, when she came into my office buoyed up, to broach the subject of Gregory. She was standing before me, holding a shoebox in her hand.

"What do you think of these?" She lifted up a pair of red sandals.

"Where are you going in those, Kansas?"

"Are they too much? I'm speaking at a fundraiser with Gregory. We're both talking about how we were affected by his incarceration, his journey into societal reintegration etc., etc. I swear I have given this speech a thousand times. But my point is that I want to look spiffy."

"I think those shoes will work just fine." Wanda was smiling, satisfied, when I posed the question. "So how is Gregory reintegrating?"

"What do you mean?" Wanda was taken aback.

"You know, is it going well? Is everything OK?"

"Of course everything is OK. Gregory is just fine and very, very busy. Half of the time he isn't even at the house. Everyone seems to want and need him, but Gregory is just fine."

That sentence was a social period, which I interpreted to mean, none of your business.

The door to that subject had just been slammed shut. There would be no more intrusion by me.

Why does God so starkly draw contrasts, like good news opposite bad news? Wanda was having another great day. She had returned to work—her first day back following a seven-day Caribbean cruise. She was raving about the never-ending food and the shore excursions as I entered the employee eating area. I smiled from the doorway and motioned for her to come. She raised a halting finger for her lunch mates, signaling she would be right back. Even as she came, she was still laughing.

"I'm sorry, Wanda, but there is an emergency phone call for you."

Her eyebrows raised as if to say, "Really?" That was the last time I ever saw Wanda. She had the call transferred to the phone closest to her. She answered the ring and then disappeared.

The content of the call was a story on the evening news and in the next day's papers. Gregory Robinson had been arrested and charged with interstate trafficking of guns and drugs. In the trial that followed, Gregory refused counsel, preferring to defend himself. He was sentenced to twenty more years and remanded back to prison.

I made several attempts to contact Wanda.

"Can we meet sometime for lunch?"

"Sometime."

"Would you like to come to the Christmas party?"

"Maybe," she said, but she never came.

"Can I come see you?"

"I'll let you know."

I called several times. I would ask her questions, promise favors, anything to maintain contact. With each call I heard her voice withdraw, receding further and further back to a place she had forgotten existed, into a pain that robbed her words. Of what value are words, anyway? Mine weren't strong enough to retrieve a friend. The day I called and found that her number was no longer in service, I knew I had lost her forever.

Faith had taken the bar in Missouri. She had been appointed as a public defender. The day I called her, Faith had just returned from defending a man accused of committing capital murder.

"Faith, I don't know what has happened to Wanda. She fought so hard, for so long, to get Gregory free, to get him home. I think this entire situation is killing her."

"Auntie, so often that's the way it works. Mrs. Robinson could not have saved him. Gregory may have been in prison far too long. People must be conditioned to accept freedom. Freedom, when one is not prepared, is toxic. There is a reason why the caged bird sings."

The dance ends.

DANCE NUMBER NINE:
PRAISE DANCING

The Song: "This Little Light of Mine"
The Dancer: Momma

The Observance

My sister and I are sitting side by side. That's the way sisters should sit. Our husbands are opposing bookends on either side of us. We do not cry. To cry would be selfish when we had received such a gift. Let the others cry. They did not know the completeness we had experienced. It had all been so perfect. To not have shown gratitude would have been a mortal sin.

Our mother's funeral mass is underway. My sister has cantors chanting the "Dies Irae." Mom would have appreciated the dirge, but she wouldn't have loved it. For her, it would have been more style than substance. Mom never fully appreciated the Latin vernacular. She was a convert. Before becoming a Roman Catholic, Mom had been a fervent Baptist and would probably have preferred a rousing rendition of "We Are Soldiers" or "Sign Me Up." Whenever I think of my mother, I smile. It's not a smile reflecting amusement. It is a smile of recognition. It is my silent way of affirming that, in the course of my lifetime, I had the good fortune to be related to and know the most complete and wonderful creation God had ever made. I was smiling now.

Was it only a week ago to the day that Mom and I had been looking at each other across the bedroom pillows?

"How are you feeling now?" The question was in response to the night before, when Mom had been ill. She was weak when she came to Chicago, but she came just the same. She had promised me she would, and a promise made was a promise kept.

Mom usually made a summer sojourn to Chicago, so that she and our family could go to Wisconsin or Michigan. When Dad was still alive, they both came. Dad had left us several years earlier, but Mom would still faithfully come for time with her grandkids and great grandkids. Under duress, she conceded she would like to see me as well.

But that summer, she didn't feel up to the trip. She had endured a painful bout of shingles and wanted to recuperate. She promised to come in the fall. God gives Chicago September because He knows what will follow. Mom had never seen a Chicago autumn with its spectacular, blazing hues. Orange was her favorite color. It was as if nature knew she was coming. Every tree seemed to be wearing orange.

I had wanted her to relish the Technicolor tree parade, but Mom was sleeping a lot and occasionally complaining of a sour stomach. Mom was always a thin woman, but she now seemed tinier than ever. Her prominent cheekbones protruded from her face, betraying some distant Indian heritage. In the middle of the night, when I woke and covered her, it was as if I were sleeping with a delicate little wren.

I had baited Mom to Chicago with the promise to make her favorite corned beef and cabbage dish. I did, but after two bites, she felt too full to eat it. I heard the same when I served her warm cherry pie. We were all packed to head for Saugatuck, Michigan, to take in those awe-inspiring fall sunsets, when Mom collapsed into the family room easy chair. It swallowed her diminutive frame.

"What hurts you, Mom?"

"I'm not hurting. I just don't feel well."

Plans to travel to Michigan were scrapped. We would make do at home. When Mom complained again, I suggested a trip to the emergency room. Her large brown eyes, now saucers in her face, bucked.

"Are you kidding? People die waiting to be seen in emergency rooms."

Concerned, I asked to sleep with her that night. I wanted to cuddle next to her the way I had as a child. It was morning now, and we were awake, staring across the pillows. Who in heaven had fashioned her? Mom was ninety and had not a wrinkle.

"Do you feel like getting up?"

She seemed to want to, but she was not sure if she could.

"Let me get you dressed. When you're dressed you'll feel better. If you like I'll take you to the park. It's like an autumn arboretum."

Dressing Mom was like dressing a doll. I found loose-fitting pants and a blouse with a lace front. My favorite part was combing her hair. It was thin now and long. I braided it and laid it across her shoulder, tied with an orange bow.

"This looks silly." She laughed as I stood her before the mirror. "Where is that blame walker? I need to get around."

I wanted to feed her breakfast, but she still wasn't hungry.

"I'll give you a piece of chocolate if you eat a spoon of oatmeal," I bartered. Mom took two mouthfuls and then put down her spoon. "I'm not hungry," she repeated.

"How about Ensure? Could you drink that? It's two chocolates if you do."

Mom made a face. "I don't think so." She ensconced herself in the easy chair that swallowed her.

"Do you want to look at one of those ministers on television?"

She smiled. "No, not today."

"They may have some of that gospel singing."

"Not today."

"Do you want to read your Bible? You love to read your Bible."

She gave me an accommodating smile. "Maybe later. Let it stay there." Mom patted the book on the side table. "I think I'll just sit. The sun feels so good and warm. I just want to sit. What are you going to do?"

"I have to review a draft proposal. But I can sit here with you, in the sun, and read it."

"That would be nice."

Several hours passed. It was just Mom, me, silence, and the sun. She was so still. I called to her.

"Mom."

"Yes, sweetheart."

"I was just checking."

"Checking what?" She opened her eyes. "Oh my! When did we come here?"

"Come where, Mom?"

"Here, in this place, this big white house. When did we come here?"

"What big white house, Mom?"

"This is so beautiful."

"Mom, Mom, we're not in a big white house."

"So beautiful." She swooned.

"Mom." I shook her shoulders.

She looked at me. "What is it?"

"We're not in a big white house. We're in my house."

"Sweetheart, sweetheart, I know where we are."

I gave her a puzzled look. She slipped back to sleep. I was glad Mom was with me and we were alone together in the warm sun. The phone rang. Mom stirred.

"Keep resting, Mom; I'll get it. The phone is right here."

It was my sister. "How's it going up there? What happened, you decided not to go to Michigan?"

"Mom seems weak. We decided to just take it easy and stay home."

"So how is she now?"

"I don't know. I'm having a hard time getting her to eat."

"I know. She doesn't seem to have an appetite."

"Can I tell you something strange?" I began whispering.

"Like what?"

"Mom thought we were in a big white house."

"In the White House? You mean where Obama lives?"

"No, a big, beautiful white house."

"Where would that be? Was she asleep? Maybe she was dreaming?"

"I don't think she was asleep."

"Umm. I don't know. Go figure. Listen, remember Randall Cox?"

"The Don Juan Randall Cox, the Marquis of the Mattress, whose motto was, 'I'm a love machine; come see me do my thing. All are welcome eight to eighty, blind, crippled, and crazy.'"

"That's the one. A legend in his own mind. Well, I saw the love machine at Peach Tree Restaurant. Girl, now the brother looks like a washing machine. The only way he'd get a woman today, she'd have to be a hostage."

My sister always had the juiciest gossip, the most ridiculous stories to prompt the most unharnessed laughter. It was one hour, at least, before our frivolous conversation began to subside.

"Hey, is Momma there?" My sister remembered. "I need to tell her Mrs. Dixon wants her to pray for her. She said her arthritis is acting up, and the last time Momma prayed for her, it went away."

"She's right here. I think all our foolishness put her to sleep."

I walked to the chair and lightly shook her.

"Mom, it's your crazy daughter. She has something to tell you about Mrs. Dixon."

My mother did not move. Her mouth was slightly ajar. While I was laughing in the sun, my mother had tiptoed into that big, beautiful white house.

The Dance

The Light Is White

Where ever there are sunbeams, starlight, or morning moons, I can find you. You come through the light wearing your powder-blue Lilli Ann suit. The one Daddy gave you and a hat designed by Mr. John, full of net, ribbons, and flowers. This is your special hat. The one you saved for those occasions where you wanted to dress to impress. In the hat box, it would have been comical, but atop your head, framing your luminous bronze-colored eyes, it is a coronation.

Your visage softens everything. Which is why as a child, the most secure place in the world to be was in your eyesight. My mind spins in the light. You are coming closer. The fragrance envelopes my nostrils. It's not a perfume. It's you. Your body emits its own fragrance. It's called Mom. I recognize it even when I don't see you. I know it. Where is the atomizer? I want to spray it on me. It's Mom. It is your signature fragrance. Even before your lullabies or your caresses calmed my whining, I knew the scent. You are in the light. There you stand, smiling and perfect. The hat and suit dissolve. It is a dress, floral and cotton. You beckon. I reach for your hand. I am four.

We are twirling, the three of us: you, Lorraine, and me. We are going around a mulberry bush that isn't there. What, oh what is a mulberry bush?

"Ashes, ashes, we all fall down." Our hands release. Laughing, we tumble to the ground. We are rolling about in the grass.

"Careful, girls," you caution as we roll. "We can't let the chiggers get us." And down the hill we go.

Where am I now? Bouncing on your knees. You are singing.

"Mr. Froggie went a courtin' and he did ride, uh-huh, uh-huh. Mr. Froggie went a courtin' and he did ride, a sword and a pistol by his side, uh-huh, uh-huh." I knew the song enough to sing parts of it with you. When the song ends, you spread your legs apart and I fall into the swing of your skirt. You are holding my hands.

I recite a poem by Robert Louis Stevenson. "The rain is raining all around. It rains on fields and trees. It rains on umbrellas here, and it rains on ships at sea."

You taught me this poem, which I memorize and recite that night at dinner for Daddy. I must be a big girl now. You said this is a poem. I usually recite a nursery rhyme.

I have been sent to the Mr. Switch bush. Mr. Switch's bush is round and short. I have to pick my switch. Bad girls are sent to Mr. Switch's bush. I pick the smallest switch I can find. I cry all the way from the bush to you. I hand it to you. You switch my legs. I jump and jerk to the stinging.

"I hate Mr. Switch," I tell you.

"Don't hate Mr. Switch. He makes you better. I'll bet you won't do that again." I poke out my mouth, not affirming or denying. You are right. I won't do that again.

I crack the bedroom door. The light through your window makes you a silhouette. I go stand beside you. Fringes of lashes draw your lids closed across your eyes.

I whisper, "What are you doing?"

"I am praying."

"Why are you doing that?"

"Because I am talking to God."

"Who is God?" You and I are now the same height.

You smile. "God is goodness. There is no other name. No other word."

"Where is God?"

"Here, there, everywhere."

"I don't see him."

"I know, but he is here, and this is how we talk to him. We get on our knees. We never talk to God the way we do other people. When we talk to God, we say, we pray."

"Why do you pray?"

"I pray because God is my father and he loves me. Do you want to pray?"

I think about it a moment. "No thanks. I'm going to go pray to Daddy."

My mind finds the light again. You are standing. You are embracing a yellow crocheted receiving blanket.

"Momma, is there something inside?"

"Lift out your arms. This is for you." You tell me to sit on the sofa. Now I am extending my arms.

"Here you go. Now you won't be lonely anymore."

It is the baby sister I had asked you to get me. You must have gone to the Parkview.

"Can you get me another diaper, your sister just made poop. Can you warm her bottle for me? She has applesauce all on her highchair. Will you clean it, please? Get the Mexsana powder, and let's put it on her back; she has a heat rash. She's colicky. She won't stop crying. She has a fever. Will you hold her and burp her?"

"Momma, can we take her back to Parkview?"

The Light Is Refracted

It's Christmas Eve. There you are in lounging pajamas, showing me how to set out cookies and milk for a White Santa, wearing a red suit, steering eight flying reindeer who will land on top of our roof, which has a chimney the size of a Del Monte can, to bring me toys. You said this is what happens for good little girls, and I believe. It was a stretch, I admit, but a more convincing proposition than a bunny bouncing around with a basket full of colored eggs and not getting shot for someone's supper. But you said it was true, Momma, and so I believe. I even believe when you confided, following the loss of my first tooth, that a five-inch fairy had been commissioned to pick up useless teeth and leave five cents in return.

What you told me, Momma, was kooky but easier to believe than what I learned in catechism. Sister said there were three people in one God. Now, how does that work? What in the name of God is original sin? Father Henley told us, in second grade, that we are born with it. We caught it from a woman named Eve. Eve ate an apple, and God got mad. I've never seen that woman in my life, and I for sure don't want any more apples. God should take her to see Mr. Switch. Father tells the class we have to make a confession. That I have to be sorry for my sins. I have to learn prayers to say for my confession so that my sins will be forgiven.

I memorize the Act of Contrition. I wait in the pew for my turn to go into that spooky, dark closet, and I say, "Bless me, Father, for I have sinned, but I did not eat that apple." I tell you about my first confession. Your laugh is a lilting melody. You swallow me in a deep hug and say how proud of me you are. I want to go to confession again.

"What is heaven like, Momma? Sister Mary Peter said if we are good and have been baptized, when we die we will go there." I'm not excited about heaven. I don't want to die. I'm only eight. We are in the front porch swing. It is a July evening and too warm to be inside.

"Heaven is a place where we will all be together with God, our father. It is a place where we will live with the angels and saints. We will always be happy and safe in heaven, and I will never leave you. I think heaven is a big, beautiful white house." I'm reevaluating the situation. I want to go to heaven.

The Prism

The empyreal white light passes through the prism. Shafts of colors splay like a holiday fan. Everywhere I walk is yellow. You are handing me a card. It is my membership in the Look It Up Book Club.

"Momma, the bookmobile is coming. I'm going to get some books."

We don't have a neighborhood library, but there is the bookmobile. It crawls down the street stuffed with enchanting stories of girls who live in strange places of which I have never heard. Lorraine and I climb aboard in awe of the many books, stacked like jewelry boxes, holding precious stories. We are ten-year-old jumping beans. Every week we ask the librarian the same question. "How many can we take? How long can we keep them?"

Every week her answer is the same. "Only two, until we come back next week."

Our eyes search the shelves. The librarian lets us hold the ones we request, dutifully reminding us, "Only two. That's all you can check out on your card. Next time you can get two more."

We are satisfied. We take our two books, race for the front porch swing, and read. When Lorraine isn't there, I take my book like a passport to bed, where I can escape. Sometimes, Momma, you would do a read around with me. You would read a page aloud, and I would read a page. To every character that spoke, we would assign a different voice and unique mannerisms. Sometimes, after one reading, I would request a second one.

"Reading can be fun," you explained, "and it is important because you learn new words and their meanings, you broaden your world, learning about things you would otherwise never know, and you make a friend who lives with you for a week. But there is more to life than fun."

"There is?"

"Yes, there is. There is work, and work may be more important than fun."

Ah yes, work. Definitely not always fun. Work consisted of taking the trash and garbage out, every day, to the metal barrel and galvanized garbage pail at the rim of the backyard. I got to burn the trash, which possessed some element of mystery, but the garbage haul was a grind. It wasn't hard. It was just nasty. It held no intrigue except in the summer, when the maggots emerged from nowhere to roam the ruined food.

Momma, you believed girls needed to learn girl's work, like bed making, dish washing, and hanging out the clothes. There it is, standing erect in the yellow light. My mind sees it now. It's our backyard clothesline. Our bedsheets are hanging, billowing in the breeze. You remove the clothes pins and put them in your apron pocket. As the sheets droop off the line, we wrap ourselves in them, becoming white, sun-bleached mummies.

"Smell the sun, baby. Did you know the sun has a fragrance?"

I draw in a deep breath, inhaling the sweet scent of the sun. In bed that night the sheets are still emitting that special perfume.

"I smell it, Momma. I still smell the sun."

"Of course you do, baby. Let your nose fill up with the smell of the sun, and you'll never be afraid of the dark."

The Light Is Red

It's high school. I don't call you Momma anymore. Momma sounds too baby-fied for a sophisticated, upper-class junior. I am not yet considered cool, but I want to be. You embarrass me when my new White friends and their mothers stop to pick me up and you talk about the Bible. All they asked was, "How are you?" Isn't it enough that you read it all the time, go to Mass every Sunday and rosary on Wednesday? Stop! No more talk about the Bible. Not cool! Lorraine's mother doesn't talk about it, and she plays piano for her church choir on Sunday. What is this you are telling me? You have holy water stored in used Jean Nate bottles? Please stop! You are so not cool. I don't want my friends and their moms to talk to you. They will think I'm the biggest square. Please, not the holy candles again! You have them strewn around the house in every color and size: green for prosperity, white for protection and healing, and blue for wisdom and sleep. Isn't it enough for you each Sunday after Mass when you burn the red votive candles? Only pyromaniacs want this much fire. Dad tells you repeatedly you will burn the house down. It's bad enough when we are awake, but they are flaming in their glass canisters throughout the night. When my friends' moms bring me home, I have them drop me at Parkview. I say I have to pick up something. Don't you get it? I want a cool mom like Mary Cecilia's. Her mom talks about American Bandstand and hairstyles; you are talking about how prayer can change things and miracles.

own spiritual epiphany. I understood you better now. "Is there anything else I can do?"

"Sweet baby, don't you know by now that nothing lasts forever? Everything is for just right now. Each of us has just to keep doing what we have to do, and God will make a way. So you keep going to school and helping out with your tuition working at Milgram's. I'm going to keep praying that Internal Revenue doesn't fire me, and that Miss Lottie still needs me every Saturday, at least for right now."

Mom, you are so right. Nothing lasts forever. Not even pain.

I will graduate college. Daddy will get a job on the City Council, the first African American to be so seated, and you will stop working Saturdays.

The Light Is Blue

I stand at the altar, looking back at you in the pew. You are a rapture of soft pink. I think my mother is more beautiful than the bride. Two nights before, like a whisper, you softly tapped my door.

"May I come in?"

"Is that you, Mom?"

"Yes, I want to give you something."

"Come in." I sat up, removing the tea bags I had applied to my eyes all week to make them glisten when I marched down the aisle. You sat beside me.

"Well, I said give, but I meant borrow. You know, something old, something new? Well, this is something borrowed." You took my hand and slipped a rosary in it.

"It's supposed to be blessed by the Pope. I don't know for sure, but Madge said, when the church took the trip to Rome five years ago, that it was. Of course, I didn't take the trip, but I don't think Madge would lie." I fingered the beads. It was dark, but I understood the configuration. The Apostle's Creed, the Our Father, the Hail Mary's, the Glory Be's, and the amazing mysteries, simple when spoken but so potent in prayer.

I don't pray the rosary much anymore. The fingering of the beads and the constant repetitions seem medieval to one as future-focused and secular as I now believe myself to be. But not you, Mom. Every Wednesday you pray the rosary. I have seen you at church kneeling, as instructed by Christ, gathered with two, three, or more.

What have those beads done to you with their mystical chants? Your face serene, at peace, only your fingers moving; what have those beads done to you? Why is their magic more powerful than Valium? What have those beads done? I hear you now as we sit invisibly in the darkness.

"Ah, sweet baby, you seem so in love." Mom, you are so right. I have the large diamond engagement ring, my engagement picture has been published in both the *Kansas City Star* and the *Kansas City Call* newspapers. My wedding banns have been read in church; my wedding dress was on sale, but it is a couture delight, and wedding presents are arriving. To top it off, my godmother has lent me her pearl necklace. I have ascended into Hollywood heaven. The only word to describe me is ecstatic. I had told myself each time I was a bridesmaid that marriage was not for me. I had told myself that I didn't need a man in my life, that I had to find myself, but here I am in the middle of the night, drunk on the Cinderella fantasy of happily ever after, and I never ever want to become sober. "Sometimes I think I could levitate right off this bed and hit the ceiling." A chuckle races from my throat.

"Really?"

"I know. It sounds crazy, but those songs are right. Love makes you fly, lifts you up." I flap my hands like wings in the night.

"Really?"

"Uh-huh." I am flapping my hands.

"Well, you just keep on flying for a few more months."

"No, no. Not a few more months. Forever."

You put your hands on mine, slowly lowering them to the covers. "Baby, listen to me; love is heavy. It is not light. It is a hard thing. It makes you want to turn away from it sometimes and leave it alone. Sometimes love is ugly, and it scares you to look at it, but you stay and you stare and you work it because it is the very best of who we are and allows us to bring forth our very best. So promise me that when you stop flying and hit the ground that you will stay and work through the hard things so that you can stare and see the best of yourself."

What kind of prayer is that? "Mom, what are you talking about?"

"You will see. Just promise me."

I feel your hands pressing warmly on mine. I want to explore your point, ask you what could be so hard about love and marriage, horse and carriage. Haven't I watched you and Dad all these years?" But it is my wedding eve. Keep it simple stupid. "I promise." A simple reply.

Again, Mom, you are right. It's our daughter's birthday. There you go, round and round. It's that old Mulberry bush. This time it's my daughter's hand you are holding. I see her laugh and fall down. There's no grass. It's the family room carpet in our new home. My husband and I have a jumbo mortgage, two new cars, furniture bills, and daycare costs that exceed my college tuition. Love is heavy.

There I am, wearing a navy-blue silk dress. I like my sister's outfit better. My outfit went straight from the mannequin to me. Hers looks custom made for her. But you, Mom, are glowing. You are wearing an orange dress with a matching jacket. People are hugging you and bearing gifts. It's your retirement party. You're leaving. Miss Lottie didn't last long. You continued to go most Saturdays because she needed you, but one day she just came undone and was sentenced to a senior living facility. You don't have to work anymore for anyone. The United States Government rewards your service with a pension. How sweet it is. We watch the slideshow Dad prepared. It's a photo gallery showing how a pretty young woman becomes an elegant matron. There is a chorus of oohs and ahs and laughter. My sister and I make speeches. She cries. I try to tell jokes. Neither work well.

When the guests leave, the four of us sit in the grand lobby of the banquet hall while our husbands go for the cars.

"What are you two going to do now?" I ask my parents.

"We're taking a cruise," Dad pipes up.

"You took a cruise last year," my sister reminds them.

"So what?" Dad counters.

"Each time, we go someplace different. Your momma on the water is not the same person she is on dry land. Let me just say we need to be on the water, because when we are, your momma is hot. I mean burning." Daddy's laugh is wicked. Mom is embarrassed.

"Would you just hush with that nonsense." She slaps his knee. Daddy squints repeatedly for emphasis. "Burn-ing."

"Too much information," my sister teases.

"Stop, now I mean it." I see the cautioning mom reminding that children, even grown ones, are not adults and are not admitted to adult conversations. So stop, Daddy. Change the subject. Dad shrugs as if to ask, so what did I do? "It was a beautiful party. I thought the old girl might cry. But I knew she wouldn't. This woman is tough. I told you how it is. She only gets wet on the water."

Nuclear mortification. The three of us with bulging eyes and open mouths dare not respond.

Then comes Dad's rejoinder. "What are you three thinking with your dirty minds? I meant swimming. She goes swimming."

Mom clasps her heart. Daddy feigns consolation. "I just meant, you know, your breast stroke."

Mom pulls away. "Your mind is sitting with the devil tonight. You best ask God to help you with your mind."

"I will, sweetheart. I will," he pledges, "but first I want him to help me with my body." There it is again, that wicked wink.

I see you sitting there, expressionless. I ask myself, how long, how long will you sit in blank repose? He is gone; left us five days ago. Later this day, others will come to gawk and mumble. Some will approve his countenance and say he looks great. Others will whisper that he does not look at all like the man they knew. It is all immaterial. He has left. He is gone. You sit with a vacant man. Will you cry tomorrow? I doubt it. If not today then tomorrow will, for sure, be deprived. You're on dry land: no water, no tears. Have you left, too? Your bearing, so straight and statuesque, suggests that you, too, may have escaped, leaving this plane for another. Have you found him? If so, now say goodbye. You must come back to us. We are calling. Momma, you must come back.

You stand straight as if you are starched. I know some parts of you, but not all. I can never tell when you are happy. You smile and you laugh, but are you happy? I know for certain the meaning and measure of most of your moods. I have experienced the duration and intensity of funny mom, exhausted mom, worried mom, quiet mom, and playful mom. I file through my index of mom moods. Happiness is not there.

My sister takes your arm to make a bow for your shoulder. Your empty eyes turn toward her. You are still not there. Maybe tonight, maybe tomorrow you will return. We will wait for you, never asking where you had gone. Some places are for parents only, not their children. You are Momma. You will not desert your children. We will wait for you.

Time passes. I stare at the vessel that is you and wonder, when you do return, who will you be? Will Daddy's death shrink you, turn you inward? Will you feel incomplete minus a man? Will my sister and I be enough? We are waiting.

The Light Is Orange

"Prayer Warrior." The sun is setting. An orange glow flattens across the Missouri sky.

I look at my sister pouring through old photos and letters on the dining room table. I return from my reverie and remember. We're selecting pictures for a collage that will be projected at Mom's wake.

"I'm sorry. Did you say something?"

"Of course I'm saying something. I've been saying something. Let's get a grip here, girl. It's going to get worse before it gets better. Allow me to repeat myself, and this time pay attention. I said Momma was a prayer warrior. Remember people would call her that? The ladies at the church, that place where she volunteered, her neighbors—everybody would call her that. I've been just reading these letters and thank-you notes. Look at all of this. They're to Momma, thanking her for her prayers and saying how her prayers helped them, even healed them." My sister pushes her glasses back up her nose and picks up a letter.

"Just listen to this. 'I don't have words to express how grateful I am for your many months of long, unflagging prayer. My son's cancer is now in remission. Your prayers, more than any others I am sure, go directly from your lips to God's ear. He hears you and he answers.' Here's another. 'You are a miracle worker. Harold has completely left that chippy alone. It's like he broke from a fever when you told God to have Satan unlatch him. Christ Jesus heard your every word.' Here's another one. 'You are for sure a prayer warrior, marching in the army of the Lord. When I pray with you I feel the spirit, like an electric current, moving from your body through mine.' You're really not going to believe this one. It's from Mrs. Vaden. Remember her, the neighbor with the glass eye? She writes…"

I'm leaving my sister, drawn to the dazzling orange light. It's our house. I unlock the door and step in. I'm home. There you are, Mom, standing in front of the floral living room chair. Two women are with you. You three are singing, "When I have done all I can, I just stand." The song ends. You sit in the chair. The other women sit near. "We're going to go to God now." You open the Bible on your lap, but you are not reading. You lower your eyes and begin to pray.

"Father God, we come to you today as suffering women. We are alone and afraid."

I hear soft murmurs of "Uh-huh," and "Yes, Jesus."

"Sister Sullivan here is in pain, Father God. Her job is gone, her husband is sick, and she may lose her house, Father God. Now I know I don't have to tell you this, because you know all things."

"Yes, he does," swoon the ladies.

"See all things."

"Yes, yes."

"Hear all things. But we come to you, today, again because we know you care. Know that you love us. Know that you and only you can lift Sister Sullivan out of her torment, bind her wounds, and make a way for her somehow."

"Somehow," the ladies echo. "Somehow."

"We know this because your word has taught us to have no anxiety about worldly things. We know this because you have taught us if we bring everything to you in prayer, if we come like supplicant children on bended knee and lay our burdens at your feet, you will lift our burdens and make them light."

Mom, your voice is rising, gaining volume.

"For it was you, Father God, who said, my yoke is easy and my burden is light. Just call upon your name, just ask, just knock, that's all, just knock and it shall be opened to you."

You had been churning in your chair, but at this moment you rocket up, issuing what could be perceived as a challenge to the almighty. In one hand you are clutching your Bible; in another you raise a clinched fist. My Catholic mother has just been hijacked by her Baptist roots.

"Well, here we are, Father God. Here we are." Mom stomps a foot. "Do you see us Father God? Here we are, gathered together to beg this favor. Can you hear us?" This is a loud adjuring. "Can you hear us?" The women begin doing some form of praise dancing.

Again they charge, "Can you hear us?"

In case God has forgotten, Mom, you remind. "You told us so yourself, heavenly father. You said that when two or three of us are gathered in your name you are in their midst. That is your word, and your word is true. We are here, and so, our father, are you. Now hear my prayer. Sister Sullivan is suffering. Without you she will lose everything. Everything. Can you hear me when I tell you she lost her job, and the bank is trying to take her house? Can you imagine a good woman, your child, who every day, every hour, every second lives your word and gives you and you alone all the glory, so distressed? A woman who in prayer utters no name but yours, abandoned? Can you imagine her pain, the inconsolable pain? She is here now, heavenly father. Your child is here and in need. Tell her that you will not abandon her. Show her that you will not abandon her." Was it a prayer or the defiant child daring the father?

Mom, are you dancing? You have joined the others. Your feet are prancing to an unheard song. It's a spiritual line dance. I, an unintended onlooker, am also starting to feel an unidentified quiver in my Catholic feet. Mom, your aura is causing my soul to stir. I feel awkward. You don't see me. You are a prayer warrior, doing your war dance.

"We know that you are here and that you will not abandon her. She is knocking, Father God. She is knocking. Let her in and heal her where she hurts. Show her how you can make a way where there is no way. Show her how faith in you can move mountains. I implore you to show her how you care for your children, how you will shepherd her as you promised and keep her from want."

My mother, the preacher, the exhorter, the prayer warrior. I watch you, and I am in awe. As you climb down the ladder of your prayer, you recite the praise names of your Lord. "God the promise keeper, hear us, God the protector, shield us, God the provider, care for us. God our father, love us."

A cathartic calm enters the room and cloaks you, once again, in your Catholicism.

"In the name of the Father and of the Son and of the Holy Spirit. Amen." You make the sign of the cross. All three women say amen.

As you are taking your seat, you look up and see me at the threshold of the living room.

"Hello, baby." You are shining. "When did you get in town?"

I am back at the dining room table with my sister. She is beginning to read another stack of notes. "You know what I think?"

"What?"

"I think we should pack all of this up, along with a petition for sainthood, and send it to Rome."

"And what do you think will happen there?"

"What do you mean what will happen there? They'll make her a saint or blessed or something."

"I think she has to do some miracles for that."

"Momma can do that."

"You think so?" I have to smile. My sister is so certain.

"I know so. I didn't tell you this because I didn't want you to say I'm crazy, but I saw her yesterday."

"You saw who?"

My sister slits her eyes and whispers in a hushed tone, "Momma."

"Are you trying to be funny?"

"See. I knew I shouldn't have told doubting Thomas here."

"I'm sorry. OK." I can't restrain the full-blown grin. She is so the Mary to my Martha.

"So what did she say?"

"Please remove that revolting, mocking smirk."

"I'm not mocking, really. But you surely can understand that I'm a bit shocked to hear it. I mean we both know she's dead."

"Exactly my point. When you see dead people that is called a miracle."

"No doubt about that. But I think in order to qualify as a miracle, you have to have a notary or third-party validation of some sort that is provided to Rome."

"I understand all of that. I'm just saying, if Momma did it once, she can do it again."

"OK, so you saw Mom, and what did she say?"

"Say? What's to say? What do you want her to say?"

"I don't know. Well, what did she do?"

"Listen, you agnostic, atheist infidel, she didn't say or do anything. She just smiled to let me know she was all right."

"OK, OK, so what was she wearing?"

My sister exhales the breath of futile exasperation. "So now you want labels? I can tell you one thing for sure, my sister, you will never see her, not today, not tomorrow, not ever. What was she wearing? Oh ye of little faith."

The day drains away. The advancing evening sends the sun scurrying to middle Kansas. We are still sorting. My sister is in the bedroom. I am in the kitchen, rummaging through the pantry, when I spy an unopened bottle of wine. Minutes later I call for my sister to join me at the kitchen table. She chuckles at the site of the wine bottle on the silver tray with two wine glasses.

"I see you found Momma's Mogen David stash. It was for her little some-thing-something after prayer."

"What do you think, should we toast her?"

"Without a doubt."

I fill the wine glasses. We lift them high.

"To Momma," my sister says.

"To Momma," I repeat.

The sorting is done. Darkness and I sit alone in the kitchen. I lift my glass in the stillness to salute you once again. "Here's to you, my zealot, firebrand Momma. Forgive me for thinking that without him your voice would have been diminished."

In the morning my dark companion will have left. The light will be white, and once again I will find you.

The dance ends.

DANCE NUMBER TEN: THE SALSA

The Song: "La Vida Es Un Carnaval"
The Dancer: Catalina Mendoza

The Observance

The word is *Rosario*, which means rosary and is the way, in some Mexican communities, the death of a loved one is commemorated. Each year, on the anniversary of the person's death, family and friends gather for refreshments and pray the rosary. I have attended at least four of these rosaries for Catalina Mendoza, whom I affectionately called Cat. Cat was my hair stylist. At least those were the conditions under which we met. But by the time she died we had become dear friends. Cat's daughter, Teresita, named after Saint Teresa, always invites me to celebrate this special remembrance with her family.

For the most part, the remembrance is always the same. There is always the same honey-colored face of Catalina smiling from an ornate gold frame, the lighted white candle mounted on a brown candle holder and a bouquet of red roses in a clear glass vase. The guests are pretty much the same: Teresita's husband, Catalina's two sons and their wives, her sister, six grandchildren, a nephew, a niece, a woman I pretend to know but really don't, and Charlotte, another one of Catalina's clients.

We pray the rosary, eat several types of tamales, and drink hot chocolate. This is followed by everyone telling the same stories, year after year, of what Catalina means to them. We all laugh some. Her children might even cry. When the last tear is dried, we all expel a collective belch and promise to return for the commemoration celebration next year.

The storytelling weaves a comfort quilt that covers us all with the endearing memory of Catalina. These stories reconnect us, if only for an evening, with this vibrant and determined woman whose life was predicated on love of God, family, and country.

My stories, at the Rosario, are of the master hair stylist with the miracle hands who restored my damaged hair. The gifted stylist with the dexterous hands who in ninety minutes could do cosmetic surgery on my hair. The alchemist stylist who could mix and match colors better than Bruno Mars saying, "Don't believe me, just watch." I tell these stories with humor and panache that would have made Catalina howl resoundingly. But it was the other stories, the ones never told, that formed the binding fibers of our friendship.

The Dance

You Never Miss Your Water

My current hair stylist is Tamicka. For starters, she forgets everything. This makes conversation with her difficult because she can never remember what we said the prior week. So it means I keep starting the same conversation from the beginning every Thursday. If I say to her, "Do you remember this or that?" she will flash a blank stare and simply say no. This initially was infuriating until I realized how effortlessly talking to her had become. I could say the same thing from week to week, and for her it was always new. When we try to practice the time-honored cosmetologist art of gossip, it is a reciprocating disaster. Tamicka wants to do all the talking, which places me at a grave disadvantage because I have no idea what she is talking about. What makes matters worse is that I talk very little with her about myself. That occurs for many reasons. Primary among them is the fact that I am old enough to be her grandmother. When I try to tell her a story, she makes me feel like an ice age fossil when she utters such banal expressions as, "Was that back in the day?" or "I read about that when I was in grade school." Then there is the compounding insult that a girl wearing leggings, a postage stamp for a skirt, and two heads of multicolored hair feels comfortable addressing me by my first name. Every time, when I request she use my last name, Tamicka casts her eyes downward as if I have destroyed her self-concept. She immediately apologizes but then instantly forgets. Ultimately, I give up and resign myself to the fact that skill comes at a cost. Which explains why I stay with

Tamicka. She is technically talented. Of the four stylists I have had since Catalina, Tamicka is the best. But every week, when I sit under the dryer with a conditioner, a wet set, or a wrap, I pine for Catalina. Does she have any idea how much I miss her?

Catalina Mendoza had been referred to me by a respected colleague whose hair, one day, I was admiring.

"Girl, you need to go see Catalina Mendoza."

"Mendoza?"

"I know. I know. You're like me. I always wanted a Black stylist, someone who understands my hair and isn't experimenting. But I am here to tell you Catalina is the real deal. The woman is from Mexico or South America or something. You know they have all types of hair textures down there. And she can do them all. When she finishes with you, your hair will be as smooth as a newborn baby's bottom and twice as cute."

I wasn't unhappy with my current stylist, but my colleague's hair looked so much better. Besides, I was getting older. I had enough things changing. A shiny new hairdo might slow down some of the apparent ravages of time. I made an appointment. When I took Catalina's chair I wanted things to be perfectly clear. First, I wanted her to appreciate that I knew and understood my hair better than anyone. I could tell her what worked and what didn't. Second, I didn't want some creative artist who wanted to give me some radical new look. I knew the styles that worked best for me, and I would tell her. Third, I didn't want her constantly coming at me with a pair of scissors. My hair didn't grow as fast, now that I was older. I would inform her when I needed my ends clipped. Finally, do not try to sell me a host of products. This was not my first time at the rodeo. I knew the products that worked for me, and those were the ones I wanted to use.

I was deep into my speech. Catalina hadn't commented. She had simply placed a cape around my shoulders and was hunting through my hair, separating it into sections, pulling it through her fingers, and examining my scalp.

I had finished talking for at least three minutes when she spoke through a deep Mexican accent.

"No worries, I got you."

What did that mean? Now I was worried.

"We do the shampoo now, OK?"

She was nudging me toward her shampoo bowl. I was apprehensive. She had the skill of a dentist in lowering her chair. My only other course of action would have been to break and run. When I was in the shampoo bowl, I made another attempt to impress my instructions upon her. She seemed not to hear me over the running water. Her shampoo felt like an agitator whipping around my head. Then came the hot and cool rinse and a slathering of I don't know what. Next, my head was out of the bowl, in a cap, and under the dryer. As I sat there for five minutes, I pondered the possibility that Catalina didn't understand English. Perhaps she had not understood a word I had said. I descended, again, into the shampoo bowl, and returned to her chair.

"This time we do a wet set. Not too much heat. You's got to understand, your hair can't take that." She swabbed more of that solution, found the right-size rollers, and did her set. While I sat under the dryer I promised myself I would sue Catalina if things didn't turn out right. Forty-five minutes later, Catalina was escorting me to her chair to remove the rollers. She was humming something to herself but said nothing to me.

When Catalina finished, she spun me around to face her mirror. The reflection that greeted me was astonishing. The woman staring back was super chic. The smart bob signaled that I was still young enough to be dangerous but wise enough to know better. Was it perception or reality? The drab winter sparrow, properly pampered and gilded, was now a spring robin ready to fly out onto the streets of Chicago.

For several seconds I stared at the woman who stared back at me. I gently touched my hair, then I shook it. My motor was starting to race. Get ready, world.

"What do you think?"

For a moment I had forgotten that I had arrived at this image only with assistance. "I think, Catalina, that you are a sorcerer with supernatural powers."

She didn't quite understand the compliment. "Is that good?"

"Very, very, very good."

"You come back then?"

"Put me down in your book, same time every Thursday."

That was how it all began: one dynamite hairstyle by a nonnative speaker for a fading female who needed a life lift. From that seed blossomed a friendship and mutual trust that endured until the day she died. I would never again question anything Catalina wanted to do to me. When she came with scissors, I surrendered. When she wanted to push away the gray with hair rinse, I submitted. If it was conditioning time or perm time, I subjected myself to whatever it was, because when the hair magician was through and she spun me to the mirror, I simply adored the woman I met on the other side. Good work deserved acclaim. I became an apostle for Catalina, telling anyone who would listen about the wonders she had wrought. At one point over a dozen of her patrons were my referrals. At its apex, a day at the salon was a conference, with professional women of all stripes gathering to trade survival tips and add value to their beauty experience.

It is impossible to see someone for two to three hours a week on an average of fifty-two weeks and not become attached. Most things we do, not counting work and sleep, don't last that long. Think about it. A meal is over, Mass is over, and if you're my age, your man, unless he is medicated, has been over. Only your stylist endures.

And so together we journeyed deep into each other's lives. Each Thursday, I would enter the salon with the expectation of sharing. It's like the old-fashioned serial movies I watched on Saturdays as a kid. The last frame always climaxed with something suspenseful, but that was all right because I knew the story would resume the following Saturday.

Getting to know someone is always an adventure because you never know what your encounters will uncover. For that reason, you start with safe subjects.

"What music do you like?"

Catalina liked Julio Iglesias. I liked Lionel Richie.

"How many children do you have?"

Catalina had four. I had two. We traded recipes. Catalina gave me hers for pozole. I gave Catalina mine for sweet potato pie.

And then it goes deeper. You began to share private feelings and confidences. I learned that Catalina lived in Chicago with her two sons. She had no other family here. One son drove a school bus. The other one was a student at Daley College. Her husband was an invalid in Jalisco, Mexico. Her two daughters, Anastacia and Teresita, had remained there to care for him. She and her sons constantly sent money home for the family.

Catalina was a fervent Catholic. Six years ago, when she was still living with her family in Jalisco, the doctors had diagnosed her husband's medical condition as terminal. In response to that diagnosis, Catalina prayed to our Lady of Guadalupe to heal him. In exchange she promised to say a rosary every day in Our Lady's honor and to cut off all her hip-length hair, sell it, and donate the proceeds to the poor. Her promise furthered prescribed that each time, for the rest of her life, when her hair swept across her hips, she would shear and sell it, giving the proceeds to the poor.

As she told me this story, her hair was just beginning to touch her shoulders. Over the next eighteen months, I would watch it snake down her back until once again it was a pixie. None of this seemed to trouble Catalina, and the deal seemed to be working. By my account, the Lady of Guadalupe had gotten the long end of the stick. Jorge, Catalina's husband, was alive but completely incapacitated. He could not travel, forcing Catalina's daughters to remain behind as his caregivers.

Most of Catalina's tips and income went to their upkeep. Still, Catalina's gifted skills as a beautician enabled her to model a considerable number of hairstyles, as her own hair perpetually phased from short to long and back to short again.

Better Than Canterbury

One of the most rewarding things about friendship is how you learn to hear. Upon first meeting Catalina, her heavy accent was an obstacle, but as our friendship deepened, her accent grew fainter to my ear and, over time, disappeared. As our understanding of each other evolved, I was no longer hearing Catalina with my ears. I was hearing her with my heart. As much as I might have wanted to, I found I could not mock or criticize her for her filial love of the Christ and his mother. No one I had ever met was as fervent or as consecrated in their faith as was she. Catalina's devotion and unabated demonstration of that love left me speechless.

Here's an example: Lent was concluding. For all the forty days, Cat was fasting. She took only toast and tea for breakfast, chicken broth for lunch, and a small meal in the evening.

"I only eat meat on Wednesday and Sunday," she reported. "The money I save, I give to the poor. What did you give up?"

I pretended I hadn't heard the question. Cat did not probe. This was the beginning of Passion Week, and Cat was bubbling.

"Do you remember I told you I was planning a special surprise—something I always wanted to do?" She crossed her chest, holding a comb in one hand and a brush in the other. Her eyes turned upward.

"Yes I do remember."

"It's going to happen. I have enough money, and my sons and I are going to do it."

"What is it you are going to do?" She leaned into my face, hers illuminated by the vanity lights behind us.

"We are doing the pilgrimage to El Santuario de Chimayo. Can you believe it? Me and my sons, we are going to do that pilgrimage. Do you know what that means?" Her questioning stare said I should have known, but I shook my head indicating that I did not.

"Oh girl. This is the big pilgrimage. Miracles happen there. I've seen pictures of the crutches on the walls. There are canes and walkers left behind. Blind people see. Sick people are cured. Real miracles! Listen, this is no little thing. Thousands of people from all over the world do this pilgrimage. Are you saying you never heard of it?"

I began to feel slightly ashamed and embarrassed. It seemed I had missed critical Catholic intel. Catalina's excitement was a runaway train. There was no stopping this story.

"Remember passion time last year? I told you about the Via Crucis in Little Village. That was when my son Miguel, on Good Friday, had the honor of playing Jesus. Remember how I told you he carried that heavy cross all the way to St. Adalbert Church, and people were flogging him with straps and crying, 'Crucify him, crucify him'? Remember how I told you this woman played Mary, Christ's mother, and how we were all crying real tears?"

"Yes, I do remember that." Who could forget?

"Remember how I told you hundreds of people marched in a procession down the street behind the horses and the burros?"

"I do remember."

"Remember I told you when we got to the church, they planted the crucifix and hung up my son?"

"That I definitely remember."

"Well, girl, this pilgrimage is a thousand times more than that."

Catalina was scaring me. What could possibly be a thousand times more impactful than that?

I would have my answer that Thursday following Easter as I sat in her chair for a relaxer. Cat's expression, speech, and body language were describing an ecstasy.

"First, there were thousands upon thousands of people. Not like the Little Village procession. I mean thousands…maybe fifty…maybe a hundred."

"You mean thousands?" The number seemed unfathomable.

"Yes, yes I do. All walking, singing, and praying. People everywhere clogging the streets, carrying crosses. All going to El Santuario de Chimayo."

"That little bitty church you were telling me about?"

"Yes. But you have to understand, that teensy tiny church is holy ground. Everyone who is suffering and hurting wants to get on holy ground. I know I did."

"Well, did you get there?"

"Of course, we all did." Believe me, anyone who is trying to go to our Lord and his blessed mother can get there. You'll never guess, though, what I did when I entered that holy church." I couldn't imagine.

"I got on my knees, and I crawled down the church aisle to the altar, and there I laid my petition before our savior."

"You crawled down the church aisle on your knees?" Was she kidding?

Catalina's response was defiant. "Yes, I did."

I was searching for what to say. My retort was weak. "Cat, that had to hurt."

She dismissed my concern sweetly with a smile. "No, girl, not in the least. Don't you know when you're filled with grace, nothing hurts you?"

The chemicals in the relaxer were starting to burn me. "Cat, I think we should do the shampoo."

"OK, OK, but just one more thing. I've been waiting all day to give you this." I began to rise. Cat placed a plastic ziplock bag in my hand.

"Here. This is for you." I turned the bag over several times.

"What is this?"

"It's holy dirt."

"Holy dirt?"

"Yes, holy dirt. I put a plastic spoon inside just in case you want to eat some."

"Dirt?"

"Miracle dirt, girl, miracle dirt." My head was on fire. I was pushing back into her shampoo bowl.

"Now, Cat, now!" As the cool water rushed into my hair, washing away the tingling, I wondered, just how often does our human existence intrude upon our spiritual experiences?

Sanctuary City

Catalina and I were scampering through the Chicago Pedway. It was February and freezing. I didn't travel this underground corridor that connects retail in the loop to other business enterprises until the weather was unbearable. We were booted and bundled. Cat had something to tell me, and she wanted us to be as incognito as possible. I loved conspiratorial adventures. I couldn't wait until Cat found the rendezvous spot for our meeting. The rendezvous spot was not much, just a Subway sandwich shop. It was not even dark, with people moving like shadows. But this place was warm and would have to do. We procured our sandwiches and began the winter strip down. Wounded soldiers wouldn't be wrapped this much.

"So tell me. Come on, what's up?"

We were in a booth sipping cold cokes. Only God knew why. Cat's face was as earnest as I had ever seen it. "I want you to know something."

"Great, because I want to know." I was percolating with curiosity.

"I really mean this when I say, from the depths of my heart, you are one of the few people in the world I believe I can trust. You are someone I can tell everything, someone who would help in my time of need. I prayed on this…asked Our Lady of Guadalupe to guide me, and now I am sure you are the one."

"I am?"

"I believe so. No, I know so. My heart tells me I can ask you this favor."

Christ in heaven! Was she going to ask me for a loan?

Catalina leaned in closer. "You are my dear friend for sure, right?"

How does one answer maybe to that question? "Of course." I succumbed.

"See. I was right."

I began to calculate her possible ask. Cat reached across the table and took my hand. A passerby gave me an awkward glance. Things were getting weird.

"Will you take my Teresita and keep her, just for two months? That is all I need."

"Your Teresita? You mean your daughter?"

"Yes, my daughter."

"But I thought she was in Jalisco with your other daughter. What's her name, Anastacia?"

"She is, that is true. But after my Jorge passed away, Anastacia got a great job in Guadalajara. This leaves Teresita, a young woman, alone way too much. I think it is not good and could be dangerous. My baby is naïve, and she is beautiful. Yes, I have family there and friends, but I tell you the situation is unsafe. I have to bring her to Chicago. My problem is that I have not room for Teresita. My apartment has only one bedroom. My sons, Miguel and Paco, sleep in the living room, and they have a friend, a student at Daley College, who lives with us as well. I know I need more room, and I'm working on everything, but I have this lease. All I need is a few months and I'll have things all worked out. Will you help me?"

Catalina's plea was so sincere, and she wasn't asking for a loan. "Of course I will."

Cat squeezed both my hands, tears in her eyes. "I have learned something in this life. Some people feel your pain. Others help you carry it. You help carry, my friend, and I owe you my life."

"Well, let's start small—maybe some deep conditioners."

"Yes, yes of course." Tears were streaming down her face. "And some relaxers, whatever you want."

"It's a deal."

Telling my husband was a bit of a sticky wicket.

"Are you trying to tell me we will have a Mexican refugee coming to live with us?"

"I prefer to describe her as the daughter of my friend."

"Why can't her mother take care of her own daughter?"

"It's a long story, but she doesn't have the room."

"So what are we now, an orphanage?" My husband was pacing. He was clearly annoyed. "I have to admit, this is one of your better capers. You're bringing in some south-of-the-border tortilla to live with us for how long?"

I couldn't admit it, but even I was beginning to rethink it. "A month and a half…two months."

"You're bringing in someone's child you have never met, your hairdresser's child, who by the way I have never met, to live with us for two months, and you couldn't even ask me how I felt about it? I'm sorry, are you saying something?"

I cleared my throat. "I just said hair stylist. That's what they call themselves now. Hair stylist, not hairdresser."

"Oh, that's smart! You want to define terms while I'm addressing a core concept in our marriage: communication, or in your case, the lack thereof. Somehow, it seems to me that you feel all decisions you make regarding our two lives are unilateral. You make them all, and I am supposed to do what, say thank you? Thank you for bringing a perfect stranger into the house where I live to cohabitate with us for two months. You know I really don't have words for this."

He seemed to be doing fine with the words he had found. I knew, though, that he was right. I had gone too far. I resorted to the only tool I had left. I began to cry.

"What's wrong with you?"

"Nothing." I dabbed my eyes.

"Are you crying?"

"No. No."

"Well, don't cry. It's not worth all that. I'm just trying to have you recognize that we're a team, and when you make these crazy decisions, I should be consulted."

"You're right. I'm so sorry."

Was he kidding? What woman in her right mind would consult her husband on any matter when she knew his answer would be no? The Jesuits were right: "It's better to beg for forgiveness than to ask for permission."

"Well, since it seems we're going to be living with Miss Taco Bell, what do we get out of it?"

"You know when you're helping a friend, it's not exactly bartering."

"What do we get out of this?"

"I get free shampoos, conditioners, and wet sets."

"That can't be all?"

"No."

"Well, what else?"

What else indeed. Let me think. Let me think. "Well, she's also going to help out with chores, do some domestic work."

"Like we've got a Mexican housekeeper?"

"Teresita's is not exactly a housekeeper. Maybe a little dusting, some washing, making the beds, and she may even help with dinner."

At that suggestion, my husband raised a halting hand. "Absolutely not! You know I have irritable bowel syndrome. The last thing I want is little Miss Chiquita around my food. I have to draw the line here. Mamacita does not cook. Got it?"

My husband found his way to the recliner. The evening news was beginning. I heard him grumbling. "I can't believe this. I just can't believe this."

The day I brought Teresita home, my husband was dozing in his recliner.

"Honey," I called. "I have someone I want you to meet."

Emerging from his sleepy fog, my husband entered the living room. As he drew closer to us, I felt as if he were a recent eye donor recipient who could now see.

"Well, hello." He reached for Teresita, his hands cupping hers. Teresita did a slight curtsy and dropped her head, hair sweeping forward like a curtain. Unable to speak a word of English, this delicate girl-woman with doe-like eyes and a disarming smile had just brought Mr. Macho to his knees.

"She doesn't speak English, honey."

"I just want you to know we are so glad you are here."

"She doesn't speak English, honey."

"You are welcome here."

"She doesn't speak English, honey."

"You are safe here."

"She doesn't speak English, honey." Were they handcuffed?

"Our home is your home."

"She doesn't speak English, honey."

Mi casa es tu casa. Teresita bowed an acknowledging, grateful head, still holding her luminous smile. Good move. I was so grateful my husband remembered the name of the Mexican restaurant where we were frequent diners, otherwise he could not communicate.

"No one will harm…" And suddenly the welcoming litany and monotonous hand pumping stopped.

"Excuse me. I'm sorry. You two carry on."

My husband was bolting for the bathroom. Infatuation had been overtaken by irritable bowel syndrome. Such are the vagrancies of life. Still, my lips bent in a broad grin at the thought of my husband, astride the commode, Teresita's champion.

That evening, after serving up my version of tacos, I stopped by Teresita's room. I should have knocked but forgot. She was on her knees praying her rosary. She spontaneously left her beads and ran to hug me.

"Muchas gracias, señora, muchas gracias."

I hugged the sweet woman-child and shut the door. I entered my own bedroom to find my husband snoring contently. There is much to be said for a silent woman who smiles.

I had to admit things were going well. It was hard not to be enchanted by Teresita. Who can possibly be irritated by someone who says nothing, smiles continuously, only tries to help you, and is lovely? Cat never came to the house but called every day. Each Thursday, when I arrived for my complimentary hair appointment, I filled her in on Teresita.

"She's spoiling my husband rotten. She brings him his house shoes and his coffee. All he can do is look at her, entranced. The truth is, she spoils me as well. She makes all the beds, dusts, vacuums, and has learned how to operate the washer and dryer. Cat, I'm not asking her to do these things. I swear. She just does them."

"I'm so glad to hear that. I, for sure, don't want her to be trouble."

"Trouble! She's a delight."

"Thank you. Thank you. It won't be much longer. I am working through some things, and within a few weeks she can come to me."

"No hurry, really. Teresita is just a sweetheart. When she is not cleaning the house, she is watching television. She is trying so hard to learn English. She's coming along. It's just too hard by herself. If you like, I could maybe get her into an ESL program."

Cat was uneasy. "No, no. Not now. I will be ready for her soon, and then she can go to school near me."

"Makes sense." I leaned back in the shampoo bowl, basking in one of my many conditioners.

My husband was hopping around. It was not irritable bowel. "She's got to go, got to go."

"Who, Teresita?"

"Yes. She's got to go. You know I adore her, but think about what month this is."

"Oh yes." It was becoming clearer. "It's March, and I do know what that means. March Madness."

"And you know what that means?"

"Jerome is coming."

"Exactly. Which means she's got to go."

Jerome was my husband's older brother, a Texan, and a fully vested federal employee for the United States Border Patrol. Very few people even knew that Teresita was living with us. It had been just over three weeks. Unaccustomed to the cold and afraid to venture out into uncharted territory, Teresita stayed inside, immersing herself in American soap operas and telenovelas. My husband and I never discussed whether or not Teresita was legal. He was too smitten to consider the question, and in my value system, ignorance is an excuse. But Jerome was an entirely different matter. He was a career civil servant and the self-appointed keeper of the flame of justice. Jerome always spent that last week of March at our home, with his brother, glued to the games. They would be totally absorbed as one NCAA team defeated the other, and I would try my best to further sedate them with buffalo wings and beer, but a non-English-speaking woman bringing my husband slippers and me tea would never escape him. Something had to be done. I had to call in reinforcements.

A Sister in Need Is a Sister Indeed

Why was my sister having such a problem with this request? "So you are going to drive to Kansas City and leave me with a non-English-speaking nineteen- or twenty-year-old who is supposed to stay at my house with my husband and me for a month? Is that what you are saying?"

This would be the third time I would have said it. "Yes, and I'll give you money for food and incidentals."

"And I am supposed to just saunter into my living room with Miss Tequila Nachos and say what?"

"Like I just said, that she is an exchange student. That will explain why she needs to stay a month. That will make it all appear authentic. She is staying with you and several other American families for this spring semester. Your college is participating in an exchange program, and for a month she will be staying with you. I don't see what's so hard about this."

"For a month?"

"Yes. But trust me, she is absolutely no trouble, helps out in any way she can, and is very charming. She really doesn't speak English, so you can't hurt her feelings or say anything wrong. Whatever you say, Teresita will just smile."

"I see. So I'm not only harboring a fugitive, I'm lying to my husband as well."

"Oh now, come on. You know I wouldn't ask you if I didn't need this in a big way. Plus, we're not sure she's undocumented. To be honest, I'm not sure what she is."

"Oh, I'm sorry. I forgot. This is a favor you're doing for your hair stylist so you can get free hair conditioners and wet sets."

"It's deeper than that."

"Of course it is. And what's in this for me? Let me see, if I get caught, jail time and divorce. Do you realize how crazy this is?"

"Well, not if you live in Chicago. Chicago is a sanctuary city."

"First of all, no one lives in Chicago. Read your daily papers. So to describe Chicago as a sanctuary for anything is an oxymoron." My sister paused, muttering something to herself.

"Well, I'll tell you one thing, if I do this safe-house transfer craziness with you, I am not going to lie to my husband about it. I'm going to tell him the truth. This situation is already bizarre enough without me lying to him on top of it."

"Does this mean you will do it? It does mean that, doesn't it? Oh my God! You are so wonderful, and I love you so much."

"No, you do not love me at all. It does not even occur to you that I could land in jail and my husband's reputation could be ruined by this insane escapade. I do this, and only do this, for our dearly departed mother who is looking down and wondering where your mind has gone. I am doing this for her. Do you understand?"

"I do. I do, and I love you so, and don't worry about your husband's reputation. It's already ruined. He's a Black Republican."

"Comments like that, and I…"

"Sorry. Sorry. I really do love you."

I explained the situation to Catalina, who said she trusted me and would be all right with her daughter spending a month in Kansas City with my sister. She also told me she was close to working something out for Teresita. Catalina explained things to her daughter over the phone.

It was the last week of March when I packed Teresita up and handed her off to my sister. For whatever reason, we decided to meet halfway at a gasoline station in Lake Saint Louis. My sister and I didn't say much. She just accepted the mission and headed due west. I checked in with her every day to make sure all was well. As the days wore away, I could feel her tension receding. My sister, too, was now falling in love with Teresita. Teresita had become her road dog. Together they were at the Plaza, Crown Center, the art gallery, and the movies. She even accompanied my sister to her job at the college, where she let Teresita audit ESL classes.

To be honest, I was growing a bit envious at how easily the sound of her name made my sister laugh. "That Teresita, she's such a clown."

"She is?" Strange, I had never seen the clown. Where were her rosary beads?

"That Teresita, she's a virtual blood hound. Do you know she can smell a sale a mile away?"

"She can?" Why is she roaming through clearance racks with my sister? Why isn't she at Mass praying for citizenship?

"That Teresita, she is such a nut. I let her hide the eggs for the Easter Egg Hunt, and then she went and found them all."

"She did?" You sound like the nut to me.

I couldn't wait to bring Teresita back to Chicago so I could rediscover the girl that I knew. It was four weeks later. We met at the same gas station to do the exchange. Both women had tears in their eyes. Teresita was laden with boxes.

"What did you do, exhaust your annuity?" I helped load the boxes in my trunk.

"Nah, just a few things. We caught some sales. You know how that is." Teresita was sitting in the front passenger seat, trying to collect herself. I stood outside, talking with my sister.

"You know I really do appreciate this. I really do. It couldn't have been easy. Was your husband OK?"

"Yeah, he was fine."

"What did you tell him?"

"That she was an exchange student."

"Yeah, makes perfect sense. I'll call you when we get home."

Teresita only stayed with us another week before Catalina called. Not sufficient time for me to discover the funny bone my sister had found. My instructions were to bring Teresita to the salon. When Catalina's last customer left, we stepped up with suitcases, bags, and boxes. When Teresita glimpsed her mother, she ran to her, bags and boxes dropping to the floor. Both women were crying and reciting what sounded like a prayer. I wasn't praying, but I was crying. In seconds they had enveloped me. Everyone was hugging. Two men, who I assumed were Cat's sons, appeared. It became a group hug. We wiped our eyes, and the hugging began again.

"Cat." I felt compelled to help in some way. "Can I take you guys someplace? My car is downstairs."

"No. No. Nothing more. You have helped carry me. I am in your debt forever."

The young men bowed in agreement. Teresita's arms caught me in another tight squeeze.

"I think, then, if there's nothing else for me to do, I had better try and beat this traffic." It was a clumsy exit, but it was the best that I could orchestrate. I turned and headed for the escalator.

It was odd how we never mentioned it again. Those two months were a time warp. If my sister would not have asked from time to time about Teresita, and if I had not continued to benefit from the free hairstyles and wet sets, I might have wondered if the entire visit had ever happened.

The Shadow People

It was a typical Thursday hairdo day. I had engaged in all the ritual gossip about politicians, actors, and an assortment of other people we didn't know. Cat had projected a date when she believed Mother Teresa would be canonized. I mindlessly concurred. When my wet set was finished, I burrowed into a cocoon of warm humming beneath the dryer. I was gradually pulling out of my coma as Catalina pulled the curlers from my hair. She stopped abruptly to give me the news.

"Teresita is married." We had said almost nothing about Teresita since she returned home. For some reason Cat seemed to avoid that topic and now this.

"Married?"

"Yes, married. She married an American. She's going to get a green card."

I did not know what to make of the announcement. What? No banns, no church, no priest, no sacrament? Maybe I just wasn't invited.

"Was there a wedding?" I felt awkward asking, but I wanted to know.

"No, it was at city hall. But there will be a wedding, a real one, and I want you there. You have to be there."

"Yes, of course I will be there. Who did she marry? I mean is it someone you knew? When did she meet him?"

"It's Bradley. The boy who lived with us. Remember he went to Daley and then to UIC? He has a good job now with the state."

"I see. Is she happy?"

"Of course. Who wouldn't be? She is going to be an American."

"Where do they live?"

"We all moved to a three-bedroom flat, and it's perfect."

"It certainly sounds like it."

"I will send you an invitation to the wedding."

"Yes, please do."

But the invitation never came. My broaching the subject made Catalina visibly uncomfortable.

"How is Teresita doing? How is the young couple?"

Cat would answer with one or two words and then change the subject. It was definitely something she chose not to discuss. The question of the mysterious marriage popped to the forefront of my mind every Thursday, but I pushed it back. Cat should not be dragged into an unwanted conversation about her daughter. Imagine, then, my surprise the Thursday Cat volunteered.

"Did I tell you Teresita is pregnant?"

"Pregnant? Oh my gosh!"

Cat appeared genuinely happy and proud. It had been almost five years since Cat acknowledged the marriage. That announcement was stilted and cold. This one was warm and inviting.

"I'm going to be a grandma." Cat's face was beaming.

"Cat, that is wonderful! I am so glad things are going well with Teresita and Bradley."

"No, not with Bradley, with Roberto. Roberto is from home. He is the boy she loves, has always loved. He is here now with her; they are a family. They took the basement apartment in our building."

Catalina could see from the frozen expression on my face that I did not know what to say.

"Oh, my friend, I know how confusing this all must seem. I have tried to do the right thing to protect everyone. It is not easy becoming an American, not easy at all. What I wanted most of all for Teresita was that she could come to this country and go back to Mexico as she pleased, unhampered and unharmed. She can do that now. Don't you see? Marriage to Bradley made it possible. It worked out for everyone. My sons and I have paid for his schooling. This spring he will get his master's in engineering. Big deal for him. We will all be there to cheer him on. His fiancé will be there as well. She's cute. A little blondie. I do her hair. You want to know about the marriage, right? Well, after graduation Teresita and Bradley will file for a divorce, and that's that. She's an American, and Bradley's an engineer. Fair deal, right?"

Cat leaned forward and hugged me. She then whispered in my ear. "God did not promise that he would make our way straight. He just said that he would make a way. So get ready, my friend. After the divorce we are going to have a real wedding, at a church, with a priest, Mariachi bands, everything!" Cat twirled around, laughing as she spun. She stopped and pointed her finger.

"Promise me you will be there. Bring your husband, your sister, her husband, and the kids. Promise me."

"I promise."

This world can be a pretty murky place. That's what makes a beauty salon so inviting. It's a prescribed event. You know who you are going to see, how long you will be there, and what is going to happen. You can spill your deepest thoughts, trample the people you hate, opine about people you don't know, and leave feeling renewed and looking better. It all works fine, that is, until you cross the line into the uncharted territory of becoming friends. That is a professional breach. It is like a doctor dating his patient. From that moment on things are never quite the same. You are not quite sure if you like the bargain you have struck.

Until Cat and I became friends, I never cared if her daughter could or could not be an American, never thought about what being in this country meant to her. I never questioned if her social security card was phony or real; I never thought about it. I never thought about what it meant to go to Mexico, about her fears at the border. I never thought about the daughter she had left behind. Those grandchildren she might never hold. But we were friends now. Friendship brought knowledge, and with knowledge came caring. Friendship possessed a certain gravitas, carried a definite weight. Before we became friends, Catalina was an optical illusion—someone I looked at, but did not see, someone who served me but whom I did not fully recognize. We were friends now, and I saw her even when she wasn't there.

"Things are working, my friend. I'm saving good money. We're all going to buy a three-bedroom flat. My sons, Teresita, Roberto, the children, we will all live there. Do you know what I think?"

"I have no idea."

"I think next that I, Catalina, am going to become an American, and then I think I will build or buy a hacienda near Guadalajara so I can go back and forth whenever I want and see Anastacia. That's what I think."

Catalina sent me out that Thursday with a bouncing bob, and then she died. The shop's account was that she went back to the break room, asked for a glass of water, and then collapsed. Catalina was rushed to Northwestern Hospital accompanied by two other stylists. They said she never regained consciousness.

Teresita carried Catalina home to Jalisco, where she and Anastacia interred her beside her beloved Jorge. In the casket with her were a bag of holy dirt from El Santuario de Chimayo and an American flag. My farewell was simple. I dialed her cell phone number and listened to her joyous voice.

"*Buenos días.* Es me, Catalina Mendoza. Leave a message."

Almost a year to the day I received a call at work. It was Teresita, her voice soft like cotton, her tone so naturally sweet.

"Can you come to Momma's Rosario? It's just family and close friends. We will pray the rosary, have hot chocolate, and share stories about her."

"Yes, of course, I will be there."

I hung up the phone and called my sister.

"What's up?" This was her standard hello.

"Guess who I just talked to?"

"Who?"

"Teresita."

"No, girl. I know you didn't just say Teresita. So how is her English?"

"Pretty good now."

"Well, I guess so by now. How many years has it been?"

"I don't know. Several."

"You know we could have gone to jail for that. What the hell were you thinking? I mean it's bad enough if you go to jail, but oh no, you have to destroy my family as well. It's not your fault, really, it's mine. I'm the one trapped in that second-child, always-trying-to-please syndrome. Only a fool or a second child would let someone talk them into something that outrageous.

"Come on. You're giving yourself too much credit."

"How would you know? You're the firstborn. It's all about you. What did I just say outrageous? No. Not outrageous. Damn dangerous. That's what it was, you know, damn dangerous. You do realize, don't you, that we were harboring a fugitive?"

"She was a child."

"Exactly: your hairdresser's fugitive, illegal child! What was that experience for you, the refried-bean version of the Underground Railroad? If we had gotten caught with that girl, what could we have possibly said? What kind of Black people kidnap people with no money that they can't even talk to? We don't even know half the time what we're saying to each other. I should never have let you talk me into that. I could have lost my husband."

"You'd get a better last name."

"My husband could have lost his job."

"He's a Black Republican in public office in Missouri. He's the only one. His job is safe."

Talking to my sister is medicinal. We were both laughing.

"That was crazy, wasn't it?"

"Insane," I assured her.

"But we really were trying to do something good, right?"

"We were."

"And she never talked about it?"

"Catalina? No, not ever."

"Now that was crazy."

"To you and to me, maybe, but not to her. She just wanted her daughter to be an American, whatever it took. Sometimes I think just trying to be all right can make you crazy."

To be an American. I pondered the concept's power. The chance of it would drive Catalina to abandon her husband, her home, her country, her language. America's creed dangled a promise so potent she would live in the shadows, a guarded stranger hidden in society's hem, materializing and vanishing as necessary.

"OK," my sister said, "I'll call you back." That's how we always said goodbye. The word goodbye meant nothing. "I'll call you back" meant so much more. It meant we would always stay connected. Maybe that's what Catalina had taught me. Words were overrated. Sometimes simple things like secret-keeping can plunge friends into deeper depths than words could ever say.

I examined my bag of holy dirt. Catalina didn't go to heaven; she propelled there. But His eye is on the sparrow, so He saw her coming.

The dance ends.

DANCE NUMBER ELEVEN: THE WOBBLE

The Song: "Wobble"
The Dancer: Chantilly Hobson

The Observance

You would think that we were trying to park at the United Center for a Bulls Game. Men are directing traffic, slicing the darkness with their lighted batons. But this is not a Bulls Game. It is Chantilly's visitation. This funeral home has become the destination place to be viewed if you die young in the urban ghetto of Chicago.

For many, Chicago is that gleaming white city on the western side of Lake Michigan—the urban mecca of the Midwest, signaling all that is best in middle-American culture and Midwestern pragmatism. But embedded inside of its glorious core, another Chicago is metastasizing. Deprived of economic opportunity, strapped with decaying schools, inhabited by a disproportionate number of impoverished single parents reliant on federal and state aid, this Chicago is rotting. The strong work ethic, moral fiber, and dream of a better life that had been packed into the trunks of their antecedents moving from the South has long ago vanished, replaced by a seething system of systematic racism, gang culture, double-digit unemployment, and violence. This Chicago is a wasteland of wasted people nourished on drugs and alcohol in barren food deserts, where the only things that grow are despair and guns. This Chicago is a community of nothingness. Churches are there to hear the shouts of the abandoned and to bury the dead. Much of this societal tumor can be found on the South and West Sides of the city, where these indigenous citizens have been so traumatized and mutated they can no longer recognize what the broader, beautiful Chicago calls normalcy.

Chantilly Hobson was born in this Chicago, and she died there. This is the evening of her visitation, and we are being directed by lighted batons to a parking spot at one of the hippest funeral homes on the West Side. Only the best for Chantilly.

Arriving in the foyer is like entering the theater of the dead. The couches and chairs, overstuffed and posh, are partnered with polished cherry wood and glass-topped tables. Demurely lit sconces line the walls and light the name placards at the door of each viewing room. Dropping from the ceiling in the center of the foyer is an enormous crystal chandelier. Greeting each arriving mourner is a filigree, gold-framed marquee advertising who is being featured in each viewing salon. There are at least a dozen viewings this night. My husband and I enter three viewing chambers, by accident, trying to find Chantilly. Each room is filled primarily with young men, dressed in their coffin clothes, primed for this premiere. These lives should have been a feature-length experience but have been cut down to only a trailer.

When we at last find Chantilly, she is resting on satin pillows, a sleeping child whom I cannot wake. Placed around her is her associate's degree from the school, pictures from fun times, a folded T-shirt from Great America, and her perfect attendance certificate. Chantilly's crossed arms caress the framed picture of her baby girl, Sky. Chalk up another motherless child for another grandmother to raise.

My throat seals shut the word I want to shout. It is a simple word. Only one. "Why?" Is there no true prince in the house with the magic kiss to awaken the sleeping girl? My throat is right to cap my cry. Who cares after all? The news cycles, day after day, carry the pitiful stories of the senseless violence, the loss of life, but what politicians care enough about nonvoting, noncontributing constituents? Who possesses coffers deep enough to correct not just mollify the problem? Where are the industrial titans who can build and renew? Perhaps in Africa, the wellspring of this debacle, or maybe India, but not in this godforsaken part of Chicago. There are a few strident voices that can be heard over the din, speaking truth to power. But most voices are silent.

Even here, even now, where are the mourners? Who is crying? Are we too early or simply too late? Maybe tomorrow. Perhaps then they will come to wail and cry for the little girl lost. I sign the book. We are the third to visit.

The night is young. The men are waving their lighted batons in the parking lot. Come one. Come all. Come see the circus. The night is young.

"Tell me again, what exactly happened?" We are on the freeway, that great divide between war and peace.

"There's not much to tell," I reply. "Chantilly and her baby daddy were leaving a fast food place when a car drove by. Five shots were fired. Two hit her." That, my husband, is the inglorious end of Chantilly Hobson. Pop, pop. A beautiful girl falls to the cold ground with nothing soft on which to rest her head except her delicate name.

The Dance

Isn't She Lovely

"Please interview her. She graduates in a few months. She would be great lunch relief at the front desk. I'll admit she needs some polishing, but a college work-study job would do it. Please. I'll tell you in advance she is utterly charming."

Charming. That was a rare adjective to describe most of the students we served at our school. In my meandering professional life I had held many titles. I was now the president of a small career college. The student population who typically sought admission were from the core city and wore bold social armor to avoid the perception of weakness. Weakness was synonymous with disrespect, and disrespect led to victimization in a wide variety of forms. The first rule of the street: don't get punked. Charm was taboo. Attitude was strength. Yet Sandy, the school's career services director, had said "charming." I would see her.

"This is Chantilly Hobson." Sandy ushered her into my office.

"Hello, ma'am. I saw you several times at Pizza with the President. I even asked you a couple of questions. One was about lockers. The other was about e-books. They weren't that impressive, probably, but you answered them. You spoke and used so many great words. Someday I want to be able to stand and speak the way that you do."

Her face blossomed in an evened-toothed smile. Her hand was there for me to shake. Was she ever charming! Chantilly got the job and continued to mesmerize all that she met.

"I love that receptionist. You can hear her smiling through the phone." My sister had strong opinions about this. "That other verbally challenged person who answers the phone makes me long for the preprogrammed voice. You know the one: If you want the president, dial two. If you know the name of your party, please enter the last name followed by the pound sign. Find a way to keep whoever she is. She makes people really want to come there. She really does. The other one makes me want to hurt somebody."

The employees were equally charmed. "She never says I don't know. She always tries to get an answer for you."

"You leave her material to copy, and she cheerfully does."

"She never gives you attitude. Never."

"You never find her on the school's phone talking to friends or on her cellphone."

Chantilly had also intoxicated our governing board.

"She took my coat, hung it up, and had it ready when it was time to leave."

"She charged my cellphone. I just asked if she knew who could. She took care of it and brought it back to me."

"That receptionist, she booked my reservation at the Marriott because I had to stay over. She is a keeper. You should consider hiring her."

My daily interactions with Chantilly were minimal. We exchanged greetings each afternoon as I went to and came from lunch. She transferred my calls and took messages. That was about it. Until the Christmas party, almost everything I knew about her was through third-party endorsements. At the school's annual Christmas party, the practice was to mix the employees up, forcing people from across departments and job categories to sit together. At my table were an Information Technology instructor, an admissions representative, the bookstore clerk, the student services coordinator, all of whom Chantilly seemed to know far better than I.

When I joined the table, the robust reveling reverted to a cautious reserve. This seemed to happen each year for me at each Christmas party, no matter where I sat. Frankly, it was a bit awkward, like being the probation officer at a jailhouse rock. Chantilly either didn't notice how the table's atmosphere changed when I arrived, or she didn't care.

"Hey, everybody, look who's at our table. It's Madam President. We are so lucky." Only she seemed to feel that way. My seat was beside hers. A silence draped across the table. Again, she did not seem to notice. Chantilly was spellbound by her place setting. "Can you believe all these knives, folks, and spoons? Is all of this for each one of us, ma'am?"

"Yes, Chantilly, it is."

"Well, what in the world are we going to eat with all this?" She leaned toward my ear. "Ma'am, I'm not used to all this. To be honest, most times, I never eat at a table."

"I see," I whispered back.

"Most of the time I eat out of bags from Mickey D's or boxes from Kentucky Fried Chicken. Don't get me wrong, sometimes I eat at a table, but it's not like this."

"It's OK. I'll help you. Just watch and do what I do."

"Got it."

Christmas lunch became a game. I picked up a soup spoon. She picked up a soup spoon. I lifted my salad fork. She lifted hers. When the rolls circulated, I placed one on the plate to my left. Chantilly did the same. The entire table began to play as each of us openly confessed our varying degrees of table etiquette knowledge.

By dessert the table had loosened up. The bookstore clerk was sharing her favorite meatloaf recipe when the music began. "OK," the DJ summoned, "it's time to hit the dance floor. It's Christmas, folks. You have just an hour left of me, so let's get it on." That command motivated mostly women onto the dance floor for a series of line dances.

I was at the table chatting with the IT instructor when Chantilly left the dance floor and rushed up to me. "Come on, ma'am. You taught me something. Now it's time for me to teach you."

"No. No," I protested, "I don't think so."

"Oh yes, Ma'am. Come with me. I'm going to show you something." The room erupted in laughs and applause. There I was on the dance floor, feeling more than a little embarrassed.

"Ladies and gentlemen, the president and I are going to do the Wobble. Feel free to join us." With that, everyone was on the dance floor. I had no idea what we were doing. I only knew I was having the time of my life.

When someone proposed Chantilly's name to be the evening desk relief, it was a no-brainer. Even if it meant we paid her out of the school's operating account, I was all in. Let her work the extra hours. This young woman was a winner. Besides, after six, there was very little foot traffic. The hustle and bustle in the reception area had died down. The students had their own entrance, so the front desk was mainly about info calls or an employee's spouse or child wondering when their loved one had left the building. For me it was a quiet time, a moment to recuperate in the staff lounge with a Diet Coke and glance the six o'clock news before journeying home. This relaxation ritual meant I had to enter the reception area to access the adjoining hallway to the staff lounge. Chantilly understood the moment. "It's your time to chill, right, ma'am?"

"It is indeed, Chantilly."

"Well, enjoy."

Chantilly seemed to reside in permanent innocence. There was so much about the world she either didn't know or never understood. I marveled at the novelty of her very existence. How could the tangled maze in which she lived not have blocked out the sun, shriveling her very soul? On my way back from the staff lounge I would bring her a soda.

"Take this," I said to her one evening. "There ain't nobody here but us chickens."

Chantilly erupted into a side-splitting laugh. "Nobody here but us chickens. I never heard that. Is that what old people say?"

I was stunned for a moment. Chantilly was right. I was a child when I first heard the Louis Jordan song.

"Yes, Chantilly. That's what old people say."

"You're funny, ma'am. Most people don't see it, but I do."

From that moment on, I brought Chantilly a Coke every evening. It was intriguing trying to comprehend just how her mind worked. She could say the darndest things. I had to be prepared for anything. Her questions were unabashedly naive and beautifully innocent.

"Ma'am, do you own a yacht?"

"A yacht! What makes you think I would own a yacht?"

"All rich people own yachts."

"Chantilly, I am not rich."

"I think you are. You live like a rich person or a drug dealer."

"I want to assure you, I'm neither."

"Ma'am, how long have you been married?"

"Over forty years."

"Good God, that's two of my lifetimes. Do you like being married?"

"Most of the time I do. You're with your best friend. It's a sensible way to live."

"My best friend is Tanisha. We do everything together. I could live with her. I don't think I could live with a man. I don't think it would work. My momma said she could never have lived with my dad. She tried for a while, but he was irresponsible. He's in Pontiac."

"Ma'am, have you ever gone to Disney World?"

"Yes, but not in a while."

"I want to go to Disney World. When I get my job, I'm going to go to Disney World. I want to see all the princesses."

"Ma'am, did I tell you one of my best friends got shot?"

"No, did he die?"

"Sure did."

"Who did it?"

"Don't know. Somebody just came up and shot him. That was when I took off last week for his funeral. Otherwise I would have been here. Let me show you the pictures."

"The pictures!" Chantilly was scrolling through photos on her cell phone. She thrust the device into my hands.

"That's him, ma'am. Good-looking, wasn't he?" I held the cell phone, stunned by both her matter-of-fact manner and the young man framed in the gray coffin wearing a blue tie. Chantilly retrieved the phone, continuing the conversation.

"We all dressed in blue for the funeral to match his tie." A fashion statement. The death of a friend.

The Promise Keeper

Chantilly was scheduled to graduate that spring. She would have an associate's degree in information technology. She had so many natural gifts. It wouldn't take much for this young woman to break through most of the barriers that life would present. She was attractive, and if necessary, her tattoos were placed well enough to be hidden. She had the enhanced hair, but so did Beyoncé, and everyone loved her. Chantilly's attendance was perfect, and her grades, in a challenging program of study, were mostly As and Bs. Chantilly was a person who did what she said she would do when she said she would do it, and she was a millennial. The cherry on top of it all was her wow personality. Everyone was defenseless to her charm. Even the salty older crop of employees, whenever they saw her, would smile as if to say, "She can't be from the West Side." The unison phrase used to describe her was, "Isn't she lovely?"

Over the weeks, my passage through the reception area advanced from "Here is a Coke" to engaging conversations. My intent was to inoculate Chantilly with promise. I wanted her to know the potential she possessed, the opportunities that awaited. I wanted her to understand the power of her personality, the innate ability she had to lasso people into her sphere of influence, to entrance them into wanting to help her.

Chantilly was an intent listener who received every word I spoke with wonder. Everything I voiced on any subject she seemed to be hearing for the first time. The halo effect of all this was that it made me feel completely brilliant. I would walk away from a conversation with her thinking, "Gee, I didn't realize I knew so much." That was the Chantilly effect. She gave you more than you gave her. No one smiled as much or as freely. She was a booster cable of happiness. Her smile made you smile, and before you knew it, there was joy.

We were finishing one of our many conversations, and I was smiling.

"Chantilly, Chantilly, you have your whole life ahead of you. Make it wonderful. You have the capacity to do things with your life that you can't even imagine."

I saw her mind lift with the possibilities.

"Ma'am, I will be the first person in my family to finish any kind of college. The very first. Most didn't even finish high school. Even Tanisha didn't finish high school."

"Chantilly, I'm so proud of you."

"Me too. I can't believe it. I'm going to be a college graduate and a mother."

A mother! Was Chantilly pregnant?

"Chantilly, are you expecting?"

"Yes, ma'am." She was bursting with pride. "Me and Tanisha are both pregnant. I'm going to get a job, and the two of us are going to raise our babies together."

"But what about school?"

"What do you mean?"

"Well, you're a student. You have to graduate."

Her expression relaxed.

"Oh that. Don't worry, ma'am. I'm going to graduate and have a baby. I can do both."

We were all stunned by the news of Chantilly's pregnancy. Every day for the next week felt like stormy Monday. Without realizing it, we had idealized her, lifted her up to personify and validate all that we believed we were doing right for our students. We were unwitting Professor Higginses creating our own West Side Eliza Doolittle, and now this. Chantilly was the low-hanging fruit. She was the high achiever who made everything we advertised we could do as a school come true. It wasn't just what we were doing for her. It was what she was doing for us. It's the way everyone says Bill Gates went to Harvard, even though he didn't graduate. Would it be that way with Chantilly? Was she not going to graduate, not going to be that testimonial we could promote?

I was angry and disappointed with Chantilly. Pregnant? What would make her do such a thing? She was almost out of the chaos, free of the war zone. What was she thinking?

"Chantilly." I tried to mask my anger and frustration as I framed my question. I had wanted to ask it three days earlier but found myself too distraught and disappointed to do so. "What happened?"

"What do you mean?"

"I mean, did you not have access to birth control?"

"Oh, ma'am, I don't use birth control. I've been wanting to have a baby for a long time."

"Even while you were trying to go to school?"

"Having a baby has nothing to do with going to school."

"It doesn't?"

"No. Of course not. I'm gonna finish school. I'm even more motivated now than ever because I've got to take care of my baby."

Chantilly smiled that bewitching smile. "My baby's gonna be the best-dressed baby ever. I've been looking online at Babies R Us and Buy Buy Baby. I saw the cutest Minnie Mouse dress."

"So you want a girl?"

"Of course I do. A girl always stays with you. I stay with my momma. We are gonna probably have to get a bigger apartment, though. Tanisha and I will work, and Momma will keep the girls. You don't want boys. Boys are hard to raise, get into gangs, and get killed. No, sir, not for me. I want a girl. They love you and never leave you. By the way, ma'am, did I tell you Tanisha just passed her GED? I told her now she has to come to this school. It's the best place ever."

I didn't stop by the reception desk and chat as often. Chantilly continued smiling, but as her belly expanded, I began to question if anything I said to her had ever mattered. Her pregnancy made me rethink my involvement with her. Why did I ever think I could get to know her? I could have been her grandmother. Could I ever have really known her? Did I want to? While we orbited in the same college solar system, we were not in the same world. Did Chantilly not understand the struggle, all that had gone before? Did she not realize there was still an unacknowledged social divide that she would have to bridge? Had she not been instructed as my generation had, that she would have to do twice as much to get half as far? The tragedy was Chantilly had the gifts. She could seize the golden bird of opportunity and seduce it. Why could she not visualize a tomorrow holding more for her than a baby girl in a Minnie Mouse dress? It would definitely be easier for me to stay put in my office and avoid the evening soda run.

Chantilly never asked why I stopped our Coke encounter. She just continued to smile and never missed a day of work. I was washing my hands in the ladies' room when Chantilly burst through the door.

"Got to go, ma'am. Got to go."

"Go. Go." I ushered her into a stall and returned to washing my hands.

"Thank you, ma'am," she blurted from the other side.

"No problem. Just don't let your water break in there. If that happens, I may have to deliver that baby."

"Have you ever delivered a baby, ma'am?"

"No, but I can learn."

"Wait, don't go. I have something to ask you."

Chantilly left the stall and was washing her hands.

"Ma'am, I want to invite you to my reveal party."

"To your what?"

"You know, my reveal party. Momma and Tanisha are giving it for me. I'm so excited. I bought a new two-piece yellow outfit. It's too cute."

"Wait. I'm sorry. Tell me again. What is a reveal party?"

"You know, where you find out what sex the baby is. Keep your fingers crossed. You know I want a girl. You know I do." Chantilly was broadcasting that electric smile. "I have your invitation at the reception desk. Wait, I'm gonna get it for you."

My head was in a Kansas tornado. A reveal party! Let's reveal who the child's father is and see if he can help. A reveal party! Let's reveal how you and your momma are going to make certain this child is never abused, malnourished, or neglected. A reveal party! Reveal how you plan to provide for the child's education. A reveal party, indeed! My heart was doing the Conga.

Chantilly stopped midstride. She stared at me. Her hand touched my shoulder. "Are you all right?"

"You know, Chantilly, I really do appreciate the invitation, but I don't think I'll be able to make it."

"How do you know? You don't even know when it's going to be."

"That's true, but I don't think I'll be able to make it."

I could feel her eyes searching mine for a possible reason. My mind was searching itself for one.

"I know why. It's because you think you're too old. Don't worry. There'll be several other older people there. In fact, Tanisha's uncle has to be older than you."

"Well, that's comforting, but I still don't think I can make it."

I watched the light extinguish from her eyes. Our minds had connected. Her next words were dry and heat scorched.

"I understand. I'm sure you're busy."

"I really am."

"I'm sure you are, ma'am."

Chantilly tossed the paper towel in the waste receptacle and left.

When her baby was born, the news went around the school like the shot heard around the world. Disappointed or not, everyone—students, faculty and staff—all loved Chantilly. My guilt grew deeper by the second as I watched people making gift baskets and signing cards. When had I stepped from the caring class into no class? Where was the girl from St. Patrick's who knew how it felt not to be accepted, who knew what it meant to be different? It was time to reintroduce myself to Chantilly.

The next day that young girl from my past and I walked into the maternity ward at Stroger Hospital. I carried a large bag from Macy's. That familiar broad grin stretched across Chantilly's face as I entered the room.

"Momma, look who's here. It's our college president. Come in, ma'am. Come in and take pictures with me and Sky. See. This is her. Momma, let me have her. Here, ma'am, you can hold her."

I put down the bag and caressed the warm bundle.

"She's beautiful, right ma'am? Isn't she beautiful?"

"She is beautiful and looks just like you and your mother." Both women dropped bashful heads.

"I want you to take a picture with me and Sky. Momma, get my cell phone."

"Wait," I announced," before we do that, I want to give you something. Here, take Sky."

Chantilly took her daughter and watched with anticipation as I went for the Macy's bag.

"This, Chantilly, is all for you. There are onesies, sleeper sets, and several outfits, as you can see." I held up two envelopes. "In this envelope, young lady, is a hundred-dollar gift card from Walgreens for Pampers, and in this one, a three-hundred-dollar gift card for Babies R Us."

Chantilly's feet had become bouncing springs. She seized the three-hundred-dollar gift card.

"Momma, this is for the baby bed we saw, right?"

Her mother smiled. Her hand quickly covered the space where a tooth used to be.

"Thank you, ma'am. Thank you so much." Chantilly handed Sky to her mother and cinched my waist in a tight hug. "This is the best day ever."

Her mother looked as if she might cry.

"This isn't just from me. It is from all of us."

I lied. For the first time, I felt embarrassed about our disproportionate lives. I could afford to buy these things. Chantilly could not.

"Well, then, thank everybody." Chantilly was spinning around.

"There is one thing, however, that is just from me. So Chantilly, close your eyes."

"Oh my gosh, oh my gosh."

"Go ahead, close them."

"They're closed. They're closed."

"OK. Now open them."

Chantilly opened her eyes and gasped.

"Momma, Momma, it's a Minnie Mouse dress just like the one on the Internet. Let's put it on Sky and take a picture. Ma'am, would you take a picture with me and Sky in her Minnie Mouse dress?"

While her mother was dressing Sky in her Disney frock, Chantilly exhaled for all to hear and then stated, "Ma'am, did I tell you one of my best friends was shot?"

"Oh no, Chantilly, not again."

Both women were shaking their heads. "I know. It's getting crazy out here."

"Do you have any idea who did it?"

"Not really. Floyd had some complications. Sold a few drugs. That might have had something to do with it. He and my baby's daddy were really tight."

I shook my head, wondering if her baby daddy was selling drugs, too, but I constrained myself from asking.

Again, she held her phone. "Here. This is what I wanted to show you. This is Floyd's grave. See how we spelled his name out with the funeral flowers? Can you see it F-L-O-Y-D? Isn't that pretty?"

I held the cell phone and looked at the picture.

"Just touch there. I've got several different views. Yeah. Look at this one."

Clearly, Chantilly and I existed in alternate universes. What had happened in hers? What had we all done to make a bright-eyed girl see the repeated deaths of her friends as normal?

"Chantilly, this isn't right. You do know that, don't you?"

Chantilly shrugged her shoulders. "That's your question? My question is who's gonna stop it? Look. Look. Sky has on her Minnie Mouse dress. Let's take the picture."

Up, Up, and Away

The career services director could not have not been more pleased with herself. She had gotten Chantilly a job at Google. It was entry-level by title and description, but for Chantilly, who could not name a family member who had ever held a full-time job outside of the food service industry, she had hit the jackpot.

With the start of the next quarter, following her delivery, Chantilly had returned to school. Her mother was keeping Sky, and Chantilly had picked up where she left off. Her attendance was perfect, and her midterm grades, if precursors of her final exams, forecast that she would graduate with a 3.6 grade point average. I had to admit that maybe Chantilly was right. What did babies have to do with finishing school?

Sandy hadn't told Chantilly the good news yet, as she had just received the offer information from Google's HR department. Because of her pregnancy and delivery, Chantilly had missed the spring graduation, but she planned to march across the stage carrying Sky in January.

"I'm going to take a picture of that, frame it, and put it in her room. I want Sky to always remember that if I can do this, she can do more. I want her to reach for the sky. See why I named her that?"

That day when Sandy got the news, she told me first. I had been pressuring her to cultivate more coveted career opportunities. Google was the brass ring, and Chantilly was the student who could grab it. As Sandy relayed the amazing news, I leaned back in my chair, gloating. "This is what we need to do to up our game with student placement. Connecting names like Google and our graduates sets us apart, puts us on the map. It took two women, you and Chantilly, to make it happen."

"I hear you." We gave each another a high five.

Sandy paused and then elaborated. "You know, I just got the interview. Chantilly did the heavy lifting. She answered their questions. She gave better-than-expected performances on both her written and skills tests, and she charmed the pants off them. Unlike so many of our students, that girl is not afraid to talk. She would chat with a deaf person."

We shared a knowing chuckle.

"I have to also say—and I tell this just to you—even our international students, who are IT majors, could not have outperformed her, and you know how good they are."

Another high five.

"I think we should do the PA."

I agreed.

The PA, short for placement announcement, was a hokey ritual the college devised to celebrate students who had gotten jobs while still attending school. I really wanted to perform this for Chantilly, as she had missed the spring graduation, and this little ceremony could be somewhat of a consolation prize until her winter commencement.

Together Sandy and I marched into Chantilly's classroom ringing a large school bell and crying, "Hear ye, hear ye, we have a placement announcement."

With that, Sandy walked over and stood beside Chantilly's desk. "I'm here to announce that Chantilly Hobson was just offered a full-time job at Google."

Chantilly squealed and clasped her chest. The classroom exploded in applause, whistles, and compliments like, "you go girl" and "you're the bomb." I stood half-hidden in the doorway, hoping no one could see the tears I was fighting so hard to dam.

"Stand up, Chantilly," Sandy insisted.

Chantilly stood, fanning herself with her hands.

Sandy recited her proclamation. "In honor of this outstanding accomplishment, the college awards you this gift card. Congratulations." It was short but sweet. The ensuing applause, yells, and desk banging were deafening. Everyone loved Chantilly. Sandy pleaded for quiet.

"Chantilly, do you have anything you would like to say?"

Never lost for words, Chantilly, still shaken, stood and began to speak.

"Wow. This is just the best thing ever. I think when I get home I'm gonna tell my momma, pack our bags, we're going to Disney World." There was more cheering and desk beating.

"No, seriously. I want to thank everyone here: the students, my teachers, financial aid, the career service staff, and you, Madame President. I see you hiding back there. You all don't realize it, but you have changed my life." Applause followed, but it was more contained.

"To my friends and other students, I just want to say never give up on yourselves. I know sometimes our lives and problems seem too hard to overcome. But I am living proof that if we just do what our teachers call focus and don't give up, we'll win. So thank you to everyone for everything." There it was. That stellar smile.

You're almost unchained, Chantilly. Almost there. A wonderful world is waiting for you, so make it happen. That was my thought as I pressed the elevator button and returned to my office.

"What, baby?" Was I shouting?

Sandy was oscillating in my office, her face grimaced in bewilderment. No high fives now. She was straining to explain something that even she didn't understand.

"She says she's pregnant. I know, I don't get it, either. What's crazier is that she's thrilled."

"But what about her job? This is Google, for God's sake. How long has it been?"

"Four or five months! And they love her."

"Can they fire her?" I began to pace. What was Chantilly thinking? She already had Sky. Why did she need another baby? Wasn't Google enough?

"I don't really think so. I mean not without violating some major laws. Plus, I don't think that's Google's culture."

"That just is not the way to begin a career. It is just not the way."

"I know. I know. But you need to calm yourself. She's here."

"Chantilly's here?"

"Yes. She came to give you and me a Thanksgiving present."

"What kind of Thanksgiving present? After the missile she just dropped, she thinks I want a present?"

"They're candles that smell like pumpkin pie."

"And I'm supposed to do what with those? What I want is for her to keep that job at Google."

"I know what you want, but you need to calm down. She is here, and she does want to see you."

There she was, standing before me, telegraphing that disarming smile. Chantilly had assumed the presentation position, extending her arms, holding her gift.

"Hi, ma'am. I bet you thought I forgot about all of you. I could never do that. I'm even in the alumni association. Here, this is for you."

I took the present, placed it on a table, and stormed the issue at hand.

"Chantilly, are you pregnant?" The abrupt approach set her back on her heels.

"Yes, ma'am, I am." She was on the defensive.

"So do you want to have this baby?" My aggressive tone was not being well received.

"What do you mean?"

"I mean you already have Sky. You don't have to have another one. You're starting your career."

What in the world was I saying? Even I knew I had overstepped in all ways imaginable.

"But this is my baby, ma'am. What are you saying? Kill my baby? Why, I couldn't do that, ma'am. I'm a Christian. Would you kill your baby?"

It was definitely time to retreat.

"I'm just concerned about your career. You have so much potential, and Google is such a great opportunity."

Sandy, who had been in shock since my opening salvo, began to thaw. So did Chantilly.

"Oh, is that it, ma'am? Don't worry."

The smile returned.

"For a moment I thought you were throwing shade. It's fine. Really it is. I've talked with my supervisor at Google. It's all good." She waved a dismissive hand, put an arm around me, and began to direct me to my chair.

"You need to sit down, ma'am. You worry too much, and besides, I've got some pictures to show you."

"Oh my God. No. Did someone else die?"

"What? Nobody died, ma'am. I want to show you my new boyfriend. See, look." Chantilly was handing her cell phone to me.

"Look at these. His name is DeAndre. Cute, isn't he? He's not like my other baby daddy. That boy just wasn't on nothing. He's not serious about anything. I don't even want him in Sky's life. He's too negative and going no place. DeAndre, though, is focused. I think he's gonna get a job with UPS. If he does, me, my momma, DeAndre, and the babies, we're all going to move to Country Club Hills, and then we're going to Disney World."

Three days later, Chantilly was dead. Students' Facebook pages broadcasted her death before the nightly news. I received the news in a text. By the morning news cycle, Chantilly was already incorporated and reported on Good Day Chicago as part of a crime statistic.

Is there a doctor in the house? Who takes the vital signs of a moribund people? Who can resuscitate them and bring them back? Are we collapsing the natural order of things? The future cannot precede the present.

The dance ends.

DANCE NUMBER TWELVE: THE WALTZ

The Song: "I Will Always Love You"
The Dancer: Me

The Observance

There are many ways to die. I am experiencing one of the better ones. Everything is quiet around me now. There is something about dying that lowers the volume and the lighting in a room as if too much commotion or glare could reverse the outcome. Still, I'm all about atmosphere, so yes, this is preferable. Father Callahan came by today and administered the anointing of the sick. When I was young, they called it Extreme Unction. Today, I guess dying is not considered extreme. But as Shakespeare pointed out, "a rose by any other name is just as sweet."

I had tried to do all that I could to make this as easy as possible for all of us. My husband and I had prepared wills and a trust. We had identified powers of attorneys and executors of estates. We had taken whole life and long-term care insurance. I prepared an advanced directive and prepaid the burial plot. At one point I had contemplated cremation but retreated under opposition from my husband and children. With time and knowledge, one can do things. I had selected a delicate cream frock, something that was a cross between a first communion dress and a wedding gown. I wanted a soft cloud of fabric, not a stiff, encapsulating suit. Staging matters. I wanted the viewer to imagine that at any second a divine voice would summon and I would arise, levitating through the stratosphere, me, my delicate outfit, and the clouds all becoming one astonishing vapor trail. There would be no shoes, which was a bit of a pity, but they wouldn't work with the image. The devil is in the details. So I provided the names of my favorite songs, requested that Father Callahan perform the mass, and left a cashier's check for a hired harpist and lunch at Grand Lux.

My eyes are closed, but I am not sleeping. I can hear the sobbing in the room. It is my daughter. I would have opened my eyes, but that would have only distressed us both. I would have felt compelled to ask, who had the kids? It's so dammed hard to be otherworldly when you are of this one. This is all I have known. I maybe could have opened my eyes, but maybe not. It is so much harder now. My eyes prefer to be closed. Besides, to open my eyes to ask about the children would have been pointless. I know her husband has them. My daughter and son have both lucked out. They have truly wonderful and supportive spouses. Their father had told them to "Look before you leap." They looked and made strong partner choices. I won't worry now about the grandkids. In fact, I'm not worrying about much. Things are still. It is easy to drift in and out of sleep.

This is home hospice. The nurse who came weeks ago bearing all sorts of gifts described it as a time when no one would bother me anymore. A time when people would do things for me, not to me. I had watched the last presidential debate a week before hospice began. The entire election cycle had been nothing but wrenching. There really are some things worse than dying.

My sister had come for Thanksgiving and didn't leave. I was slipping away. It could be three weeks or three months was the hospice nurse's prognosis.

"It won't be three months," I assured my sister. During the day when it is just the two of us, she will read me my favorite Robert Frost poems and T. S. Eliot's *Old Possum's Book of Practical Cats*. She becomes so animated with her readings; I can't help but laugh.

The hospice nurse told everyone music was comforting, so my son has purchased me an iPod. If I nod yes when they ask if I want to hear music, someone will put in the earphones, and off to music land I go. Sometimes my sister will place the iPod in a speaker dock so we can both hear the music. When songs play that we both love, she will stand at the foot of the bed and sing to me. This always makes me laugh. She is so demonstrative and forever off key. I have refused a hospital bed, and the hospice nurse has conceded that if that was my wish, it would be granted. I am propped up with a foam wedge when I choose to sit. My sister asked for a matching foam prop. She sits there beside me, much of the day, chatting about our shared history. When she knows we are absolutely alone, my sister plugs in a small pot of wax and treats my upper lip and chin. No reason to look bad.

In the evenings my daughter comes from work and sleeps beside me. Her breathing is like music, sweet and low, still playing the same song I heard when she was swaddled and lay across my chest. Dying should not be an isolated activity. It should be an intimate shared event. It should never be consigned to the callous, uncaring hands of paid providers, but laid in the warm lap of those who truly care. What stranger could ever say to you, "It's OK to go," when they don't even know how you came? That send-off should only be voiced from the throat of one with personal knowledge sent on word vessels constructed from love. To say "go" should arise from the belief that the one you love is moving toward a destination and to a God who will make all things new. For if there is no immortality, then life becomes unintelligible. I read that someplace. It is what I believe, and so I close my eyes, listening to my daughter weep. I want to say don't cry, but that never works. I understand the crying.

The parade of the probable, those I would expect to visit, began two days ago. People really don't know what to say. Still, they come. Some talk as if nothing is happening and they will see you next week for lunch. Others express shock. I say to myself, "You think you're shocked?" There are the hand claspers who seem to prefer your hand to theirs while you are searching for ways to unclamp it. There are the naysayers who repeat countless times how they can't believe it. There are the uplifters who call for miracles, the prayers who pray for you, the gift bearers who bring things you will never use, the beautification crowd who tell you that you look amazing, and the weepers who can only be removed from the room by forced extraction.

The room is silent again. I don't need to see to know who is there. I know who sits in the silence. There is my sister. She takes my hand and lets it go. I hear her tell my daughter that I am sleeping. My sister has tried the last two days to control the traffic flow. Telling people who stayed too long to go. Telling others not to cough or speak so loudly. To those who are uninitiated, my sister may seem bossy, but I know the life she has led and can attest that she is strong. I will sorely miss her and she me. The bond that makes us sisters is essential to the way we self-identify. It is how we achieve balance.

I know my husband is there, sitting in the small chintz chair. He is sitting there and staring. I cannot see him, but I know the stare. It's the look he wears when we've gone too far in the car, but he won't ask for directions, or when he looks at the bank balance and can't understand where the money went. We were going to make a million dollars when we came to Chicago. We were small-town people moving to the Second City. We had big plans. A million dollars or bust! I'm glad we didn't make the million. We had something more than money. We learned to work together, struggle together, and be together through good times and bad. We learned the hardship of commitment, the glory of love, the reward of children.

Money would have changed all of that. Money fortifies risk, weakens communication, and reduces tolerance. It makes new words like "conscious uncoupling." If we had money, my husband might have wanted to trade up and acquire a trophy bride. He might have desired a really beautiful woman or, worse, a White woman. You know what they say in Brazil: money whitens. No, things were exactly as they should have been. My dearest husband, you could not have been a more cherished friend, a truer lover, or a more caring father. I'll give it to you. Once you took those vows, you were all in. I'm leaving now, so please don't be lonely. If there is another person who is worthy of you, please find her. I can exit knowing that I have taken the better part.

My daughter, you sit curled beside me in the bed. I am lying slightly elevated. You stroke my hair. I hear you whisper, "I love you, Mom." My sweet, sweet girl, I know you do. In so many ways for so many days, months, and years, your actions have spoken those words. And I love you. You are the me I selfishly made for myself. With you in this realm, I will never be gone. Please make me, through you, better than I could have ever been.

I see you, my son. Not with my eyes, but with my soul, and it laughs. You are my sunny, funny boy. No one makes me laugh longer or harder. So many times you have tickled my soul with humor, made me laugh out loud, shattering those imminent tears. You will never know how your presence greased the tracks of so much life pain and carried me across. No sadness now, please. Is death the ultimate loss of innocence? If so, then fill the loss with joy and smile again for me, my beautiful boy.

What is happening now? Where am I? Am I kneeling? Am I in church? Is that you, Sister Agnes?

"Do you remember what I taught you?"

"Yes, Sister."

"Please say it."

"Oh my God, I am heartily sorry for having offended Thee, and I detest all my sins because I dread the loss of heaven and the pains of hell, but most of all because I have offended Thee, my God, who art all good and deserving of all my love. I firmly resolve, with the help of Thy grace, to sin no more and to avoid the near occasion of sin."

I finish my Act of Contrition. Sister Agnes pulls me close.

"Was that good, Sister?"

"Very good, my child. Now, there is just one more thing, and we are finished."

"What is that, Sister?"

"I want you to pray for a happy death."

I took a deep breath and prayed.

"You may go now" was all I heard.

The Dance
Man Plans; God Laughs

I had planned a fun-filled retirement until death intervened. Things were actually going pretty well. Our kids were out of college and married. The kids and grandkids came to visit enough for us to love them and stayed away enough for us to miss them. The mortgage was paid. We now had to contend only with the rising property taxes, which exceeded the monthly mortgage. We had been concerned about our 401Ks following the 2008 bust, but they were rebounding. It was time to live a little, to travel. We had considered a time-share in Arizona for the winter, but then began seriously contemplating a two-bedroom senior living condominium off the ocean in Sarasota. Old friends, also retiring, began to resurface, and we were eager to see them. My husband and I began exploring the city in ways we had never been able to before: Navy Pier, restaurants, the museum campus, architectural tours, theaters. It was fun being a tourist in our own town.

As spouses, we had seriously dialed back the "I'm going to leave you" threats of our budding marriage days. This was our September song, and we were now totally codependent. Our survival was at stake. One of us could not hear; the other could barely see. There was continuous interplay about who could remember what. Sometimes he could remember. Sometimes I could. Sometimes neither of us could, but we both knew what we meant. Then there was the matter of expiring body parts. Knees and hips were going. Our gaits had deteriorated from confident swaggers to cautious starts and stops, making sure what we saw was a curb and not just a simple line in the street. The medicine stockpile was contained in boxes marked by days to make certain we remembered what to take and when. We trekked to the health club three mornings a week to ride stationary bikes and walk around the indoor track. By no means were we complaining. Our days were full and stimulating. There was much to look forward to.

It's funny how you never think of yourself as old. You look in the mirror, and you just see you. Others see you, and they stand back, open doors, smile deferentially, and you know something is dreadfully wrong. Boy Scouts rush up to help you cross streets. Your primary care physician begins to ask, Are you still having sex? Do you need a pill for incontinence? She didn't ask that ten years ago. The coup de grâce came the day my thirty-eight-year-old boss asked, "So how long do you think you can keep doing this? Companies used to have mandatory retirement."

I tried to file an age discrimination claim but stopped when my left cataract blurred the company's complaint form. In that instant I asked myself, "Why are you doing this?" My husband had retired a year ago and complained each morning as I mixed Metamucil with my oatmeal that I should as well. Why did I think the people at work needed me? No one had said they did. I still got great performance reviews, but that wasn't a compliment. I had been doing the same job since my snarky boss was eight. Screw this! I gave a one-month notice and went home.

The six months were grand. My husband and I planned the vacation of our dreams. We spent three weeks talking with travel agents and hours roaming on the computer, planning paradise. Neither of us had ever taken more than two weeks for a vacation. Just to consider a month was ecstasy.

I had worked consistently since my days at Milgram's. It almost felt like cheating to indulge one's self in a month of dillydallying. The vacation search was a three-week daydream. We imagined ourselves in every exotic world capital, at every one of the Hawaiian Islands, in every city where we had ever seen James Bond, and at all seven wonders of the modern world. In the end our vacation was simple. We would spend the month in Western Europe. It would include the British Isles, where language would be no problem. Those destinations would prime us to take on France, Italy, and Spain. Paradise collapsed into just a garden variety holiday, and it was perfect.

My life was falling into a sweet and easy rhythm. So when I got the call about a routine blood test associated with my annual exam, I was not initially alarmed. More tests would follow. The prognosis was clear and undeniable— three months. Hearing it is the hard part. It violates your ears. Acceptance is harder still. Life with all its vagrancies is all that we know. It's far from perfect but worth enduring. I was prescribed Xanax for anxiety. My sister argued that Northwestern Hospital was not the clock maker and was not empowered to say when the clock would stop. She insisted three months meant nothing. The rest of my family stood stunned and mute, searching for words to comfort me and themselves but found none. We all asked ourselves how something as inevitable as death could be possible.

My husband, feeling helpless and desperate in the face of the medical report, suggested we go away, just the two of us, take another trip, and forget about everything. I considered but declined. My life had been narrowed to ninety days. I didn't want my life dwindling down away from home. The final family consensus was that everyone would gather at our home for Thanksgiving and pretend that nothing was wrong.

Thanksgiving Day

Thanksgiving Day was a blast! I am sure it was my best holiday ever. I was visibly weak, but with assistance made it to the table. There was no longer a need to be concerned. I could spend the morning doting on myself and not the dinner. I could not care less if the turkey was dry, if the green beans were salty, or if the sweet potatoes were too sweet. If the cakes fell, I was fine. If the pie crust was tough, that was OK, too. I couldn't eat much, anyway. I never understood the psychology surrounding the concept of the last meal before the execution. Did we really believe making a menu selection was the number one thing on a convict's mind? Yet why not flirt with trivia? I decided I wanted a glamorous holiday look. My nieces, three cousins, and two sets of in-laws would join my sister, her husband, my husband, my children, a daughter and son-in-law, and a cast of children around the Thanksgiving table. I had no idea how they would handle the logistics, but that was not my problem.

I had lost my appetite for food, but not for vanity. The prior week I had given my daughter a list of items I would need: black flair slacks with an elastic waistband, a white silk blouse, and a brocade cropped jacket two sizes smaller than my regular size twelve. The jacket would give me bulk and not make the weight loss so noticeable. I also insisted on satin ballet slippers and fake eyelashes. Everyone was wearing fake eyelashes. I had wanted to but never had. I instructed my daughter to make up my face and put blush on my now-exaggerated cheekbones. I wanted red lips lined in pencil. The total facial composition should scream femme fatale.

When my sister and daughter escorted me to the dinner table, the room fell into a hush and then applause. All cell phones were pointing at me. In a matter of seconds, I was certain to be on someone's Facebook page. As I took my seat, everyone began oohing and ahhing about how beautiful I looked. Only my son and husband really meant it. The room fell silent once again, as if waiting for someone to reboot the conversation. Everyone was staring at me. I thought of saying something cheeky like, "Look on the bright side. No one will have to buy me a Christmas present," but I realized that probably really wasn't funny. Instead, I tapped my glass and announced, "Thank you all for sharing this Thanksgiving holiday with us. So now, let's dive into this good food and enjoy." That was all everyone needed, permission to forget.

In seconds everyone had returned to what keeps humanity tame—routine. Oh Christ, they were now talking about the election! The conversation swirled around the table in a firestorm of disbelief. The American electorate could not have delivered a more devastating shock to this Democratic dinner table. Donald Trump would be the next President of the United States. No more Blacks, no more women. Please no! Here you come, my self-proclaimed Republican brother-in-law, wading into this caldron of Democratic anger and hysteria, valiantly defending your man. "Double, double toil and trouble." Still, I admire your combativeness. I certainly would not have done it. The verbal abuse is going to be torture, but you hold your own. You go, gladiator, even as they drag you across the arena of the Thanksgiving table. I looked around the table and wondered if there are any closet Trump supporters in the room, anyone who secretly went behind the curtain and thought, what the hell have I got to lose?

To be honest, I really didn't care who was President. To me it all now seemed so senseless, striving and conniving to divide, build, or conquer nations. I would have no more military industrial complexes and evil empires to consider. No more rogue nations to fear. How many more coups and revolutions would it take for kings, premiers, and presidents to understand that it all ends here, with a singular salute to a solitary life? The Parker Brothers found the secret to life and unveiled it for us in Monopoly. "It's just a game, people. Get over it." Enough already. I tapped my glass.

The animated enmity ceased. The table became a mannequin frame. Oh, the power of death.

"I was just wondering, did anyone say grace?"

Eyes moved from side to side. "Grace?" They asked. "Did anyone say grace?" I knew the answer. Of course not. The politics of the day had snuffed out gratitude. Everyone had forgotten about giving thanks. Someone was singled out to stand and, mid-meal, proclaim why we were all gathered and what it meant to be family.

I smiled, grateful to God that we could now return to a more civil discourse. Perhaps we could discuss the pilgrims who came, learned to plant corn, and absconded with the Indians' land.

The aroma of Thanksgiving filled my nostrils, sending me remembering. Smells can tether you to so many bygone days and bygone people. I could not eat a thing, but I was full. I closed my eyes and inhaled memories. At this moment I believe I finally understand the reason why we love. It is because buried deep inside our primordial intellect is the absolute possibility that these people, who are so important to us, we may never see again. I look around my Thanksgiving table. I am grateful.

"Are you getting tired?" It was my husband, his hand cloaking mine.

"I think a little."

"Of course you are. We will take you back to your room."

With that, my husband and son bracketed me. As I stood, everyone else did as well. Should I say goodbye? Absolutely not. Let the living live. It's Thanksgiving. I smiled. Everyone applauded; I turned and with a tremendous amount of assistance left the room.

My husband and son placed me, like a fine jewel, onto my bed.

"I can stay with you," my husband said.

"Please don't. Neither of you. I want you to go back to the dinner table with everyone else. I'm just going to rest awhile. Come back later."

"Are you sure?"

"Believe me; I am certain." My husband sighed. Both turned and walked away. Sleep came so very easy, and with it the comforting knowledge that although I was in my room by myself, I was not alone.

Shall We Dance?

December, December, dancing, December. The early snowflakes twirl at my window and whisper that it is time for my personal advent. Is that my skin shining in the light? I'm not seeing as well. I am definitely sedated. My lids are weighty. My hands are placed across my blanket. There is a glow, a bioluminescence that I alone can see. The departing child returns a woman. Life is slipping away. She is quietly leaving the dance floor. My dance card is full but for this last waltz. I see you now. I never realized that you were so very handsome. You are taking my hand. I rise, folding myself into your arms. So strong you are, so sure. I am ready. The rapturous music begins. I drift with you, moving in perfect three-quarter time. I begin to shine. Time is ending.

I understand fully now, my darling time dancer, why you are here. As I shed my human shell, I can see. You are not a feared reaper or a fatal sting. You are my dance guide, there at my side to show me how to bow.

The dance ends.

ACKNOWLEDGMENTS

To my young friend, Letitia Asiedu, who had the patience to read my hand written manuscript through a multitude of tablets and a disarray of sheets to put this work into an electronic format and my young friend, Dr. Samra Saleem, who had the patience to navigate through the work with me and magnify the screen allowing me to set this work into the correct form for printing. A special thank you to my husband, Franklin, who always believed I could write a novel and supported me throughout this wonderful experience.

ABOUT THE AUTHOR

J.M. Curls is a wife, mother, and grandmother. She is the scion of one of the founders of Freedom Incorporated, a political organization that was crucial to the desegregation of Kansas City, Missouri's public facilities. In 1978, Ms. Curls was named one of International Telephone and Telegraph Corporation's Black Achievers and went on in 1986 to acquire the school she once directed. For over thirty years, she has been the owner and president of an associate's-degree-granting college in downtown Chicago. In 2006, Ms. Curls was awarded an honorary doctorate of pedagogy degree from Benedictine College in Atchison, Kansas. She is also a breast cancer survivor.